ALSO BY MAX MANNING

Don't Look Now

THE
VICTIM

MAX
MANNING

 sourcebooks
landmark

Published by Sourcebooks Landmark, an imprint of Sourcebooks
P.O. Box 4410, Naperville, Illinois 60567-4410
(630) 961-3900
sourcebooks.com

Library of Congress Cataloging-in-Publication Data

Names: Manning, Max, author.
Title: The victim : a novel / Max Manning.
Description: Naperville, Illinois : Sourcebooks Landmark, [2019]
Identifiers: LCCN 2018052448 | (trade paperback : alk. paper)
Subjects: LCSH: Psychological fiction. | GSAFD: Suspense fiction.
Classification: LCC PR6113.A5553 V53 2019 | DDC 823/.92--dc23 LC
record available at https://lccn.loc.gov/2018052448

Printed and bound in the United States of America.
SB 10 9 8 7 6 5 4 3 2 1

For Albert and Sean

1

The danger instinct, a twist in your gut, an inner voice whispering "Beware."

The fine hairs on Gem Golding's forearms prickle as she slows down and turns off the main road. Graffiti-scarred walls and a shuttered fried chicken shop glide past the passenger window. The area feels more run-down than she remembers. *Darkness can do that*, she thinks.

She drives slowly into the dimly lit parking lot, pulls up, and switches off the engine. The only other vehicle is parked closer to the store, its rear window shattered. For a moment, a sense of foreboding makes Gem consider putting the keys back in the ignition and leaving. Harsh fluorescent light spills through the store's glass door, and she's reassured by the sight of two youths in hooded tops and a middle-aged woman lined up at the register inside.

She climbs out and is about to lock up when her cell phone rings. She stops and rummages in the bottom of her bag. Without having to check the screen, she knows it's Drew.

"Where are you?" he says. "I thought you'd be home by now."

His concern is touching, and she smiles to herself. "Sorry. Something came up. You know how it is. I'll be back in twenty minutes. Just picking up those painkillers."

"Headache no better, then?"

"Worse. Much worse."

"You work too hard," he says. "You know you don't need to." Gem can hear the disapproval in his voice. "Drive carefully," he says.

"I always do," she answers and drops the phone back into her bag. From the corner of her eye, she glimpses movement and spins around. The man is two, maybe three inches taller than she is, and he doesn't slow as he walks toward her. There is something unsettling about the way he moves. Menace in every stride.

"Lovely car you've got there," he says with a nod.

He doesn't come to a halt until he is standing right in front of her. Close. Too close. Gem tries to walk around him. He steps to the side, blocking her way.

"What the hell are you doing?" she says, shuffling back to get as close as she can to the driver's-side door.

He doesn't answer her question. His lips twist into a mocking smile, and he moves forward. In her confusion, Gems wonders whether he has mistaken her for someone else.

She tries to walk away, but he blocks her again, and this time, she feels a surge of panic. "I'm meeting my boyfriend. He'll be here any second now."

The stranger ignores her, stepping in until she's trapped, his arms braced against the car on either side of her body. Gem's heart pounds. She wants the power of anger, but a cold fear grips her instead. She grabs her bag in both hands and offers it to him.

"My phone and money are in there. Please just take it and go."

He says nothing but swings a forearm. The blow sends the bag flying. It spins to the ground, spilling its contents. His silence is frightening. He's so close, Gem can see the dark shadow of stubble on his chin, feel his breath on her face. Sweat trickles down the small of her back. She raises her hands to ward him off, pressing her fingertips hard against his chest. His smile widens into a leer.

"What do you want?" she says. Her voice sounds different. Too high and shaky.

"What do you think I want?"

Gem shoves harder, forcing him to take half a step back. "Leave me alone."

The leer vanishes. He grabs her wrists and pins her against the car. Over his shoulder, she spots the hooded teenagers emerging from the store, each carrying a six-pack of beer.

Before she can call for help, he whips his right hand over her mouth and jams his left forearm across her throat. At the same time, he presses his body so hard against hers that from the other side of the parking lot, they look like lovers fumbling in the dark.

The youths glance over and snicker as they saunter toward the exit gate.

The man puts his mouth to Gem's ear. "Keep your mouth shut. Do what you're told, and you won't get hurt. I only want the car."

He takes his hand away, and she sucks in the cold night air. He grabs both her wrists again and twists the skin. She grits her teeth to stop herself from crying out. Her heart thumps hard against its cage, and her mind races. *He can have the car. It's only a car.* She is still holding the keys. She offers them up. "Take it and go," she says. "I don't care. Get away from me."

He snatches the fob from her hand and slips it into his jacket pocket. There is no way she's going to risk getting hurt for a car, but she's not going to let him get away with this. That's never going to happen. She'll see to it that he's caught and punished.

When the police ask for a description, she'll be ready. He must be at least six feet tall. His hat is pulled so low, she can't see any hair, but his eyebrows look black or brown. His nose is straight, his jaw strong, but the darkness disguises the color of his eyes. Underneath an unzipped black jacket, he's wearing a white T-shirt.

Sliding his right hand down and off her wrist, his fingers encircle hers, and he crushes them until she cries out. "Don't look at me," he hisses. "I said stop looking at me, and I told you to stay quiet. I have a knife. Don't make me use it."

Gem's throat tightens. He has a knife. Dipping her head to one side, she scans the ground, desperately searching for her phone. She spots it behind him, next to a pound coin and her lipstick.

"Please take the car and go," she says. "I promise I won't call the police." Her head spins as she tries to remember everything she's ever heard or read about surviving a violent attack.

Her thoughts are a jumble of contradictions. *Resist, shout, and scream, and you risk inciting the attacker. Fight back when the opportunity arises, and you have a better chance of escaping unharmed. Do everything you are ordered to do, appease your attacker, and you are more likely to get off lightly. Surrender completely, and you might increase your chances of being hurt.*

She braces herself against the car door and pushes. He is caught by surprise and staggers slightly. *Maybe I can do this*, she thinks.

"You bitch," he whispers, slamming her back so viciously, her head whiplashes against the car's roof.

That was stupid, she tells herself. *Don't be so stupid. Do what he says. Let him win. Then he'll go.* It takes every ounce of her willpower, but she makes her muscles relax, lets herself fall limp and helpless. Now he has no reason to be angry with her. He's won. There's no need for him to even think about harming her.

2

He feels her resistance fade and nods to himself. He knows he should be behind the wheel of the car and on his way by now, but he's having too much fun. The parking lot is dark and deserted, but he glances quickly over his shoulder before dragging her around the hood to the passenger side, where they'll be hidden from anyone coming out of the store.

She allows him to lead her in silence, her body language meek, like a lamb to the slaughter. It took some time, but she's got the message. Gripping her wrists tighter, he gives the car a quick once-over. It's a few years old, but he estimates that the BMW is still probably worth at least twenty-five thousand pounds. Stripped for parts, it could easily make a chop shop a decent pile of cash. He knows people who would pay him well for the chance to slice it up, but that's not the plan. Not tonight.

"You're hurting me," she says. "You promised you wouldn't."

He relaxes his grip and smiles. "I did, didn't I?"

She gives him a strange look, a mixture of relief and terror. It makes him want to laugh. How can she afford to drive a car like that? A high-flying job in the city? Her stinking rich boyfriend?

He suspects she's been dealt all the good cards in life. He got the joker, but he stopped joking a long time ago. He'd met people like her before and hated the unfairness of it all. Probably never had to fight for anything in her life. Never been tested. Things were about to change.

He widens his smile, willing her to smile back. She tries her best, but it turns into a grimace. Her teeth are so white, they almost glow in the dark. Her face is symmetrical and heart-shaped, her dark hair shoulder length. *We're about the same age*, he thinks. *Would she look at me twice if we passed in the street? Maybe*, he tells himself. *If things were different, we'd probably be a good match.* The injustice of it boils his blood.

3

Gem feels his breath hot on her neck. *Has he really got a knife?* she wonders. The thought makes her shiver. She imagines the weapon, heavy in his jacket pocket. A smooth handle, a curving blade, impatient to be used. *Maybe he's lying about the knife to scare me into obedience, to control me.* Lying or not, it's working.

His breathing speeds up, and something brushes the top of Gem's right thigh. Fingers slide up to the waistband of her trousers and back to her leg. She risks a glance at him. His eyes are closed. Her face burns with humiliation.

This is not supposed to happen, she tells herself. She wishes she'd taken the time to consider how to react in this situation, to have carefully planned her response. No one thinks it's going to happen to them. It's not something anyone wants to imagine.

Maybe there is a way. Get him talking. Reason with him. Anything not to have to make the big decision. Surely someone will walk by soon, see what's happening, and call the police.

"Please don't," she pleads. "You said you wanted the car. You can have it. Take it."

He pulls away a little. Hope flares in her chest. She babbles her words. Eager to get them out.

"I know you don't want to hurt me. Why would you? You don't look like a bad person. Please don't harm me. I'm having a baby. Please don't hurt my baby."

That is a lie, but maybe it will work. She's willing to try anything. She isn't pregnant, but Drew wants her to be. He'd be so happy if she had a baby and gave up her job. She made it clear that she wants to wait. Seven months together isn't long enough to know that it's right, she told him. He sulked for days.

The carjacker grabs a handful of her hair, pulls her head back, and looks into her eyes. "I know you're lying," he says softly. "You think I'm stupid." There is no hint of a question. It's a definite statement.

"It's true. I wouldn't lie about something like that. I'm having a baby. I'm eight weeks pregnant. I am." He shakes his head slowly, and she knows her bluff isn't going to work.

"You're lying," he says. "But you know what? Even if you are having a baby, do you think I care? Do you think that makes a difference? Get this. I don't give a shit. You think you're too smart for me, don't you? Keep me talking until someone comes to the rescue, is that the plan? Let me tell you something. It's dark and not many people walk the streets around here at this time of night. It's dangerous."

He pulls her hair harder, but she doesn't flinch. She's focused on getting out of this unharmed. He promised she wouldn't get hurt if she does what he says, but can someone who threatens to use violence be trusted not to be violent? She doesn't think so. If she lashes out, tries to fight him off, there's no telling what he might do.

Be sensible, everyone says. Don't put yourself in danger. Don't walk the streets at night on your own. Make sure your cell phone is always charged. Keep the car doors locked. She hears these words of advice. From her parents. From Drew. Drive carefully. Take care.

She doesn't remember being told what to do if someone grabs her in the dark, tells her he'll stab her if she doesn't do exactly as he says. Her eyes fill with tears, but she blinks them back. She knows they won't help. She takes a deep breath and tries to reason with him again. "Please just take the car and leave me alone. I won't report it missing. I won't claim the insurance. Please, I'd like you to have it. You can take it." His fingers dig harder into her flesh. She winces.

"You're going to let me take the car? Wow, that's so kind of you. Amazing."

For a second, his words confuse her, then she sees the look in his eyes. His anger is cold. He is in control, and that scares her more. He yanks her forward, then shoves her back.

"I'm so, so grateful. You're such a lovely person, aren't you?"

"I didn't mean it like that."

"You think you have any choice in the matter?" he says, spitting out the words as if they tasted bad.

Gem shakes her head. "Please leave me alone. You're scaring me."

"People like you need scaring sometimes."

Everything inside her tells her this is the time to scream. To scream as loud as she can for as long as she can. She opens her mouth and throws her head back, but before she can make a sound, a large hand is clamped firmly over her lips. Her head is pushed back against the car, and she feels the length of his body pressed firmly against hers.

"You stupid, stupid woman," he says softly. "Why can't you do what you're told?"

Gem's mind whirs with the realization that this is the moment she hoped would never come. The decision has to be made. Total surrender, let him do whatever he wants and hope for the best, or refuse to be cowed, find a way to fight back, and prepare for the worst.

4

SURRENDER

GEM THE VICTIM

Gem bent her knees slightly, breathed out slowly through her nose, and shrank back against the car. *Let him feel you pose no threat*, she told herself. *Once he's sure of that, he'll calm down.*

He slid his hand from her mouth, smearing her lipstick across her cheek, and gripped her free wrist. She took the opportunity to speak. "I'm so sorry. I panicked. I promise I won't try to scream again."

The pleading tone of her voice had the desired effect. He shifted the weight of his body off hers and stood taller. "That's more like it," he said. "Why would you want to make this more difficult than it has to be?"

Gem shook her head slowly, eager to convince him that she agreed she'd been incredibly stupid. "I don't know what I was thinking. I'm so sorry." She stole another quick glance at his face. A light stubble covered his chin and cheeks. His eyes were dark slits.

"I'm going to leave now," he said.

The heady rush of relief made her unsteady on her feet, and she instinctively grabbed his arm to stop herself from falling.

He grinned. "I bet you'll miss me when I'm gone." She didn't answer, and he laughed softly.

He paused for a moment, then released both her wrists. "Get on the ground," he ordered. "Get down and lie still until I've gone. Don't make me use this." He pulled the knife out of his pocket and stabbed the air with a twist. The blade glinted in the semidarkness. He hadn't lied about the knife.

Gem started to drop to the ground but hesitated. The thought of lying down made her feel sick. She'd be totally at his mercy, but then she was anyway, wasn't she?

"I said get down," he snapped. "Do it now and don't move until I've driven away. Until I've gone. Or there will be consequences."

Her eyes moved to the knife he held against his right thigh. *Don't give him a reason to use it,* she thought. *Just do as he says.* As soon as she lay on her side on the cold, hard concrete, he disappeared from view. After a few seconds, she heard the thud of a car door shutting. The engine started and Gem closed her eyes, the smell of exhaust fumes filling her nostrils. She lay motionless as the car slid past, backing out of the space before speeding away.

She scrambled to her feet, tears of trembling relief streaming down her cheeks. She was safe. It was only when the BMW screeched to a halt and started to reverse at speed that she remembered his warning. "Don't move until I've driven away."

Her mind screamed at her legs to run, but it was too late. The car crunched into her left side, sending her spinning to the ground. Lying on her back on the concrete, she stared up into the night sky. It was murky and starless.

Pain flamed across her chest with every breath she took. Something warm trickled down her nose and onto her lips, and she tasted blood. It ran down her throat, and she started to cough. She tried to roll onto her side to stop herself from choking, but she couldn't move. Then everything went black.

5

FIGHT

GEM THE WARRIOR

Fear flooded Gem's body at the thought of what she was about to do, but she did it anyway. She bit down hard into his fourth and little fingers until she felt the crunch of bone.

He snarled like a wounded animal and yanked his hand away, causing her teeth to tear through the flesh. Blood poured from the wound, and he released his grip on her to try to stem the flow.

She turned to run but wasn't quick enough. Stepping in close, he locked his right leg behind her right knee and wrestled her to the ground. Ignoring the pain from his wound, he pinned her down with his right arm, blood staining her jacket.

At the same time, he stuck his good hand in his pocket. *Oh God*, Gem thought, *the knife*. She watched in despair, expecting to feel the blade across her neck any second. She squirmed frantically under his weight, causing him to lose purchase and slide to one side.

Adrenaline surged through her veins, and her heart jackhammered. *This isn't happening*, she told herself. *This can't happen to me.* "Fucking no," she yelled as she twisted her body and rammed her right knee into his hip. He grunted in surprise, absorbing the pain with a grimace.

He pulled his good hand away from his pocket, clamped his fingers around her neck, and squeezed. Gem grabbed frantically at his hand, trying to pull his fingers away, and bucked wildly in a vain attempt to shake him off. *This is it*, she thought. *He's much too strong for me.* Her head felt like it was going to explode. She gave up trying to rip his hand from her throat and reached for his eyes. He snapped his head back, falling for the feint. She grabbed his injured hand and clawed viciously at the wounded fingers.

He cried out in pain, instantly releasing his stranglehold. Gem rolled away, grabbed her car keys, and scrambled quickly to her feet. Sprinting to the driver's door, she slid behind the wheel, immediately pressing the electronic fob to lock the doors. She reached for the ignition, her hand shaking so badly, she dropped the keys. Reaching down, she scrambled around in the footwell until her fingers closed gratefully around them. When she sat up, he was there, standing in front of the car, staring at her through the windshield.

Gem glanced over to the store. A man wearing brown coveralls and a woman holding a bag of shopping watched from behind the glass door. The man was talking animatedly on his cell phone, and Gem wondered if he was calling the police. There was no way she was going to wait for them to arrive. She started the engine and eased the car forward. The carjacker stood his ground and stretched both his arms out wide, blood still dripping from his right hand.

Gem turned the steering wheel, but he skipped sideways to block the way. She put her foot on the accelerator, and the car surged. He dodged to one side, and she jammed her foot down harder just as he darted back. She jerked the steering wheel to the right but couldn't avoid him, and he went down with a sickening thud.

Gem didn't stop. She didn't even look back.

6

SURRENDER

GEM THE VICTIM

Light seeped through the thin membrane lining Gem's eyelids as she breathed in the smell of strong disinfectant mingled with the crisp scent of clean sheets.

Before her eyes fluttered open, she knew where she was but not why. The room was small and stuffy. A gunmetal-gray patient monitor beeped beside the bed.

Gem's head throbbed, and her right arm felt unnaturally heavy at her side. She tried to raise it but stopped with a gasp when a sharp pain shot from her hand to her elbow. The pain cleared some of the fog from her brain, and a series of images emerged from the murk: a tall menacing figure, the glint of a knife, the rear lights of a car speeding toward her.

The door opened, and Drew walked in. The worry etched on his face lifted when he realized she was awake. "Thank God," he said, smiling down at her as he moved closer to the bed. "Stupid question I know, but how are you feeling?"

The sight of him and the genuine concern in his voice lifted

Gem's spirits. "You're right. It's a really stupid question," she said, her throat dry, her voice shaky. "I've been better. How do I look?"

Drew bent down and kissed her gently on the lips. "Beautiful as always. A little worse for wear, but beautiful all the same."

"For a lawyer, you're a terrible liar."

Drew shook his head. "How on earth did this happen? You seemed fine when I called you."

Gem took a moment to gather her thoughts. "I was hoping you were going to fill me in. It's all a bit hazy right now. I don't even know which hospital this is."

Drew reached down and brushed a loose strand of hair from her forehead. "Newham General. It's not surprising you're a bit fuzzy, sweetheart. You've got a nasty gash on the side of your head. You've been in a deep sleep since they brought you in last night."

"You've been here all night?"

"Right by your side."

Gem closed her eyes. An image of a tall man in a dark beanie hat surfaced, and the monitor started beeping rapidly. "My car. He took my car. I was so scared."

Drew rested a reassuring hand on her shoulder. "You're safe now. It doesn't matter about the car. As long as you're okay. That's all I care about. Your arm's broken. A pretty clean break just above the wrist, they said. You've got a temporary plaster cast on it." He edged back toward the door. "I better tell a nurse or someone that you're awake. The police are waiting to talk to you."

"The police?"

"Of course. They called to tell me you'd been brought here. They're going to want to question you about what happened. Just tell them as much as you can remember."

Drew moved to leave, but Gem called out for him again. "Will you be here when they come?"

He shifted uncomfortably on his feet. "Sorry, but I've got a meeting I can't miss, Gem. I've been here all night and need to shower and change. It'll be fine, and I'll be back as soon as I can, I promise."

Gem knew she had to tell him. The sooner the better. There was no reason she should feel embarrassed, but she did. "He touched me," she said, her voice barely a whisper. "Pushed himself against me. I couldn't stop him."

Drew's mouth tightened, and he narrowed his eyes. "He raped you?"

"No. Not that. He touched me. Groped me. His hand."

"What did you do?"

"He had a knife. He could have killed me."

Drew thought for a moment, biting down on his bottom lip. "I wasn't going to do this now, but I've said so many times that I don't like you working so late."

"I know."

"I've told you over and over again that you don't need to do that job of yours. I've never liked you driving across the city late at night. We don't need the money. You can switch to something with more regular hours."

Gem wanted to protest, tell him that she loved her job, that she'd worked hard to get where she was, but he already knew that, and she wasn't up to arguing. "I know," she said.

Drew nodded slowly. "I better get that nurse," he said.

7

FIGHT

THE DETECTIVE

Detective Inspector Elliot Day leaned forward on his desk, rested his chin on the knuckles of his fists, and watched the parking lot security camera footage for the third time.

Opposite him, Detective Sergeant Cat Shields waited impatiently for the tape to finish.

"You're not going to see anything new no matter how many times you view it," she said. "It corroborates the victim's statement, though it's a shame the worst of the violence is hidden from the camera by the car."

Day held up a hand to silence her as he concentrated on the footage he particularly wanted to see again. The quality of the film was poor, the images grainy, but Day's gaze focused on the dark-clad figure lying motionless on the concrete as Gem Golding sped away and out of the parking lot. Slowly, deliberately, the man rolled over onto his front, pushed himself onto his hands and knees, and stood up.

The image was too blurred to make out his facial features, but his hunched shoulders and the way he wrapped his left arm around his rib cage as he walked away suggested he was in a lot of pain.

Day sat back in his chair. "We need a forensic medical examiner to check her out and photographs taken of the bruises on her neck. Get someone to check hospitals for anyone fitting the suspect's description who turned up at Emergency with a cut hand and impact injuries."

Shields nodded, stood to leave, but hesitated at the door. "How are we treating this, Boss? A simple carjacking, attempted armed robbery, or attempted murder?"

Day had been asking himself the same question since he'd read Gem Golding's statement. "At the moment, all three are on the table. When we catch the lowlife, we'll see what he has to say. She said he had a knife, threatened to use it if she didn't do what she was told, and he choked her. If she hadn't fought him off, she could be lying on a mortuary slab, and we would be launching a murder inquiry."

Shields grinned. "She did more than fight him off though, didn't she? She mowed him down with her car. Could have killed him. A woman after my own heart."

She turned to leave but stopped again. "Oh, and one other thing. The victim's boyfriend, Drew Bentley, is kicking up a fuss, wanting to know when he can take her home."

Day flapped a dismissive hand. "He'll have to wait, Catherine. She can't go until the duty doctor has checked her out."

Shields made a face. "I'd prefer it if you called me Cat like everybody else."

"I'm not everybody else though, am I? I'm your boss."

Shields shrugged her broad shoulders. "Suit yourself. Do what you want."

"I usually do," Day said. "That's why I've ended up here."

The detective sergeant gave him a curious sideways look before leaving the office, and Day suspected she knew the reason for his demotion, or at least one version of the story. Police gossip travels faster than a high-speed patrol car.

Day hadn't worked with Shields before. This carjacking was his first case since moving from the city's eastern region murder investigation team to the Hackney Criminal Investigation Department. He was banished from homicide until his bosses decided he'd been punished enough. All those years of hard work and dedication to get to the top down the drain because of one mistake.

Day played the parking lot footage again, occasionally pausing the video to take notes. The suspect was undoubtedly a nasty piece of work, but there was plenty of scope for a robust defense. The worst of the violence took place on the wrong side of the car, out of view of the security camera. Gem Golding appeared to willingly walk around the car with him. She said he had hold of her wrists, but it could even be argued that they were holding hands.

The throttling hadn't been caught on camera, and although she said he told her he had a knife, he didn't produce it. In fact, a clever defense lawyer, and most of them Day had come across were extremely cunning bastards, could make the case that the most violent act caught on film was Gem Golding intentionally driving her car at the suspect.

Day had no doubt that she was telling the truth. There was something about the carjacker that made him uneasy, something malevolent about the way he moved, something troubling about his stillness when he stood in front of the car. Day had a gut feeling that if they didn't catch the suspect, they'd soon be dealing with another victim but without the benefit of a victim statement. Corpses can't talk.

He checked his watch. It was way past his bedtime, but the prospect of going home to an empty apartment held no appeal. He shifted his chair closer to his computer screen and ran the video one more time.

8
SURRENDER

THE MASTERMIND

Con Norton lay on his sofa and stared at the fuzzy image taken from security camera footage and grinned. It was him, he knew that, but no one else would have a clue.

He grabbed the TV remote and turned up the volume to listen to the news item.

"Hackney police are appealing for witnesses after a woman was injured when she was run down by a man who assaulted her before driving off in her car. The incident happened outside the Shopwise store on Roman Road, Bow, at about 10:45 p.m. yesterday. Detectives consider the suspect to be potentially dangerous and say he should not be approached."

Norton laughed and stretched out on the sofa, tucking his hands behind his head. *Potentially dangerous. That's real funny*, he thought. Potentially? Are they kidding? If only they knew what he was capable of.

That woman should count herself lucky to still be breathing. He'd been sure she'd understood. He'd warned her there'd be consequences if she disobeyed. What more could he have done?

But never let it be said that he was unforgiving. He'd seen the way she'd looked at him once she'd given up the idea of resisting. She was an attractive woman; no one could deny that. There had been something there, some spark, hadn't there. He was rarely wrong about these things. And even when he was wrong, he could usually make it right. Whether the woman in question liked it or not.

He had enough money to keep him going for at least a couple of months. He'd be able to pay the rent and stock up on food. He still had to collect the second installment, and that could turn out to be a bit tricky, but he'd find a way. He always did.

Norton rolled onto his side in a vain attempt to get comfortable. The sofa was dirty and smelled damp, like the rest of the rathole. He'd been living there for three months, which was at least two months too long. It was cheap, and his arrangement with the landlord was unofficial, which meant no paperwork, but maybe, when everything was sorted, he'd move out of east London. To somewhere nobody would find him.

His stomach rumbled loudly. He'd already decided to treat himself to a king-size meat feast pizza, but he'd have to put up with the hunger pangs until dusk. He didn't want to go out in daylight just yet, and anyway, he'd always found the streets of London more exciting after dark.

GEM THE VICTIM

Gem Golding reached for the glass of water beside her bed and took a sip. None of the hospital's breakfast choices—oatmeal, cornflakes, or prunes with mandarin segments—had appealed, but now she was counting down the minutes to lunch.

The constant commotion coming from the ward outside—strained voices, the clatter of footsteps, and the rattle of carts—made

Gem thankful Drew had insisted that she wasn't to be moved out of the side room.

She settled back on her pillow, closed her eyes, and took a deep breath. She'd been through hell. She'd never felt terror like that before, and she didn't want to feel it again. Ever. Despite it all, she'd survived. A bit battered and bruised maybe, but it could have been so much worse.

Someone knocked firmly on the door, and Gem's eyes snapped open as a tall, short-haired woman wearing a dark pantsuit and a serious expression entered.

The detective got straight down to business. "My name is Detective Sergeant Shields. The doctors say you're well enough to answer a few questions about what happened to you. Do you think that'll be okay?"

Gem nodded. "It's all still a bit hazy I'm afraid."

A smile softened the detective's face. "Don't worry. Apart from your obvious injuries, you're probably still suffering from shock. This is just an initial chat. We'll wait until you're feeling better and back home before we take a formal statement from you."

Gem pushed herself up into a sitting position, resting the plaster cast on her right arm gingerly across her waist.

Shields spotted a single plastic chair next to the patient monitor, dragged it over to the bed, and sat down. "Can you tell me why you stopped in the store parking lot, where you'd been, and where you were going?"

Gem took a moment to think. "I was on my way home. I'd been working late on a public relations campaign that's already gone over deadline. I had a splitting headache and knew we didn't have any painkillers at home, so I decided to stop and buy some."

"How did the suspect approach you?"

Gem's breathing quickened. "He came out of nowhere really.

Caught me by surprise, grabbed me before I knew what was happening. He was much too strong for me." The memory set the monitor beeping louder and faster.

Shields stretched out a hand and touched Gem's shoulder. "It's all right. We have security camera footage of the incident, but unfortunately, we don't get a really clear view of the carjacker. Could you describe him for me?"

Gem recalled making a determined effort to study her attacker's face, but all she could conjure up was his cold-eyed stare. "He was taller than me. Maybe three inches taller. Yes, he was tall and lean."

"What did he say to you?"

"He had a knife. I remember that. Said if I did as he asked, he wouldn't hurt me."

"You saw the knife?"

"I think so. He said he only wanted the car but…" Gem faltered and looked away.

"But what?"

Gem shrugged and stared silently at the foot of the bed.

Shields changed the subject. "Did you challenge him at all? Try to resist? Try to reason with him?"

"I was too frightened. Especially once I knew he had a knife. I tried to talk to him. Said I didn't care about the car. Even said I was pregnant in the hope that he'd feel sorry for me. There was nothing else I could do. I thought if I tried to fight back, it might make things worse. Anyway, it would have been futile. Do you think I should have done something?"

Shields hesitated, then shook her head. "That's not what I'm saying. No way. When you're in that kind of situation, it's so difficult to decide what to do. There is no wrong or right decision. You're the only one who can make that judgment."

Gem heard the words, and maybe she was being unfair to the

detective, but she still felt she was being judged. *Surely*, she thought, *whether your reaction is right or not depends on the outcome. If you walk away without serious injury, then it doesn't matter whether you fought back, surrendered, or simply froze.*

She'd survived by doing everything he'd asked her to. The one time she'd defied him, she'd paid the price. Gem recalled how adamant he'd been that she should lie still until he'd gone. She had a strange feeling that throughout the whole incident she was being tested, dared even. The surge of relief she'd felt when he drove off had made her careless. She'd disobeyed him and he couldn't let it go.

"I stood up before he'd driven away," she said. "That was my only mistake. He reversed the car into me as a punishment. If I'd resisted him earlier, tried to defy him, who knows what would've happened. The important thing is I'm here and I'm still breathing."

Shields stood up and put the chair back where she'd found it. "You certainly are. You got lucky. I understand you're being discharged later today. We'll give you a few days to rest, then we'll speak again and take a full statement from you."

Gem waited until the detective had left the room before adjusting her pillow and lying down. She stared at the ceiling, wondering what the policewoman really thought about how she'd reacted to the attack. *No doubt*, Gem thought, *if it had been her, she would have put her training to good use and beaten the carjacker to a pulp.*

God, she couldn't wait to get back to her home, to lie in her own bed. Why had this happened to her? Life had been going so well. She had a great career, an attentive, caring boyfriend. Gem had never thought of herself as a victim. She'd known hardship growing up, but from the moment her father had walked out on them, her mother had been determined that her only child would escape public housing, build herself a better life, and she had. She considered herself a self-assured, confident woman. But last night, she'd felt so helpless. Maybe she'd have to reassess her life, reconsider her opinion of herself. The thought made her angry, made her want to scream. Instead, she bit her bottom lip and blinked away tears.

She'd come close to telling the detective about the carjacker groping her but had held back because Drew's reaction had been so negative. It'd been clear that he'd rather not have heard it and probably wouldn't want anyone else to. She supposed she'd have to tell the police eventually. They might question why she hadn't mentioned it, but bad memories can be pushed aside.

Maybe, she told herself, *it would be better if that particular memory didn't come back.*

9

FIGHT

THE MASTERMIND

Norton rode the Jubilee line south from Stratford to West Ham, then the District Line east to Upton Park, in the traditional heart of London's East End. The journey took fifteen minutes, and every rattle and bump shot pain across his chest.

Despite being after 11:00 p.m., the cars were still packed with passengers, and the permanent grimace on his face and the way he clamped his left arm around his torso attracted plenty of curious glances.

The police had released a computer-generated image of the carjacker's face, and Norton had seen it on the TV news earlier that day. It looked a bit like him, but he didn't think he had anything to worry about. The jawline was too weak, the cheekbones were definitely not high enough, and he was hardly going to walk around wearing that beanie hat.

In a sprawling city of eight million people, he'd always found it pretty easy to fly under the radar. The anonymity on offer made it easy to cheat, intimidate, and manipulate without fear of retribution. That's why Norton loved London.

The twenty-minute walk to Newham General Hospital was less painful than the Tube ride. Norton knew the narrow streets of that part of the city were dangerous to walk late at night. He also knew that only ordinary people worried about stuff like that, and he was far from ordinary.

Even though he was obviously injured, a group of youths milling around on the corner of Glen Road fell silent as he approached and parted tamely to let him pass. If he wanted people to know they should be wary of him, they knew. It happened as naturally as breathing. He couldn't explain it, but physically, it involved a tensing of his shoulder muscles, a forward tilt of his head, slower breathing, and a cold stare. There was more to it than that, of course, much more: a special energy, a powerful force. It didn't control him and he didn't control it. It was him. He was it.

At the same time, if he needed to, he could make most people, men or women, like and trust him. Norton smiled to himself. It was a rare gift, and he used it to his advantage.

He hadn't been inside a hospital for twenty-five years. Not since the day he was born. He couldn't remember a thing about it, and that was probably a good thing. By the time he reached the Emergency Department, he'd sworn never to step into a hospital again. The place smelled of vomit, disinfectant, sweat, and fear.

The triage nurse, a slim brunette, looked up from her desk with weary disdain. "Name please."

Norton knew that the police would probably have alerted hospitals in the area to watch out for a man fitting his description with impact injuries. He'd held out for two days, despite the fact that every breath he took sent a painful reminder down the right side of his chest that the bitch had defied him, fought him, and gotten away.

He was banking on the hospital's night staff being too busy and too exhausted to think about anything other than how long they had left until the end of their shift.

"John Joseph," he said, flashing the nurse a smile.

"What's wrong with you, Mr. Joseph?" she asked, her slender fingers fluttering across the computer keyboard.

Norton stepped closer and looked her directly in the eyes. "It might not seem like it, but this is an emergency. I need to see a doctor quickly."

The nurse frowned and blinked rapidly, her cheeks flushing under the directness of his gaze.

"Are you in a lot of pain?"

"Do you think I'd be here if I wasn't?"

The nurse flinched, and Norton raised a hand in apology. "I'm sorry. I really am. I know you are all under pressure in a busy hospital like this, and I think you do a fantastic job, but I'm in agony. Stabbing pains in my chest. I could die. I really need to see someone as soon as possible."

He smiled again, and this time, the nurse smiled back before typing up his symptoms. "Please sit down," she said. "We'll get to you as soon as we can."

Norton nodded and walked over to the seating area. It was heaving with feverish, groaning, bloodstained bodies, broken men, women, and children waiting patiently to be called for examination. Their weakness disgusted him.

Twenty minutes later, he was stretched out on a hospital bed, stripped to the waist. "I hear you think you're going to die," the doctor said, a wry smile on his chubby face.

"I don't think it. I know I am. We're all going to die sometime."

The doctor looked a couple of years older than Norton, but he was five inches shorter and at least thirty pounds heavier. "Too true," he said. "But I'm sure you'll have to wait a while. Of course, some patients like to exaggerate their symptoms to try to jump the line."

Norton said nothing. He wanted this over with as quickly as possible.

"You have some severe bruising on the right side of your rib cage. How did that happen?"

"I'm not sure. Got drunk and fell over, I think. Can't you just do an X-ray or something to check it out?"

The doctor pressed his fingertips on the bruised area. Norton jerked away from the touch, but he didn't cry out.

"An X-ray would be a waste of time. Looks like you've got a couple of fractured ribs. They'll heal, but there is nothing we can do in the meantime except give you something for the pain." The doctor pointed at the bloodied bite wound on Norton's right hand. "That looks extremely nasty. What happened?"

Norton slid off the bed and slipped his shirt back on. "My dog bit me, didn't it? It hurt like hell at first, but it's not so bad now. Flea-bitten mutt wouldn't harm a fly normally. Don't know why, but it just went for me. Had to have it put down."

The doctor raised his eyebrows. He wasn't fooled. "We see a lot of dog bites in here. If a bite gets infected, it can be serious. I'll have to give you something for that."

———————

Norton stepped off the Jubilee line train at Stratford and headed for the gate, weaving his way along the crowded platform. Forty minutes ago, he'd left the hospital with a course of antibiotics and a box of painkillers stuffed in his jacket pocket. And the whole of that time, he'd been thinking about the woman who'd bitten him and run him down. *I bet she's pleased with herself*, he thought. *I bet she thinks she's safe.*

His ribs were going to take two to three weeks to mend, and the antibiotics were probably going to upset his stomach. All because of her. *It's not over*, he told himself. *It's never over until I win.*

Norton increased his pace as he walked past the southern perimeter of the Queen Elizabeth Olympic Park, the giant silhouette of the London Stadium dominating the skyline. Each step sent a jolt of pain across his chest, fueling his fury.

He deserved compensation for his suffering, he told himself. The deal he'd made hadn't included broken ribs and infected bites. He had a right to demand more, and that was exactly what he was going to do.

Norton nodded to himself and grinned as an idea formed in his mind. Oh yes, more money would ease his suffering, but that alone wouldn't be enough.

No one gets the better of me. It's not allowed. The thought of what was to come sent a warm, pleasant sensation flooding through his body, temporarily soothing the pain in his ribs.

He'd be home soon, and although he felt tired, sleep would have to wait. He had a campaign of action to plan.

Norton grinned again. He was already feeling much better. Did he really need this medication? Probably not. *Embrace the pain. Use it*, he told himself. Pain is fuel, and he knew exactly how to burn it.

10
SURRENDER

GEM THE VICTIM

"We've found your car," Shields said, stepping over the threshold into the hall.

Gem ushered the detective and her male colleague into the living area and invited them to take a seat with a sweep of the plaster cast on her right arm.

"This is Detective Inspector Day," Shields said. "My boss."

Gem greeted Day with a nod. He didn't look much older than Shields, but the shadows under his eyes suggested he'd been missing out on his beauty sleep.

"How are you feeling now?" he said.

"Much better for being back home, and this is healing well," she answered, pulling back her dark hair to reveal a stitched wound across her left temple. "I'm told the scar will be small and almost invisible." She lifted her right arm and wiggled the plaster cast. "I'm having to put up with this for weeks though."

The two detectives smiled and exchanged glances. "As DS Shields said, your BMW has turned up, but it's not going to be any use to you or anybody. It was found burned out beside the canal at Hackney Wick. Nothing but a twisted shell of metal."

Gem frowned. "Why would a carjacker destroy a valuable car?"

Day shrugged. "You're right. The cars are often stripped for parts to sell. Occasionally, it's all about the thrill. In your case, the suspect seemed a particularly violent individual who was more interested in terrorizing you than taking the car."

Gem recalled the strength of the man's grip, the heat of his breath on her neck, and shivered. The thought that he was still out there walking the streets terrified her. "How likely is it that you'll catch him soon?"

Day gave Shields an almost imperceptible nod. "We're doing our best," she said. "Our press office is arranging appeals for information and witnesses. We've got security camera images of the suspect, but the quality is so poor, it's almost useless." Shields hesitated and looked across at her boss.

He rolled his eyes, and Gem could see he thought his colleague should stop pussyfooting around and get to the point. "We were wondering how your memory of that night was," he said. "I understand it was a bit hazy when you came to in the hospital, but if you're ready to answer a few questions and give us a description of the suspect, that would be great."

Gem wanted to help; of course she did. There was nothing she wanted more right now than for the carjacker to be caught, but she wasn't sure about talking to the detectives without Drew present, and he wouldn't be home for a couple of hours.

The thought of reliving what had happened that night made her feel physically sick. Her memories had returned in the form of vivid flashbacks, often when she was lying in bed unable to sleep, but the truth was she couldn't be absolutely certain whether the snapshots were real or imagined. She closed her eyes and took a couple of slow, deep breaths.

"If you're not up to it right now, we can wait," Day said. "We can come back when you're feeling better or arrange for you to come to the station."

Gem shook her head and held up a trembling hand. *There is no point putting it off*, she told herself. *It has to be done, so why not get it over with?*

"I think I can remember most of what happened," she said, her voice hesitant. "I'll do my best."

"That's great," Day said. "But tell me if you're finding it too difficult, okay?"

Gem nodded.

"Why did you stop at that particular store so late at night?"

Gem had asked herself the same question many times. If only they'd had painkillers at home. If only she'd been more careful. She'd been stupid stopping in that part of the city at that time.

"I was on my way back from a work event and had a splitting headache. I knew we had no painkillers at home and had bought some in that store once before, but that was in daylight."

"So you got out of the car, and then what?"

Gem clasped her hands, twisting her fingers. "The parking lot was deserted, but I could see there were a few people in the store. He came out of nowhere, out of the dark. Walked right up to me, smiling, as if he knew me, like a friend. Before I could think, he pushed me up against the car. He had a knife and said he'd hurt me if I didn't do what I was told."

The words poured out so quickly, Gem struggled to catch her breath.

Day offered her a sympathetic smile. "Take your time. There's no rush."

Gem took the opportunity to compose herself. She knew the detective would force her to think about things she'd blocked out.

She'd survived the carjacking without serious injury, but if she could revisit that night, would she do things differently? Probably not. For the first time since the attack, she understood that the choice she'd made that night would change her, was already changing her. She didn't know how exactly, but she could feel it.

Day encouraged her with a nod. "You said he told you he was armed with a knife. Did you actually see the weapon?"

Gem closed her eyes briefly, flinching at the image of a curved blade glinting in the darkness. "I think I saw it. Yes, I did see the knife. The blade was curved, and the handle was black, I think. I was so terrified, I couldn't think straight and…"

"That's okay," Day said. "That's good. Very good. What about the attacker? Could you give us a description?"

When the carjacker had pressed close to her and stared into her eyes, Gem had thought she'd never forget that face, never be free of the look he'd given her, but her mind had already started airbrushing his features.

"He was tall, definitely tall, and lean. He was strong, so strong there really was nothing I could do. It would have been crazy to try. He was wearing a dark beanie hat, pulled down, but the hair I could see was darkish too. Clean-shaven, I think, maybe a bit of stubble. I don't know what color his eyes were, but they were deep set. I'd say he had an east London accent and I…I don't know."

Day glanced across at Shields, and she shook her head. "That'll do for now," he said. "If you recall anything else you might think is important, you know where we are. You've been great. Really helpful."

Gem stood at the sitting room window and watched the detectives get into their car and drive off. She hated being stuck at home, but Drew had called her office and told them she'd need at least a week, maybe even two, before she'd be well enough to return to work.

That had angered her. She'd had to make decisions for herself at an early age. The day before her ninth birthday, she'd finally allowed herself to believe that her father hadn't abandoned her because she wasn't clever enough or pretty enough. He'd left because *he* had a problem, *he* wasn't good enough. Since then, she'd always prided herself on her independence.

Sure, she understood Drew thought he was doing her a favor, but she'd snapped at him for interfering when he'd told her what he'd done. He'd be happy if she never went back to work at all.

Gem walked into the kitchen, filled a glass with tap water, and swallowed two of the painkillers the hospital doctor had prescribed for her. She didn't want to upset Drew, but she wasn't staying cooped up at home for two weeks. Besides, she'd set her sights on earning a promotion, so the sooner she got back to the office the better. She'd been putting off telling Drew because she knew how he'd react.

She loved her job, and she didn't want him to get used to the idea of her waiting at home for him like some kind of Stepford wife. There was no way that was going to happen, and he was just going to have to accept it.

THE DETECTIVE

It was only three miles from Gem Golding's Shoreditch home to Hackney police station, but the traffic on Dalston Lane crawled at a snail's pace, and Day had to fight a strong urge to get out of the car and walk. Shields had been driving for ten minutes, and the station was still two miles away.

Day stared out the passenger-side window at the busy restaurants, wine bars, and cafés. Gentrification had seen Georgian terraced homes torn down and a rapid increase of property prices in the area.

"What sort of salaries do you think they earn? The mortgage on that house must be huge."

Shields braked as the traffic slowed to a standstill. "I think public relations pays quite well, and Bentley is an employment lawyer. Advises people who've been fired on the best way they can screw compensation out of their former employers."

Day nodded. He'd considered getting legal advice about fighting his demotion but decided not to push it. He'd been lucky to be allowed to stay on the force at all, and he knew it. The traffic started moving, and Shields shifted into gear. She didn't elaborate further on Bentley's work, and as the silence stretched, Day sensed her thoughts had also turned to his stalled career.

"I guess you know the reason I was kicked off the murder investigation team?"

Shields flicked him a cautious sideways look. "I think every cop in the city has heard what happened. Some version of the story anyway."

Day grunted. He knew well enough what police officers were like when it came to gossip. "Tell me what people are saying about me, and I'll tell you if they're right. What about that for an offer?"

Shields changed gear but said nothing. Day understood that she probably didn't want to offend a new boss, especially as they hadn't worked together long enough to form any kind of understanding.

"I'd like to know what story is going around," he said. "Don't worry though. I won't shoot the messenger. Even if the message is a pile of crap."

Shields kept her eyes on the bumper of the car in front. "Well, er, the word is that you assaulted another murder squad detective and threatened to throw him out a window."

Day let out a long sigh. "That's surprisingly accurate. Spot-on actually. Do the gossipmongers know that the window was on the third floor of New Scotland Yard and that my wife had left me, taken our son, and moved in with the bastard?"

Shields shot him another look and shook her head.

"Well, they do now," Day said.

11

FIGHT

GEM THE WARRIOR

Gem ran the bath as hot as she could bear and added the bubbles, stirring the water with her fingertips. She closed her eyes and breathed in deeply through her nose as the sweet aroma of orange and vanilla filled the room.

She lit the candles placed around the bath and climbed in, lying back slowly until the foam covered her shoulders. After a few seconds, she reached behind her, lifted the large glass of chilled chardonnay off the ledge, and took a long sip.

As a child, she'd have a bath once a week. A quick soap, rinse, and out within minutes. Now, it was her favorite place to relax and pamper herself, and she definitely needed pampering after everything she'd been through.

She'd given a full statement to the police, and they'd assured her and Drew that they would be doing everything possible to bring the carjacker to justice. Gem took another sip of wine. She supposed she should feel proud of herself, challenging a violent criminal and getting away unscathed, but the whole episode had unsettled her.

As the only child of a single parent, she'd not had an easy child-hood, but she'd never before had to face that kind of physical threat, and even though she'd come out on top, she knew that it could so easily have ended differently.

She'd driven out of the parking lot on such an adrenaline high, she'd almost felt invincible. That feeling hadn't lasted long. She'd never describe herself as naive, but the cold realization that there were people in the world who would harm her and find pleasure in it made her feel more vulnerable than she'd ever felt before.

Because of that, she was in no hurry to go back to work, which surprised her. She loved her job and was working toward climbing the ladder and maybe even setting up her own company one day, but since the attack, she couldn't even think about launching a new product or promoting the opening of a nightclub.

Gem looked at the nearest candle and studied the flickering blue and yellow flame. Violent crime was widespread across the city, with sex assaults, armed robberies, and street stabbings reported in newspapers and on the TV every day, but like most people, she had never imagined anything like that would happen to her.

She took a deep breath, slid down the bath, and slipped her head under the water. After a few seconds, she surfaced and smoothed her hair back over her ears. That night, she had made a split-second decision to fight. Had she done the right thing, or had she simply gotten lucky? What scared her the most was that if it happened to her once, it could happen again.

THE REPORTER

Matt Revell switched off his cell phone, flipped it onto his desk, and grinned from ear to ear. He had spent a lot of time, effort, and a fair chunk of his expenses cultivating police contacts across the city, and he loved it when it paid off.

He swiveled in his chair, scanning the two rows of desks in front of him. As always, the newsroom buzzed with reporters either yelling or whispering into their phones, while others tapped frantically at their keyboards, their eyes fixed determinedly on their computer screens.

Some of his fellow newshounds were friends, others no more than professional acquaintances, but they had one thing in common. They were all his rivals. They were constantly chasing stories that would be given the most prominent slots in the paper, desperately seeking the thrill of seeing their byline at the top of the report.

Poor suckers, Revell thought. If only they knew. A story guaranteed to be splashed across the front page had just fallen into his lap. He could imagine the headline: *Woman Fights Off Carjacker, Then Mows Him Down*. Or maybe *Courageous Victim Fights Off Knifeman*.

Revell knew the sub-editors would probably come up with something snappier, but all he really cared about in the end was that they spelled his name correctly.

He stood up and headed for the news desk, a swagger in his step. The first move would be to let the news editor know that his brilliant journalistic instincts had produced the goods yet again. Then he'd start the ball rolling by putting in a call to the Metropolitan Police press office.

THE DETECTIVE

Day opened his office door and yelled across the squad room. "Shields, I need a word in here now."

He watched the detective sergeant rise from behind her desk and walk over to the watercooler. Slowly and deliberately, she filled a plastic cup, drank half of it, and poured the rest away before heading for his office.

Day held the door open for her, a sheepish smile on his face.

"Sorry about that," he said. "The press room has just called, and to say I'm pissed off is an understatement."

Shields sat down and arched an eyebrow. "What's happened?"

"There's been a leak on the Golding case. Some smug reporter on the *Daily News* knows the full story, how she fought back and ran the carjacker over. I bet the paper's editor is wetting her pants with excitement. Not-so-helpless woman takes on violent attacker and triumphs. The press loves that kind of bullshit."

Shields thought for a moment. "They won't be able to name her if she is a victim of sexual assault."

Day nodded. "Of course not, but we haven't classified this as a sexual offense yet, have we?"

"What are you thinking?"

Day walked over to the window and searched the gray sky for an answer. "The press guys suggest we cooperate and go all out with coverage. The story's going to be out there anyway. That way, we may have some control, and maybe someone somewhere will come forward with some information."

"What's your instinct?"

"I think they're probably right. We've had nothing of any use from the police e-fit sketch and limited press release we've put out. I don't think this suspect is going to go away. He's not going to hold his hands up and decide to be a good boy from now on. Sooner or later, he's going to do the same again, and next time, the victim might not be so lucky."

Shields pursed her lips. "We can't do the big news story, a TV press conference, without Golding agreeing. That's a big ask. If I were in her shoes, I'd think carefully about putting myself in the public eye."

Day turned away from the window, walked back, and slid behind his desk. "I'm not sure you're right, Cat," he said. The emphasis he put on the short form of her name made Shields smile.

"She stood up to this guy and took him on, didn't she? I'd be surprised if she was too shy to speak out about what happened. I'd like you to pay her a visit and ask her to step up. Explain to her the benefits of extensive media coverage and how it will increase the prospect of catching her attacker. I've got a feeling she'll be up for it."

12
SURRENDER

GEM THE VICTIM

London Fields was one of Gem's favorite places to walk on weekends, especially when Drew agreed to go with her. The morning had started off gray, but by midday, the hazy spring sun had burned away the cloud cover.

"This bloody plaster cast itches like crazy," she said, nodding at the sling that held her broken wrist against her chest. Drew laughed and squeezed her good hand. Since the attack, she'd noticed that he'd been extra attentive and had started coming home from the office early so they could spend more time together.

As they passed the high wall encircling the park's popular outdoor swimming pool, the air ringing with the sounds of voices, laughter, and vigorous splashing, they exchanged smiles.

"I'll cook dinner tonight," Drew said, squeezing Gem's hand again.

"I can help, you know. I'm not completely useless, even with only one fully functioning arm."

"There's no need. I want to treat you. I've got a bottle of your favorite wine too."

Gem leaned in and kissed him on the lips. As they pulled apart, she decided to take the plunge and break the news. "I think I'm going to go back to work next week. I know you want me to take at least two weeks off, but there's no need."

Drew said nothing, but Gem felt his grip on her hand tighten.

"I'm going mad being stuck at home, and apart from the discomfort of this plaster cast, I'm feeling fine. I can work at my desk and don't have to attend any evening events until the cast is off."

Drew stayed silent, but after a few paces, Gem felt him relax.

"If that's what you really want to do, it's fine with me," he said. "After what happened, I'm going to worry about you, of course, but we can't let the bastard who attacked you control our lives, can we?"

Gem sighed. Drew was trying so hard not to show it, but she knew he'd prefer her to not work at all, or at least switch to a job that was less demanding. He'd never been able to explain to her properly why he felt like this. In the past, whenever she challenged him on it, he'd claim he worried about her being out late, that things were going so well at work that he'd be getting a huge pay raise. Inevitably, they'd end up arguing. Gem had often wondered whether his strangely old-fashioned views were the result of his years spent in foster care. He refused to talk in detail about his time in the children's home, but she knew he'd never been part of a family, never had a proper home life.

Maybe he was at last trying to come to terms with the fact that the size of his salary, and his feelings about her late hours, would never influence the way she wanted to live her life. That wasn't who she was. They'd been together long enough for him to know how much she loved her career and how hard she'd worked for it. He'd have to suck it up.

"I'm glad you feel that way," she said. "If I'm going to get the promotion I want, I need to show I'm dedicated. A broken wrist isn't going to stop me."

Drew put his arms around her and hugged her tight. "If you're happy, I'm happy. I'm just relieved that you survived your encounter with that madman and are getting better."

Hand in hand, they headed along a path they knew would take them through the park's wildflower meadow. They hadn't spoken in detail about the attack in the four days since Gem had been discharged from the hospital. Drew always seemed to have something urgent to do whenever she brought the subject up. Since he'd raised it this time, she grabbed her opportunity.

"Tell me if I'm wrong, but I got the feeling in the hospital that you thought I should have done more, should have put up some kind of resistance."

Drew turned and looked her directly in the eyes. "I was upset about what had happened, so scared for you, that's all. He caught you by surprise, and he was armed. What else could you have done? I don't know what I would have done if he had seriously harmed you, or worse. It honestly doesn't matter what you did or didn't do. You're here now, and that's all that I care about."

Gem nodded, grateful that he had thought things through. The problem was, no matter how hard she tried, she couldn't shake the feeling that she should have put up more of a struggle. Not put her life at risk, nothing like that, but she would have liked to have shown more defiance. If she had, maybe she wouldn't feel so damn guilty.

She sensed Drew's discomfort, but she had things she needed to tell him. "Believe me, I wanted to kick him, scream, and bite him. I really did. But a voice in my head kept telling me to be careful. Don't make him angry, don't drive him to do something he hadn't thought about doing. I felt so helpless. He had a knife. I was so terrified, I think I froze."

Drew didn't say anything. He stopped walking and wrapped his arms around her again. She buried her face in his chest, but her eyes stayed dry. She was determined not to succumb to fear. Never again.

"The worst thing is that monster is still out there, wandering around the city, biding his time before choosing his next victim," she said. "He gets a kick out of terrifying and hurting people, pure and simple."

THE MASTERMIND

Con Norton sat on the grass, his knees up, his back propped against the trunk of one of the many plane trees surrounding the park's green spaces. From his vantage point, he watched the couple embrace. *So romantic*, he thought. It made him want to puke. Though maybe everything wasn't quite as it seemed. He had a pretty good idea what Bentley was up to. Using the girlfriend's ordeal to cement his position, make himself indispensable. No doubt he was being incredibly understanding about what had happened. Would she be stupid enough to fall for it? *Probably*, Norton told himself.

If only she knew what her loving partner was really like. As slippery as an eel and twice as fishy. A man who couldn't be trusted to honor his promises. A deceiver and betrayer.

Norton wondered what the boyfriend would think if he knew the truth about what had passed between him and Gem that night. The chemistry he'd felt had been unexpected but, at the same time, undeniable. He'd frightened her, but not in a bad way. She'd never admit it, at least not until he had had the chance to explain, but she'd felt something too. He had no doubt about it.

She'd done everything he had asked her to do, without complaint. She'd submitted to his will, and he hadn't wanted to hurt her. Not really. She'd even promised not to call the police.

When he'd pressed close to her, he'd felt something stir. It wasn't purely physical. There was so much more to it than that. Then the stupid bitch had to go and spoil it, didn't she? He'd had to punish her for her transgression. What else could he have done?

Norton rubbed the stubble on his cheeks and chin with his fingers. He'd been growing it for only three days, but it was already thickening nicely. A beard was a quick and easy way to alter his appearance.

Everyone makes mistakes, and he was prepared to give Gem another chance. Lucky for her, he happened to be that kind of person. The boyfriend posed a problem, but problems can be solved if you're prepared to do what's necessary. Nothing and nobody would be allowed to come between Norton and Gem. She wanted him. She just didn't know it yet.

He stood up, dusted himself down, and flexed his back. The couple had emerged from behind a clump of tress and were making their way toward the park's Lansdowne Drive exit. They were walking slowly, arm in arm.

Norton snorted a humorless laugh and followed.

THE DETECTIVE

Sitting in his car outside the Victorian terraced house, Day pulled his phone from his jacket pocket and fired off a one-word text message to his wife: Here.

Walking up to the doorstep, knocking, and engaging in polite but extremely awkward conversation was out of the question. He couldn't trust himself to behave in a civilized manner. Not yet. Maybe never. He'd arranged to see his boy, take him out for the day. He didn't want to set eyes on—or worse still, have to talk to—anyone else in that house.

The front door opened slightly. Tom slipped out, ran to the car, and slid into the passenger seat. Day reached out a hand and ruffled his son's hair. It had been only a week since he'd seen his boy, but he looked at least an inch taller.

"I don't know what they're feeding you, but it's working," he said.

Tom beamed. "Where are we going, Dad?"

Day shrugged. "Well, we've got plenty of time. I've got to bring you back by 5:30 p.m. I thought we might go to Greenwich Park, walk up the hill, then find somewhere nice to eat lunch. What do you think?"

Tom sniffed and rubbed his nose with the back of his hand. "Sounds boring. Why can't we go bowling or something and have a burger? I'm starving."

Day started the engine and pulled away from the curb into a gap in the slow-moving traffic. "It will be good for both of us to stretch our legs," he said. "A walk will give us a chance to have a chat."

Tom didn't argue. He sat in silence until a set of lights up ahead turned red and Day braked to a halt.

"Dad?"

"What?"

"Can I ask you something?"

"Of course. I can't guarantee I'll give you an answer though."

"Are you and Mum going to get divorced?"

Day's throat tightened, and he swallowed hard. This wasn't the sort of chat he'd had in mind. "No. I mean, I don't know what's going to happen. We'll have to sort things out when we're ready."

Tom frowned. "Rob said you and Mum will have to get divorced. That you won't have any choice."

The lights changed, and the traffic started to move again. Day stared ahead, gripping the steering wheel so tight, his fingers turned white. *Who the hell gives a fuck what Rob thinks? Nobody with any sense, that's who. What the hell does that miserable asshole think he's doing, discussing stuff like that with my twelve-year-old son?*

He looked across at Tom, forcing a smile. "Nothing's been decided yet. When it has, then we'll make sure you know what's going on. I promise. It's between Mum and me, and we'll sort it out. It's got nothing to do with that, with him, with…" Day faltered. He couldn't bring himself to utter the man's name.

13

FIGHT

GEM THE WARRIOR

Gem had been expecting the doorbell to ring, but the double chime still startled her. She walked down the hall, feeling more nervous than she'd expected. She and Drew had lain in bed talking into the early hours about the wisdom—or otherwise—of agreeing to be interviewed.

Drew had argued that talking to a reporter about what had happened would be a huge mistake, whipping up interest in something they'd be better off putting behind them. *Mark my words*, he'd warned her. *You feed one hungry wolf and it won't be long before the rest of the pack closes in.*

Reluctantly, in the end, he'd accepted that Gem wasn't going to change her mind. She believed that no matter how difficult it might be, speaking out about the attack was the right thing to do. If it helped just one person unfortunate enough to find themselves in the same situation, then it'd be worth it.

She opened the door to the half smile of a man wearing a smart gray suit with a white shirt and red tie, the whole ensemble slightly out of kilter with his unruly mop of dark hair. She estimated him to be about her age, maybe younger.

"Matt Revell, a reporter for the *Daily News*," he said. "I spoke to you on the phone about an interview."

Backing away a fraction and tilting his head, he gave Gem the impression that he half expected her to have had a change of heart and had prepared himself to be disappointed.

"Of course," she said, waving him in. She led the way to the living room and sat down on one of the two white leather armchairs. After a moment's hesitation, the reporter perched on the edge of the sofa.

"Thank you so much for agreeing to do this," he said. "It's a fantastic story. I know the police have already told you that speaking out could assist with the investigation, but it could also help other people who find themselves in the horrible predicament that you did."

As a public relations executive, Gem dealt with journalists all the time, but this was different. She was the story. She knew the reporter would be hoping for plenty of gory details and an angle that would get the story splashed across the front page. If he didn't get exactly what he wanted, then he wouldn't be averse to a little spin.

"Would you like a coffee?" she asked.

"If it's okay with you, I'd rather get started straightaway." Revell pulled a digital recorder from his jacket pocket, switched it on, and slid it onto the oak coffee table between them.

Gem stared at the device.

"We record everything nowadays," Revell said. "It protects us both from any dispute about what was and what wasn't said, and it's much easier than scribbling down everything in shorthand. I never could get the hang of that."

"Of course, I'm happy about being recorded. I think this is an important story and I want it to be reported accurately. I don't want my words spun, or angled in a way that distorts the truth. You understand that, don't you?"

Revell raised his eyebrows and gave her a look that suggested the thought had never crossed his mind before reaching out and nudging the recorder slightly closer to Gem's side of the table.

"I already know the nuts and bolts of what happened. What I'm really interested in is the fact that you fought back against a violent attacker. Fought back and won."

Gem ran her hands along the arms of her chair and dug her fingertips into the leather. This was going to be harder than she'd thought. She lifted a hand to her neck and slid her fingertips gently across the skin. The bruises had faded, but her throat was still tender.

"It's hard to describe how terrified I was. He said he had a knife. The truth is, I had no idea what to do. No one ever tells you how to react when you're attacked. You know this type of thing happens all the time, but you never let yourself imagine that it's going to happen to you."

"Did you see the knife?"

Gem shook her head.

The reporter held up a hand. "Sorry, but could you please say yes or no for the recorder?"

Gem nodded. "Yes. Sorry, I mean I'm not sure if I actually saw the knife, but he told me he had one, and why wouldn't I believe it?"

Revell sat back in his seat, but only for a second. He edged forward again, eager to ask his next question. "When did you decide that you were going to put up a struggle? That you were going to risk everything and fight back?"

Gem paused for a moment and took a deep breath, her mind a jumble of shadowy images. "I don't think I actually decided anything. I panicked and didn't know what to do. I'd heard such conflicting advice about how to react in those situations and had never thought it through. I was so badly prepared. I had no idea what to do."

The shrill sound of the house telephone ringing in the hall interrupted them. Revell smiled. "Do you want to get that?"

Gem hadn't been expecting a call. Drew always phoned her cell. She shook her head, and they waited in silence until the ringing stopped. Revell jumped straight in with another question.

"Can you remember when and why you fought back against an obviously very violent, extremely dangerous attacker? Weren't you worried that it would make things worse? That you might end up getting seriously hurt, or worse?"

Gem rubbed her hands back and forth on the arms of her chair as she recalled the terror she had felt that night, the feel of her attacker's hands on her body, his fingers tightening around her throat.

"I knew that if I resisted, I could make things worse, of course, but I was also frightened about what he would do to me if I submitted. He said he wouldn't harm me, that he was only interested in the car, but there was something about him that made me feel he wanted to hurt me, whether I did what he said or not." Gem could hear herself breathing and took a moment to compose herself.

"You decided to fight rather than surrender because you thought your life was in danger either way?"

Gem shook her head, then remembered what Revell had said about the recorder. "No. It's not as simple as that. I told you before, I don't think I made a decision to fight. Not consciously. It just happened. I don't know what it was. Something deep inside, instinct maybe." She paused again and made an effort to breathe slowly.

Revell sat back on the sofa and stayed there. "Take your time," he said. "You're doing great. If you can remember exactly what you did, how you got away, that would be good."

Gem could remember. It was all there, every detail, inside her head. She had tried to bury the memory, but it always resurfaced, like a recurring nightmare. What she couldn't do was forget. That's what she wanted. What she longed for. She desperately needed these memories erased. They were doing more than scaring her. They were changing her. Eating away at her confidence, her strength. She'd never known her father, but she'd been brought up to be strong. *Be fierce*, her mother had told her. *Be fierce and better yourself.* She'd stood up to the carjacker; she'd been fierce. But since that night, the memories, the flashbacks, the thought of what might have happened had shaken her confidence. The last thing she wanted was for what happened to change her for the worse, and she'd told Drew that speaking out publicly might be the first step to forgetting.

"He pressed me against the car and rubbed the top of my thigh with his hand. I could hear his breathing getting faster. That's when I thought—well, knew—that he wasn't going to leave me alone and take the car. He put his hand over my mouth to stop me screaming. I bit him. Hard. He got mad and tried to strangle me. He was so strong, I almost blacked out. I went for his weak spot, dug my nails into his wounded fingers, and it worked. I ran to the car, got in, and locked the doors."

Revell waited for her to go on, but she stayed silent. He prompted her. "Then you started the engine and drove the car right at him. Ran him down because you wanted to punish him for what he'd done to you. You wanted revenge."

Gem frowned. *What's he suggesting?* she thought. *That doesn't make sense. Where had this come from? Surely the police don't think I ran the attacker down deliberately.* She was considering how to respond when the telephone rang again.

This time, she welcomed the interruption. She stood up. "Sorry, better get this one," she said. She picked up the receiver. "Hello?"

No one answered, but she sensed a presence on the end of the line. "Hello, can you hear me?"

The silence was broken by the faintest whisper of breath.

"Hello?" Still, no answer came. "What do you want? Stop calling me." She slammed the phone down and returned to the armchair.

Revell had switched the recorder off. He quickly reached forward and pressed the Power button. "Do you want me to repeat the last question?"

Gem didn't answer straightaway. Her thoughts were still on the telephone call. She could have sworn someone had been there. She looked down at the red light flashing on the recorder and then back at Revell.

"Saying that I ran him down because I wanted revenge is spinning it a bit too far. I didn't intentionally drive at him. I don't think I did anyway. I didn't want to hurt him. I'm not like that. But he got in my way, and I wasn't going to stop. My only thought was to get out of that parking lot as quickly as possible. He tried to prevent me from driving off. Jumped in front of the car. I put my foot down, but I didn't really mean to hit him. Don't expect me to feel sorry for him though. The bastard can't have been hurt that badly, because he got up and walked away, didn't he?"

The reporter looked at her for a moment. She could tell he either didn't believe her or didn't want to believe her.

"Surely there must have been some satisfaction, some feeling of justice being done when you saw him go down?"

That was true, of course. She hadn't intended to use the car as a weapon, but the moment of impact, the thud, had felt good. Gem was media savvy enough to understand that admitting this to Revell might not be sensible.

"I think we've been through everything," she said. "It's not been an easy experience for me, and I'm pretty tired."

Revell had a lot of good stuff, enough to blow every rival newspaper out of the water, but it was obvious from his pained expression that he wasn't quite ready to leave.

"One last question, if that's okay?" Gem didn't refuse straightaway, so he carried on. "Based on your experience as a victim of an extremely violent crime, what advice would you give to women who find themselves in the same situation? Submit? Or should they follow your example and resist?"

Gem closed her eyes and dropped her chin to her chest. The question was impossible to answer, dangerous even. She desperately wanted to help women who found themselves in the situation she had, but she didn't know how to, and that made her angry. She felt like shouting her answer at the top of her voice, grabbing the recorder off the coffee table and hurling it at Revell's head. She took a moment to compose herself and think carefully before meeting the reporter's gaze.

"First, this isn't an issue that only applies to women, you know. Far from it. Men often suffer violence, and they have the same decision to make. Second, I don't think I can give anyone advice about what they should do if attacked. Even the so-called expert advice seems contradictory. Each situation is different, each attacker is different. Only you can assess the danger you are in and the best course of action. But you could think carefully about what you might do if it happens, maybe attend self-defense classes, give yourself options. Be ready."

Revell blinked hard, nodded, and reached for the recorder. "That's great. Perfect. I've got a snapper waiting outside to take a couple of pictures."

"Wait a second," Gem said. "Leave the recorder on."

She had fought off her attacker, and that was a positive thing. It should make her even stronger, but as the days passed, she felt more vulnerable than ever. She still had a fight on her hands, and she thought that if she said it, then maybe it would be true.

"There is one more thing I want to say. I want to make it clear that I'm not a victim. I've been victimized by my attacker, of course, but I refuse to be a victim."

After Revell and the photographer had gone, Gem poured herself a white wine and put her feet up. It was early in the afternoon but not too early. She had drunk half the glass when the telephone rang again. She ran into the hall and snatched it up.

"Hello. Hello? Who is this? Hello?"

Gem's breath caught in her throat. Silence. But not dead silence.

14

SURRENDER

THE DETECTIVE

Day sat at his desk and flicked through a hard copy of the Gem Golding file. His team was struggling to make progress on the case. The electronic facial identification technique, or e-fit, of the suspect sent out to newspapers and television had sparked a flurry of calls to the hotline, but all the leads fizzled out.

If they didn't get a breakthrough soon, he'd have to consider putting the investigation on the back burner. He grabbed the telephone and dialed through to the press office. The call was answered immediately. Day had dealt with Helen Moody on a couple of murder cases and admired her no-nonsense approach.

"Just the person I need," he said. "I wanted a word about the Gem Golding carjacking."

"Hang on a minute while I get the folder up on my screen."

Day heard her fingers skipping lightly across a keyboard and pictured Moody at her desk, the phone wedged under her chin, her lips pursed in concentration.

"There's nothing new scheduled at the moment. The last press release went out with the e-fit. Have you got a new line or more information you want us to push?"

Day wished he had something fresh to offer. "Unfortunately, no, but we could do with a little more coverage on this one. We desperately need new information or a witness to come out of the woodwork."

Moody fell silent. Day could almost hear her brain whirring. "The problem is the press isn't really turned on by this story. Yeah, the suspect reversed the car at her, but she escaped with a broken wrist. I think the press see it as a run-of-the-mill carjacking. They may be right, but we need more information to crack this case. You know what they're looking for. Is there anything juicy we can give them?"

What the hell do these journalists want? Day thought. *Blood? A rape? A murder?* Those were exactly the things he and his team wanted to prevent by putting the suspect behind bars as soon as possible.

"Everything suggests that the man we're after is an extremely violent, incredibly dangerous character who is not suddenly going to start behaving like a Boy Scout. It pisses me off that the press is not interested enough to help us. I bet they'll be wetting themselves with excitement when he kills someone. Desperate to print everything we offer them." Day paused, giving himself a moment to calm down. "Sorry, Helen. I know you aren't to blame, but it's bloody frustrating."

"I know, but look, let me think about it. I'll make some calls to a few news desks and try to whip up a bit more interest. We might be able to squeeze another appeal for information out of them."

THE MASTERMIND

Con Norton opened his eyes and gritted his teeth. He hated being woken. Swinging his long legs off the sofa, he sat up and listened.

The knocking was loud but at the same time hesitant, as if the caller was secretly hoping that nobody was in.

Norton swore, stood up, and stretched his back. He didn't have to answer the door to know who'd ruined his nap. Only one person ever called around to see him. The one person who knew where he lived. The knocking started again. Norton walked slowly to the door and yanked it open.

"What the fuck do you want?"

Kev Finch looked up at Norton, eyes wide with apprehension. A small man with narrow shoulders and heavy hips and thighs, he looked a decade older than his tenant although they were both in their late twenties.

"Er, hi, Con. Sorry to bother you. Hope this isn't a bad time."

"It is, actually. An extremely bad time."

Finch blinked, momentarily lost for words. "Sorry."

"You woke me up. An afternoon nap is a crucial part of my beauty regime. I take it very seriously. There's got to be a reason I look so good, right?"

"Sorry," Finch said, clearly unsure whether he should laugh and nervous about making the wrong choice.

Norton winked and let out a low chuckle. "Only joking, mate. You're welcome anytime. You do own the place after all."

"I didn't mean to wake you, mate. If I'd known you were catching some z's, I wouldn't have knocked."

"Don't worry about it. What can I do for you?"

"It's about the rent."

Norton flashed his landlord a smile. "What about it?"

"You haven't paid it."

Norton had moved into the pokey apartment above Finch's kebab shop three months ago. It had been a private arrangement, worked out after Norton overheard Finch moaning to friends that he was having troubling finding a tenant. Needless to say, the agreement didn't involve a rental agent or the tax man. It meant Norton didn't have to sign any paperwork or provide ID, and Finch avoided paying fees and tax. The rent was low, but Norton resented paying up, even when he had the cash.

Early on in their relationship, Norton had realized that two things drove Finch: greed and fear. Greed gave him the courage to knock on the door and ask to be paid what he was owed. Fear made him sweat like a man who suspected his tenant wouldn't think twice about beating him to a pulp. Occasionally, Norton liked to encourage that belief.

"You know I lost that job?" Norton said.

"Yeah, you told me. I still need my rent though."

Norton stared at the little man. He reminded him of a cockroach, the way he scuttled around the place. He stifled a powerful urge to knock Finch down and stamp on him until he cracked. *Not yet*, he told himself. *Not until you've found somewhere else to stay.*

"I'm a bit short of cash right now. I need a little more time. Trust me, I'll have your money in a week or so, that's all."

As a result of the carjacking, he had plenty of cash, and he had been promised more. He simply didn't want to share any of it with this excuse for a human being.

Finch wiped a line of sweat from his upper lip and dried his fingers on the front of his Hawaiian shirt.

"I need it soon, mate. I've got bills to pay, kebab meat to buy."

Norton nodded and smiled as if he truly appreciated the situation, but when being nice to someone didn't work, he got bored very quickly. He placed a hand on one of Finch's puny shoulders and squeezed it gently. The unexpectedly friendly gesture earned him an embarrassed smile.

He grinned back and dug his thumb into the cluster of nerves between the little man's neck and shoulder. Finch squealed like a pig and tried to squirm away. After a few seconds, Norton released his grip.

"You are making me angry now, and making me angry is like smoking. Hazardous to your health. I can't pay you right now. Don't you understand English? I'll come find you as soon as I have the money."

Finch stepped back and turned away. His head bowed, he rubbed his shoulder as he descended the wooden staircase.

15

FIGHT

THE DETECTIVE

Day stood by the window watching the rain ripple the surface of a puddle spreading across the parking lot entrance. What a comedown. How had it come to this? His old office at New Scotland Yard had a view across the Thames.

Not for the first time, he wondered whether he'd been wrong to accept the stinging humiliation of demotion for the sake of clinging onto his job. Maybe he'd have been better off leaving the force, starting afresh.

Deep down, he knew the truth. His obsession with hunting killers had contributed to the breakup of his marriage, and the way it had ended had led to him being unceremoniously kicked off the murder investigation team.

He'd lost his family. How careless. He needed to stay in the force. Needed to belong to something, even if it meant having to grit his teeth and accept going back to investigating muggings and burglaries. Day clenched his fists. His life had crashed and fallen apart in a way he'd never expected, but he wasn't prepared to give up. Not when there was still a chance that he could scoop up the pieces and put them back together.

His thoughts were interrupted when the door flew open and Shields entered carrying a copy of the *Daily News*. She dropped the newspaper onto his desk with a flourish.

"They've certainly gone to town on this one," she said. "Pages one, four, and five."

Day stepped closer. The front-page headline screamed *Warrior for Women Fights Back*. Beneath it sat a large headshot of Gem Golding, and next to that a subheading: *Victim Fights Off Pervert, Then Mows Coward Down with Car He Tried to Steal.*

Day glanced at Shields. "Pervert?"

She nodded. "That's right. She talks about how the attacker groped her, effectively waiving her right to anonymity as a sexual assault victim."

Day scanned the front page again. "It's a bit too hysterical for my liking. Too sensational. Why can't they stick to the facts?"

Shields crossed her arms and shrugged. "What did you expect? It's the *Daily News* after all."

Day flipped pages until he found the double-page spread inside. This time, the main headline asked the question *Stand Up and Fight, or Surrender to Survive?* The feature was illustrated with another photograph of a somber Gem Golding and a grainy still from the security camera footage of the incident showing the back of the attacker's head.

In addition to the interview with Golding, there was another report by Matt Revell focusing on the confusion and conflicting advice about what to do if you are attacked and an article featuring tips from a self-defense expert. Next to the article, a large graphic of a faceless man, decorated with red dots, helpfully showed readers exactly where they would find an attacker's eyes, neck, and groin.

Day sat down, pulled the newspaper closer, and skimmed the text. The force's press office had put out a statement advising the public that the first thing any victim of violent crime should look to do is run away. If circumstances meant that was impossible, then hand over any valuables the attacker demands. Day noticed that there was no advice to readers about what to do if the person attacking you wasn't interested in your property or money, if the only thing he wanted was you.

The statement had been edited down to a couple of paragraphs and tacked on the end of the center spread. Day knew that ninety-nine percent of *Daily News* readers had the attention span of a goldfish and would give up reading well before they got to the last third of the article.

He shook his head slowly and pushed the newspaper aside. "You know what's going to happen now, don't you?"

Shields had a pretty good idea what her boss was getting at, but she didn't bother replying. It was clear he was going to explain whether she needed telling or not.

"What's going to happen is that shit is going to hit the fan, and we're going to have to clean up the mess. We're going to get a rash of incidents across the city where victims are badly beaten, stabbed, or even shot because they read this junk and decide it would be great fun to put their lives at risk by standing up to the bad guy and refusing to hand over their stuff."

Shields stayed silent. Day understood she was waiting for him to calm down before she said anything. He hadn't been sure about her when they'd first met, but he was warming to her.

GEM THE WARRIOR

Gem finished off her banana muesli and sneaked a look across the table at Drew. They'd both used their tablets to read the interview on the newspaper's website while eating breakfast. She had rushed through the article and finished first. Drew had been more thorough. After reaching the end, he made no comment. He turned off his device and focused all his attention on his bowl of cereal.

Gem knew a bad sign when she saw one. Her boyfriend was the kind of person who loved to voice his opinion about anything and everything. In anyone else, she'd describe it as an irritating trait, but his willingness to say what he was thinking was one of the things that had initially drawn her to him.

She let her spoon fall into the empty bowl with a clang. "Okay then, come on. Tell me. What do you think?"

Drew pushed his half-eaten breakfast away. "To be honest, there's too much unnecessary detail for my liking."

Gem waited for him to say more, but he fell silent and stared pointedly at his wristwatch. It was the groping that rankled. She knew that.

"I told the truth, that's all. I want people to know exactly what happened."

"Why? Why is that so important to you?"

Gem hesitated. She needed to choose her words carefully. She wanted Drew to understand her motives, whether he agreed with them or not.

"It can only be a good thing if people, both women and men, talk about and think about how best to respond when threatened with violence. I almost froze, and I dread to think what would have happened if I had, but in the end, I got lucky. Why should I stay silent? I didn't choose to be attacked. That savage chose me, and I want people to know exactly what happened."

"Well, they do now. There's no doubt about that." Drew stood up, lifted his glass of orange juice, and downed it in one gulp. "I need to get going. Got an early meeting."

Gem stayed sitting at the table as he disappeared into the hallway and ran up the stairs. After a minute or so of pacing and door
banging, she heard his footsteps pounding down the staircase. He
stepped into the kitchen, his black leather backpack hitched over
one shoulder.

"Do you want me to walk you to the gym?"

Gem shook her head. "It's what I say about him groping me,
isn't it?"

Drew slid his backpack off and lowered it to the floor. "I don't
see why you had to mention it. You're the woman who fought off a
violent attacker. You fought back and escaped. That's a great story.
Good positive stuff. I think some things are better kept private."

Tears pricked Gem's eyes. She wiped them away. "Why should
I be embarrassed about what he did? I've got nothing to be ashamed
of. I'm not guilty of anything."

Drew walked over to the table, pulled her gently to her feet, and
hugged her. "I'm sorry. I didn't mean to upset you. What happened
was terrible. Such a shock. To be honest, my head is all over the
place. I feel guilty that I wasn't there to protect you. I can't think
straight."

Gem pressed her face into his chest. "It's okay," she said. "I'm
going to be okay."

He squeezed her tighter, and for the first time since the attack,
she felt safe.

"I'll try to get home early tonight," Drew said. "We can talk
more about what happened if that's what you want."

She nodded and kissed him softly on the lips. As he turned and
scooped up his backpack, the house telephone rang.

"Can you get that?" Gem said, her stomach churning.

Drew frowned, checked his watch, and strode into the hall.

Gem stayed sitting at the breakfast table and listened.

"Hello? Hello?"

Gem held her breath.

"Hello? No. We don't want solar panels. I told you, we don't want or need solar panels."

Drew put the phone down, ran back into the kitchen, and gave her a peck on the cheek. "Got to go," he said and headed for the door, slamming it behind him.

Gem breathed out.

It took her less than ten minutes to walk to the gym. A member for three months, she'd joined as part of the January wave of people riven with guilt over their festive season indulgence.

It was strange how she and Drew were so different, she thought. She'd always enjoyed exercise, particularly running, but he always had an excuse not to join her. He'd be too busy or too tired and liked to point out reports in the media about the health dangers of breathing in traffic fumes while jogging.

It had always amazed her that he kept so slim, but then he ate well and definitely drank less wine than she did. Gem was a party girl and proud of it. Work hard and play hard had always been one of her favorite sayings. Drew preferred drinks in a quiet bar and romantic dinners. One of the things that used to regularly set them bickering was Drew's obsession with keeping the house spotless. He despaired at the way she liked to leave wineglasses, magazines, teacups, and dirty plates scattered around the house. She'd laugh off his complaints and advise him to loosen up and relax a little.

In the end, they'd reached an informal truce. She'd try not to leave stuff lying around, and when she did, he'd clear it away without moaning. They were certainly very different characters, but their relationship worked, most of the time.

Stepping into the gym's reception area, she spotted a copy of the *Daily News* spread open on the counter. She flashed her membership card and charged through the swing doors before the skinny blond receptionist could even think about engaging her in conversation.

A few minutes later, she emerged from the changing rooms, clutching a bottle of mineral water. She walked through the main gym, drawing curious glances, and headed for the weight training area. Her upper body strength was poor. That was going to change.

She sat on a rubber warm-up mat, crossed her legs, and took a sip of water. What had happened to her must have been traumatic for Drew too. He'd need time to come to terms with it. At least he was prepared to talk it through. That was important. Perhaps tonight would be the right time to mention the silent telephone calls. Once she'd told him, then they could both go to the police.

Over the past week, she'd had at least three calls a day, sometimes four or five. They always started after Drew left for work and ceased after he returned home. She had tried not answering and leaving the telephone off the hook, but not knowing whether he was calling was almost as disturbing as listening to him breathing.

Gem thought of the caller as a *him*. It wasn't an assumption. She knew. It wasn't a random *him* either. Every time she held the phone listening to *him* not speaking, she could feel his body pressed against hers, his fingers tightening around her throat.

She trembled at the memory, fear-fueled anger flooding through her. She'd fought him off, drawn his blood, and escaped unharmed. Now she knew, with chilling certainty, that it wasn't over.

16

SURRENDER

GEM THE VICTIM

Gem studied herself in the mirror. She loved her new look, despite Drew's reaction when he had walked in last night. The angled bob was stylish, he'd conceded, but he'd been less impressed with the change of color, insisting that copper didn't suit her complexion. She hadn't realized he was such an expert on skin tones. Tough. He was going to have to put up with it.

Once he'd stopped sulking about her new hair, Gem had broken the news that she was going back to work the next day. She had expected an argument, but he hadn't tried to change her mind. Instead, he'd sulked a bit more, pointing out that he'd gotten used to her being at home a lot more and would miss that. Gem allowed herself a smile. Since her discharge from the hospital, they'd made the most of the opportunity to spend time together. They'd done a lot of talking, about the past and the future, and had a lot of early nights.

Gem picked her cell phone off the bedside table and checked the time. She needed to get a move on if she wanted to avoid being late on her first day back.

She had reached the bottom of the stairs when her cell rang. It was her manager. "Hi, Melanie. I'm on my way."

"Ah, Gem. How's the arm? Better, I hope? Have you left the house yet?"

Gem wondered why her boss, someone who was usually brisk and articulate over the phone, sounded so flustered. "I'm leaving right now. Should be with you by nine if the traffic isn't too bad."

"Well, er, the thing is, there's been a change of plan. We've decided that it'd be better if you took a bit more time off. We don't want you to rush back when it's not necessary."

Gem grabbed the banister with one hand and lowered herself into a sitting position on the stairs. "Why? What do you mean better? What's happened? I really don't want more time off. I'm looking forward to getting back to work."

"Nothing's happened. I'm not saying this as your boss, Gem. I'm saying it as your friend. The last thing I want is for you to come back too soon. You've had a terrible experience. Maybe wait a few weeks, at least until your cast is taken off."

Gem frowned. That didn't sound like the Melanie she knew, the woman who regularly insisted that holidays were for wimps and that only losers worried about work-life balance.

"What about the wine bar launch I've been working on? It's opening next week, and the client will expect me to be there."

"Don't worry about that. We've got someone in to help on a temporary basis."

Gem stood up, felt dizzy, and sat straight down again. "You've brought someone in to take over my clients? Who is it?"

Her manager laughed, the sound shrill and unnatural. "You don't know her, a friend of a friend. Loads of experience in hospitality. Anyway, she's not taking over your clients. Don't be silly. She's helping out until you return."

Gem closed her eyes as panic fluttered in her chest. She didn't simply want to go back to work; she needed to. Sitting at home all day wasn't doing her any good.

That night, in the darkness, she'd bowed to the carjacker's will. Maybe that decision had saved her; she had no way of knowing. What she did know was that she wasn't going to let that moment of threat, fear, and submission cast a shadow over the rest of her life. That would be her way of fighting back.

"I'm ready to return today," she said. "One hundred percent ready. In fact, I've already ordered a taxi. I might as well pop into the office, even for only a couple of hours. I could ease my way back in, help the new girl out with the wine bar project. The truth is, I need to keep occupied right now."

Melanie didn't respond.

Gem filled the silence. "I promise to take it easy initially, but I really do feel that, psychologically at least, getting back to work as soon as possible is the best thing I can do."

Gem listened to more silence and sensed her boss was wavering. "I'll be there in about forty minutes," she said and ended the call.

She stood up and grabbed the banister to steady herself, her stomach churning with an unfamiliar queasiness. Nothing was going to stop her going back to work. She couldn't change what had happened in that parking lot, but she could choose to move on with her life.

THE MASTERMIND

Norton slouched in the doorway of a men's clothes store at the northern end of Chancery Lane, his right shoulder resting against the inside edge of the shop window. He'd been watching and waiting for close to an hour and was prepared to stay there all evening if necessary.

As a child, he'd always been someone who got bored easily, and boredom had often led him into trouble. Over the years, he'd learned to be more patient, to concentrate on the task he'd set himself. He no longer regarded watching and waiting as tedious. It was preparation, and he knew that preparation was vital if he wanted to succeed.

There was no question that Bentley was as sharp as a razor, and he'd always been quick to let other people know it. But sometimes he could be too clever for his own good. Norton allowed himself a smile. *That arrogance will be his downfall,* he thought.

Gem Golding had no idea what her precious boyfriend was really like, how twisted and controlling he could be. Bentley was a master at hiding his lies, his deceitfulness, his disloyalty.

She definitely deserved someone better. She needed to be rescued; she just didn't know it. Yet. Norton would bring her around to his way of thinking. He'd learned a long time ago that you can convince anyone of anything if you are determined enough, if you are prepared to do whatever is necessary.

He zipped up his jacket and slipped his hands into the pockets. The sun was dropping fast, dragging the temperature down with it. He was weighing up whether to risk fetching a coffee to keep himself alert when a familiar figure emerged from the red terracotta Victorian building opposite.

He slipped back into the recess as Bentley strode north toward Chancery Lane Tube station. Norton waited a few seconds before following at a safe distance, confident that he could stay anonymous among the hundreds of commuters streaming into the station. It was easy to hide your face on a jam-packed Tube train, and Norton was looking forward to the task of following Bentley to the home he shared with Gem.

The mere thought stirred his blood, adrenaline rushing through his veins. He loved the thrill of the hunt. Almost as much as the kill.

17
FIGHT

THE REPORTER

The fluttering in Matt Revell's stomach surprised him. During his five years as a national newspaper reporter, he'd developed thick skin and a nerveless disposition, but he'd never been summoned to a private audience with his news editor before.

Tania Duffield didn't stand or even turn her head when Revell entered the room. A stick-thin woman in her forties with dark hair tied back in a severe ponytail, she carried on staring out the window at the spectacular view over Canary Wharf and across the Thames to Greenwich.

Revell couldn't remember the last time he'd seen her away from her desk. She seemed to always be hunched in front of her computer monitor, fingers jabbing at the keyboard, or on the telephone bawling out a reporter, usually for committing the ultimate sin of not getting the story.

"What's this about?" Revell said, determined not to give his news editor the satisfaction of seeing that he was nervous.

Clasping her small hands, Duffield turned to face him. "Are you going to stand there all day?"

Revell pulled back a chair and sat down. He had no idea what he'd done wrong, but he was prepared to deny everything. Never admit to making a mistake and never say sorry. He'd learned that much. It crossed his mind briefly that he was about to get the sack, be told to clear his desk and leave the building immediately, but he knew that task would normally be the privilege of the paper's managing editor.

"What's this all about? What is it exactly that you think I've done?" Revell stared across the table.

His boss's green eyes shone with a mixture of contempt and amusement. Duffield held up a hand. "Calm yourself down. What are you getting so worked up about?"

Revell shrugged. She looked pretty harmless, but every one of the paper's journalists was wary of Duffield's infamously sharp tongue, even sharper mind, and ruthless nature. As a young reporter, she had garnered a reputation for being prepared to do anything in pursuit of a story, and now she expected her news gathering team to show the same level of dedication.

"I'm calm. Don't worry," Revell said. "I'm just curious why we're here, why we've had to sneak out of the newsroom for this meeting."

Duffield raised a hand to her forehead and smoothed it over her hair until she reached the base of her ponytail. Revell wondered whether it had been scraped back so tightly because someone had told her it worked like a nonsurgical face-lift.

"I've brought you here because I want to congratulate you on the Gem Golding story. It's a great read. To be honest, I can't remember when we had a better one. We've had a fantastic response from readers, especially online."

Revell raised his eyebrows a fraction. This was the last thing he'd expected. He'd been pleased with the interview, and a few of his colleagues had even made the effort to mutter their appreciation as they passed his desk, but Duffield didn't do praise. Usually, if you avoided being summoned to her desk and accused of writing like an amateur, then you could pat yourself on the back and assume you'd done a decent job.

"Oh right. That's good," he said, shifting in his seat. "Thanks for that. Nice of you to say so."

Duffield smiled. That surprised Revell even more than the praise. He'd never seen so many of her teeth. They were small, white, and pointed.

"You're not very good at accepting compliments, are you?" she said.

"I think the problem is I'm out of practice."

Duffield twisted in her seat and looked out the window. Revell did the same. The spring sky was the color of faded denim. Below, the glinting Thames looped around the cityscape. While they admired the view, Revell was still trying to work out why the conversation needed to take place in private. Perhaps Duffield didn't want people to know that she was capable of handing out plaudits? She had a reputation to protect.

The silence stretched, and Revell assumed the meeting was over. He slid his chair back and rose to his feet. Without turning, Duffield pointed a manicured fingernail at him. "Sit," she said.

Revell thought about barking, sticking his tongue out, and panting but decided against it. Instead, he sat and waited.

Duffield faced him. "Surely you don't think I summoned you here simply to tell you what a good boy you've been?"

Revell widened his eyes, feigning surprise. "Let me guess. I'm getting a pay raise? No? Maybe a promotion? Or both?"

Duffield didn't even blink. "I want you to follow up the Gem Golding story. The public can't get enough of it. We sold an extra thirty thousand copies of the paper and have a record number of hits online."

Revell had thought long and hard about a follow-up, of course, but he'd reached the conclusion that he'd squeezed every last drop out of the story. "I wish I could come up with something, but it's run out of steam. The police investigation isn't going anywhere. Until they identify the attacker, there's nothing new for us."

Duffield smiled again.

Shit, Revell thought. *That's twice in two years, and both of them have come in the last ten minutes.*

"What if we set the agenda on this story? Imagine if the *Daily News* beats the police to it. We track down the attacker and reveal his identity. That would be the scoop of the year, wouldn't it? A sure-fire award winner."

Revell leaned forward, rested his elbows on the table, and sniffed the air, searching for a whiff of alcohol on her breath. The news editor had a stool permanently reserved at the nearest bar and without fail would be sipping from a large glass of white wine within minutes of the first edition going to press, but he'd never known her to drink this early in the day.

"That sounds great," he said. "But I've told you I'm in the same situation as the police. That *Warrior for Women* angle was fantastic for us, but the story has hit a dead end."

Duffield shook her head, and Revell could tell she was fighting back the urge to smile for a third time. "Far from it," she said. "This is confidential information, and you are not to discuss it with anyone but me. We've had a call from someone who claims to know the name and address of the man who attacked Gem Golding."

Revell's jaw dropped. "You're kidding me? You think this caller is genuine?"

"I've spoken to him, and I think there's a chance that he's telling the truth. He claims he knows the man well and recognized him from the e-fit the police put out."

"Who is he? Is he in London? Why hasn't he gone to the police with this?"

Duffield held up a hand. "Calm down," she said. "Sit back and listen and I'll explain."

Revell took a deep breath and nodded. His heart was racing. If this was true, he wanted the story. He wanted it badly.

"We don't have the caller's name yet, but we have his cell phone number. He wants money for the information. I've told him we will pay him, but not the ten thousand pounds he's demanding. He claims he deserves danger money because the suspect is, in his words, 'a real evil bastard' who wouldn't hesitate to cut his tongue out if he discovered he was being sold out."

Revell nodded, his mind working overtime, trying to figure out where the operation could go wrong. If he could pull this off, it would make his name. He'd be able to demand a promotion and a pay raise, and if the *Daily News* didn't make it worthwhile for him to stay, he'd have his pick of the paper's rivals, maybe even a move into television news.

"As you did such a good job on the initial story, I want you on this one, but like I said before, I don't want anyone else knowing. That includes our colleagues. The last thing I want is for this to be leaked."

"Where do we stand legally? Shouldn't we be telling the police all about this call? We definitely should give them the cell number, shouldn't we? They'll be able to track him down."

Duffield shook her head. "Come on now. You're not going soft on me, I hope. Don't make me reconsider picking you for the job. When we have all the facts, including the identity of the suspect, they will be presented to the police. Fortunately for us, that will happen just before we go to press to reveal how we tracked down the man who attacked the avenging angel and handed him on a plate to the police."

Revell unbuttoned his shirt collar and loosened his tie. "What happens next?"

"You set up a meeting with the contact and do what you're good at. Keep him sweet and get him talking. Are you in?"

"Shit yes I'm in."

18
SURRENDER

THE BOYFRIEND

Drew Bentley strode briskly across Spital Square. To his left, a gap in the skyline gave him a partial view of the bulbous Gherkin tower. His morning commute always started with the fifteen-minute walk from home to Liverpool Street station, as long as it wasn't raining.

He crossed the road, dodging through the rush-hour traffic, and walked along Primrose Street. Up ahead, the distinctive crisscross steel beams of the Broadgate Tower glinted in the weak sunlight.

The energy on the streets of London always gave him a buzz, setting him up for another day advising disgruntled executives how best to screw as much money as possible out of their former employers.

Drew's thoughts wandered back to breakfast. He'd bitten his tongue and kept his thoughts about Gem's new look to himself. What the hell was that "new hair, new woman" crap all about anyway? Still, he was confident that if he was subtle about it, he'd eventually get her to see sense.

She had been excited and more than a little nervous about returning to work. He'd offered her words of encouragement, and she'd been grateful to receive them. He thought it wise not to tell her he'd been hoping that after the attack, she'd come around to his way of thinking, ditch the job, and think about having a baby.

Drew had always disliked her working unsocial hours. In fact, he wasn't convinced that *work* was the right word to describe a never-ending round of parties marking the launch of new products.

He stepped on the escalator and descended into Liverpool Street station. The concourse teemed with commuters, the murmur of voices growing louder like the hum of a swarm of angry bees. At the bottom, he headed straight for the Underground station. Three uniformed police officers, two men and one woman, all wearing stab vests, stood near the entrance.

As Drew approached, he caught the eye of a man leaning casually against a ticket machine, paused, and did a double take. The man looked straight at him, eyes like slits beneath a baseball cap. Behind the dark beard lurked something familiar, something unsettling. Drew moved on, feeling the weight of the man's stare on his back. He hurried to the electronic gate, swiped his transit card, and walked through with a furtive glance over his shoulder.

As always, at that time in the morning, commuters crowded onto the westbound Central line platform, shuffling their way to the front to await the next train. Drew shuffled forward in the crush of warm bodies.

A deep rumbling signaled the approach of a train, and the people at the front moved a fraction closer to the edge of the platform. The train rattled out of the tunnel and ground to a halt. The carriages were already crammed with passengers, but when the doors slid open, the front row of commuters expertly squeezed themselves in.

The train departed, and Drew found enough space to step up to the front. More bodies pushed in behind him, shoving him past the yellow safety zone and uncomfortably close to the platform's edge.

A distant vibration prompted him to peer into the mouth of the tunnel, but there was no sign of headlights in the blackness. The bodies behind Drew swayed forward, forcing him to brace his legs and steady himself.

He turned his head, straining to see the cause of the swaying. The bearded man with the baseball cap he'd seen outside the station entrance was elbowing his way through the crowd toward him. The man stopped two rows behind Drew and bared his teeth in something resembling a smile. Drew looked into his eyes, and his legs turned to jelly.

A train emerged from the tunnel, and Drew twisted his torso in a desperate attempt to back away from the edge, but the line of commuters behind him stood their ground, making it impossible for him to move.

He watched the juddering lights of the driver's cab hurtling along the platform toward him. Beads of sweat ran down his face, and his heart jackhammered in time with the rattle of the train. As he opened his mouth to shout for help, the bodies directly behind him surged forward, and the knuckles of a clenched fist pressed the small of his back. The movement was swift and subtle, the impact just enough to shift his weight.

The screech of steel wheels braking on steel rails drowned out his scream as he fell forward, arms flailing.

THE DETECTIVE

Day had given up eating breakfast at home. He'd discovered that sitting at his kitchen table, staring at empty chairs, was a great appetite suppressor. It wasn't just the fact that Tom and Amy weren't there to laugh at his jokes or affectionately mock his attempts at creating the perfect poached egg. He'd never had a problem being alone, but being lonely in your own home was a different thing altogether. A strange, disturbing feeling, he didn't like it at all. It felt dangerous.

The smell of grease hit Day the moment he walked through the doors of the police canteen. The place echoed with the clang of cheap cutlery and the boisterous chatter of a group of uniformed officers sitting at two tables in the center of the room.

He resisted the fried breakfast option, ordering poached haddock with baked beans on toast, along with a coffee to wash it down. He carried the tray to an unoccupied table next to the canteen's only window, sat down, and tucked in.

The Golding case was going nowhere fast. The newspapers were already bored with the story and didn't appear to be interested in helping generate fresh leads. Apparently, an attack in which a woman was threatened and injured and her car stolen wasn't considered "sexy" enough to warrant more than token coverage.

Day took a sip of coffee and made a face. It smelled great but tasted like donkey piss. One more day, then he'd have to pull his officers off the carjacking. They had a backlog of muggings, stabbings, and sexual assaults to keep them busy.

Picking up his drink again, he lifted it to his lips before remembering how bad it had tasted and put it down. He was considering a trip to the nearest decent coffee shop when he spotted Shields heading for his table like a woman on a mission.

Watching her approach, he realized, for the first time, how she moved like an athlete, her stride balanced and rhythmic. As she neared Day's table, she almost broke into a run.

He raised a hand. "Hey, Cat," he said with a half smile. "Can't a man finish his breakfast in peace?"

Shields rested her hands on the back of the chair opposite her boss, and he could hear her breathing hard. "I thought you'd want to know as soon as possible," she said.

Day pushed his plate away, curious now. "Know what?"

"It's Drew Bentley."

Day paused to let the name register. "Gem Golding's boyfriend? The lawyer?"

Shields nodded.

"Come on then. Tell me. What about him?"

"He's dead. Jumped in front of a Tube train this morning apparently."

Day slid his chair back, stood up, and started walking toward the door. Shields followed. Leaving the canteen, they turned left, heading for Day's office. "It's being reported as suicide, you say?"

Shields lengthened her stride to keep up with her boss. "Seems so. By all accounts, he turned to look the train driver in the eye before diving onto the track."

Day stopped outside his office door, turning to face Shields. "Has Gem Golding been informed?"

"We've got people there right now," Shields said.

Day didn't usually get excited about suicides. Normally, a detective would be assigned to establish the facts and then pass the evidence to the coroner. That wasn't going to happen here, no way. There had to be a link between the carjacking and Bentley's death. Day didn't believe in coincidences.

"I want all witnesses to the incidence questioned and detailed statements from them about what they saw, including the driver of the train."

Shields nodded. "I'll get someone on it right away."

Day's mind raced. "I also want copies of all the CCTV footage of the platform where it happened and Bentley's route to that plat-form, and I want it quickly."

"I'm on it," Shields said as she headed for the Golding incident room. She'd taken a few steps when Day called out to her.

"We're also going to need to talk to Gem Golding," he said. "I know we've got to be sensitive about this and that she's going to need some time, but I don't want to wait more than a day or two at the most."

19

FIGHT

THE MASTERMIND

Con Norton sat at his favorite table in his favorite café and sipped his mug of tea. Cath's Cafe, in Stratford, served the biggest, best, and cheapest all-day cooked breakfast in east London, but he wasn't there to fill his belly.

He looked down at the copy of the *Daily News* spread out on the table in front of him. He'd read the article so many times, he could recite it from memory. *Warrior for Women, Coward, Pervert.* The words jumped out at him, each one stinging like a slap in the face.

A cold rage filled his chest. He welcomed its power like an old friend and smiled. Lifting a hand, he rubbed at his beard. It needed a trim. Instead of being a barrier to hide behind, it was starting to attract attention.

He read the interview with Gem Golding again. Slowly this time, taking in every word, every nuance. True, he hated everything the woman said, how the reporter chose phrases designed to humiliate, but at the same time, the media interest stirred something deep inside him.

They were writing about *him* in the newspapers, talking about *him* on the television. For once, the world was taking notice of *him*. It felt good. He'd always known that his time would come. At last, he'd rippled the pond, and he had no intention of stopping now. He wanted to turn those ripples into waves. *Someone needs to teach that woman that she'd be better off if she keeps her mouth shut*, he thought. She'd gotten lucky, that's all. If she had any sense, she'd thank God, the devil, and the universe that she survived, show some humility, and keep her accusations to herself.

The reporter would have encouraged her to twist the truth, Norton knew, but she should have refused. She was a deceiver, dissembler, faker, pretender. Her lies rattled around in his head. The things she had said about him could never be forgotten, would never be forgiven. What a liar, a shameless liar, that woman had turned out to be.

Norton switched his attention to the reports spread across pages four and five of the newspaper. He had to admit that the headline had a certain ring to it. *Stand Up and Fight, or Surrender to Survive?*

Beside the byline, at the top of the lead story, was a headshot of the reporter. He had a youthful, smug face. The sort of face Norton truly believed deserved to be punched on sight. *This Matt Revell thinks he's smart*, he thought, *but he's missing the point completely. Victims are born, not made. They're destined to become fodder for predators.*

Norton's eyes flicked back to the main headline, darting from the word *Fight* to *Surrender* and back again. *Fight…Surrender… Fight…Surrender…Fight…Surrender.*

His upper lip developed a twitch that turned into a smirk. The smirk quickly became a smile. *If only they knew*, he thought. *Do they know? Of course not. They couldn't possibly.* The truth was simple. He was setting the agenda. He led the way and even the media followed blindly. *It's undeniable*, he thought. *I am in control.*

The newspaper coverage would probably achieve what it was designed to do: spark off a debate and attract hundreds if not thousands of readers to the paper's website, where they would be asked to take part in a totally pointless vote on how victims should react when threatened with violence.

Norton read the *Fight or Surrender* headline one more time. The power of the words made him smile. Sometimes plain crazy equaled sheer genius.

He loved playing games. Especially those he was destined to win.

20
SURRENDER

THE DETECTIVE

The Fighting Dogs pub wasn't a police haunt. That's why Day liked it. He could enjoy an end of shift pint in relative peace. In his experience, most off-duty detectives didn't believe in moderation when it came to beer. Things got rowdy. Quickly.

He bought himself a pint and sat in one of the three unoccupied high-backed booths set against the wall opposite the bar. The pub oozed character, elegantly decked out with chandeliers and book-cases and what appeared to be genuine Victorian mahogany wall paneling. Day counted five other customers, all men drinking on their own. It was early, and he knew the place would liven up as the night wore on.

Shields had accepted his suggestion that they meet up, with a warning that she had a pile of paperwork to sort out first. Day took a sip of beer and began thinking through the Bentley case. The guy had been a successful employment lawyer, a high earner living in a big house with his girlfriend. Why on earth would he dive under a Tube train? It didn't add up.

He'd been in good health, with no history of mental health issues. Maybe it was only a matter of time before they uncovered a good reason someone like Bentley might decide to off himself. Secret gambling debts? An affair gone wrong? Day thought it possible but highly unlikely.

Officially, the death was still being treated as either suicide or an accident, and Day was happy to keep it that way. For now. The last thing he wanted was to have to hand the case to the murder investigation team. He was more than qualified to deal with it.

Bentley's mangled body had been scraped off the track two weeks after his wife had been viciously assaulted by a carjacker. Day's gut instinct told him there had to be a connection. He didn't believe in good luck or bad luck. No, in his opinion, it was simpler than that. He believed in good people and bad people.

If asked to take a guess, he'd say Gem Golding was probably a good person. He didn't know her well enough to be sure, but he'd no reason to think otherwise. Bad people were his specialty. Bentley had been harder to read, and Day would withhold judgment on the lawyer's character until the investigation into his death was complete.

He wasn't looking forward to interviewing Golding tomorrow. Over the years, he'd knocked on the doors of dozens of people who'd lost loved ones in the worst of circumstances. If you stuck with the job long enough, you got used to dealing with grief.

Everybody had their own way of handling the negative emotions surrounding violence and murder. Day had no idea how other detectives did it, and he didn't want to know. He guessed that some eventually developed an immunity to tragedy and suffering, a hardening of the heart that enabled them to shrug it off.

For him, it was different. It was all still there, inside his head, hidden away in a little mental filing cabinet. As long as he kept the drawer shut and locked, then everything would be fine.

Day took a gulp of his pint. It tasted good, so he took a bigger one. He put the glass back on the table and pushed it away. *Better slow down,* he told himself. This was meant to be an after-work drink and get-to-know-you-better chat with a new colleague, not a drinking spree with an old mate.

He needed to keep a clear head. His team was no nearer to getting a breakthrough on the Golding case. The suspect had abandoned a valuable vehicle and set it alight. That didn't add up. If the only point of the carjacking was to terrorize a lone woman, then he was an impulsive, twisted predator who needed to be locked up. Day had a feeling that the case would turn out to be more complicated than that. On the security camera footage, the suspect appeared confident and calculating rather than impulsive. That was worrying.

People like that rarely emerged fully formed from a law-abiding existence into a life of crime. They didn't suddenly turn bad. They were rotten to the core. If they could identify the suspect, he'd probably turn up on the national police databases as a past offender.

Day knew from experience that the alternative was worse. If the man they were hunting had never been caught before, it would suggest he was intelligent, a meticulous planner. That would make him more difficult to find and extremely dangerous to know.

His cell phone rang, the birdlike trilling drawing disapproving glances from drinkers seated at the bar. Day checked the caller ID, his heart sinking when he saw the name. He'd been looking forward to a bit of female company before having to face going home. He liked Shields. She was a straight talker and had even started to crack the odd smile at his jokes. In fact, she was the only detective at the station who understood that they were jokes.

"Don't tell me," he said. "You're standing me up. You'd rather shuffle bits of paper around your desk."

"It's not that, Boss. Something has come up. You're needed back here right now."

Day jumped to his feet and headed for the door, his phone still clamped to his ear. The tone of his sergeant's voice had set alarm bells ringing. "What is it? What's happened?"

"It's the CCTV footage from Liverpool Street Tube station. The Bentley accident."

Day stepped out onto the street. He had an idea where the conversation was going, but he didn't want to jump the gun.

"Don't keep me in suspense," Day said, dodging smartly to his left to avoid a collision with a rotund woman carrying bags of food shopping. "What are we looking at?"

Shields didn't answer immediately, causing Day to check his phone's screen to see if they'd been cut off. "Well, that's not exactly clear," she said. "But there is definitely something going on. Something weird."

Day arrived back at the station to find Shields at her desk, her eyes firmly fixed on her computer screen.

Seeing Day approach, she stood and gestured impatiently for him to take her seat. "I've been going through footage from the London Underground CCTV center and have come up with some interesting images."

Day looked up at his detective sergeant. "Come on then. Get on with it. Let's have a look at what you've got."

Shields leaned across the desk and clicked on the editing menu along the bottom. Day found himself looking at a crowd of commuters crammed together like sardines in a tin. The camera angle showed clearly that the front row of commuters had shuffled past the yellow safety line until they were standing right on the edge of the platform.

Shields clicked again and jabbed a finger at the screen.

"That's Bentley right there. Can you see?"

"There's nothing wrong with my eyesight," Day said. "If you can see him, I can see him. Now, what am I looking for?"

"Just keep watching and you'll see."

The footage started running again. The crowd on the platform swayed forward, and panic flashed across the faces of most of those teetering on the edge of the platform, including Bentley. They seemed to steady themselves for a second before the crowd surged again.

It appeared to Day that all the people standing at the front were in danger of toppling onto the track. He glanced up at Shields. "That looks pretty unsafe. Are we looking at an accident here?"

"Keep watching, Boss. There's more to come."

Day turned back to the screen in time to see Bentley twist his head and look back over the crowd. His eyes widened, and his body stiffened. He seemed to be struggling to turn and move away from the edge of the platform, but the pressure from the bodies behind made it impossible for him to move.

Day could see the lights of the train shuddering at speed along the track. At the last minute, Bentley stopped trying to turn back, appeared to look directly into the cab of the train, and plunged forward.

Day looked at Shields, then back at the screen. He wasn't sure what he'd seen, but his sergeant had been right. Something was off.

"Run that clip again, would you?" he said. When it reached the point where Bentley turned to look back, he told Shields to pause the footage and leaned closer to study the expression on his face.

"He looks scared. Really terrified. It's a shame we're not able to see what he's seeing."

Shields touched Day lightly on the shoulder, and he could feel her excitement. "Keep watching," she said. "There's more."

The scene on the screen was replaced by footage from a camera looking down on the platform. The angle meant no faces could

be seen, just the top of hundreds of heads. Day easily picked out
Bentley as he strained to look back. A figure wearing what looked
like a dark baseball cap appeared to be pushing his way quickly
through the crowd, heading toward Bentley. Day realized that was
the explanation for the swaying. The figure stopped behind Bentley.
A few seconds later, the man in the cap clearly lunged forward and
Bentley plunged to his death.

"What do you reckon then, Boss?" Shields said.

Day frowned. "You can't see an arm reaching out to Bentley.
There's no clear contact, but it looks like a push to me. The shape
of Bentley's body as he falls and his flailing arms suggest that too. It
certainly appears as if Bentley recognizes the person moving through
the crowd toward him. More than that, he seems frightened by
what he's seeing. Maybe it's just that the crowd is unsteady and he's
scared of falling off the platform."

Shields shook her head. "I don't think that someone who was
planning to kill themselves by diving in front of a train would be
worried about falling off the platform in front of a train."

Day paused to think about what he'd just seen. To him, Bentley's
death looked extremely suspicious. This was no suicide.

"There is one more bit of footage I want to show you," Shields
said.

The excitement in her voice told Day this was going to be good.
He looked back at the screen at a side view of passengers standing
on an escalator taking them up to the station's exit gates.

Shields pointed at a tall figure in a black cap. He had a dark beard
and wore a brown leather jacket. "We're pretty sure this is our
man," she said. "The man who seemed to terrify Bentley and who
was standing behind him before he fell in front of the train."

Day moved closer to the screen to get a good look at the man's
profile. *Is there a chance this is the man who attacked Gem Golding?* he

wondered. The images from the parking lot security camera were fuzzy, and the heavy beard disguised the jawline, but there was something familiar about the man's posture.

Shields touched Day's shoulder again. "This footage was taken two minutes after Bentley supposedly jumped. The escalator is taking people out of Liverpool Street Tube station. He hasn't wasted any time getting out. He was very close to Bentley when he toppled onto the track, but he didn't wait around to tell anybody what he saw."

Day stood up and headed out of the incident room. "Thanks, Cat. Excellent work," he said over his shoulder.

Shields followed him into his office. She took a seat while Day stood with his back to her, staring out the window into the darkness of the parking lot.

Shields let the silence stretch before speaking. "Maybe we should think about handing this case to the murder investigation team, Boss."

Day didn't answer. He took a deep breath, rested his hands on the windowsill, and dropped his chin to his chest.

"It's looking more and more likely that Bentley's death was not suicide or a tragic accident," Shields said. "By rights, we should release the files and pass them on to your old squad."

Day lifted his head and turned to face her. He knew she was right. He also knew that sometimes, doing the right thing wasn't always the best thing.

"I'd like a bit more time to take a closer look at the Bentley case. If it's linked to the attack on Gem Golding, and I'm pretty sure it is, then we're entitled to investigate it, aren't we?"

Shields tilted her head and raised an eyebrow. "I think that's stretching it a bit, Boss. I know you want to work your way back onto the murder investigation team, but breaking the rules isn't the way to do it."

Day gave Shields a half smile. He hadn't known her long, but he also knew he could trust her not to go telling tales behind his back. With some people, you just knew. She was talking sense, but catching killers, seeing a victim's family find some solace in the fact that justice had been done, was an addiction, an addiction that had cost Day his marriage.

"Back me up on this one. Let's see what we come up with in the next few days, and I'll let you call me Elliot instead of Boss."

Shields kept a straight face, but Day detected a hint of a smile around her eyes. "I suppose, like you say, because of the connection to the Gem Golding inquiry, we could justify it if we really had to."

Day nodded. He had judged her right. In addition to being as smart as a whip, she wasn't afraid to take a risk.

Shields stood to leave. When she reached the door, she hesitated. "There is one thing that's been bothering me about the CCTV footage we've just seen."

"Go on then. Tell me."

"The man in the cap. If he did kill Bentley, if he deliberately pushed him off the platform, he would have known he would be caught on London Underground's CCTV system. Apart from wearing the baseball cap, he didn't seem to care about being seen. Unless it was a spur-of-the-moment thing, he could have chosen somewhere less visible to kill Bentley. That strikes me as stupid."

Day had thought the same thing, but he'd come to a different conclusion. This man wasn't stupid. Far from it. Some people kill because they don't possess the intelligence to solve their problem in a different way. They strike out in a blind rage, unable to consider the consequences. Others, the rare ones, kill because they can and because they enjoy it.

"To be honest, I don't think this person cares whether he was caught on camera," he said. "He probably believes he's too clever to ever be caught by the likes of us. You saw yourself that in the crush of bodies on the platform, it was impossible to see any contact between the suspect and the victim. It would have needed only the slightest nudge to send him over the edge. I think the suspect chose this method of murder because he wanted to be seen on CCTV. It's calculating. He's taunting us. He thinks he's untouchable."

21
FIGHT

THE MASTERMIND

Norton rubbed his chin, the skin dry and itchy. He hadn't slept well. The Golding interview had been on his mind. Was she deliberately trying to provoke him? He'd even considered that the police had put her up to it, encouraged her to try to enrage him, make him careless. Eventually, he'd dozed off at about 4:00 a.m., after he'd planned exactly how he was going to make her pay for what she'd done.

The silent telephone calls would stop. They were starting to bore him. He had another, much bigger game to play. Fight or surrender. Live or die. That woman had no idea what was coming her way. By spouting her lies to the papers, she had chosen to goad him, challenge him. That was an unwise thing to do. Her fate was sealed anyway, but the level of pain inflicted was up to him.

Heading west along the southern perimeter of Victoria Park, Norton stepped to the side as a couple of cyclists sped past. The place was already filling up with east Londoners eager to make the most of the spring sunshine. Norton preferred the park in the winter. In his opinion, the trees were at their most beautiful stripped of leaves, grabbing at the clouds like giant, twisted skeletal claws.

He pulled out his phone and checked the time. He'd probably hang on to the prepaid burner for another week or two at the most before getting rid of it and buying a new one. You could never be too careful. He tapped the top of his right thigh, checking that the thick roll of notes was still safely in his pocket. He had enough cash to comfortably see him through the next few months, as long as he could avoid coughing up rent to his weasel-faced landlord. It galled him that he'd only been paid half of what had been agreed for the carjacking. When you lived by your wits, you couldn't allow anyone to rip you off.

Show weakness and you're done for. That was a lesson he'd learned very early in life. His parents had been weak. They'd lived in a haze of alcohol and drugs because they didn't have the strength to cope with life in the stinking tower block hovel they had called home.

He was uncontrollable, they told the social worker, so violent toward his younger sister, they were scared what he might do. He knew the truth. Getting rid of him meant there'd be one less mouth to feed. They gave him up officially three days after his sixth birthday, and although he'd screamed and flailed his arms in rage, later, when he'd been crying himself to sleep in a strange bed, he'd been glad. He hated them, hated their weakness, their disgusting lack of control.

22

SURRENDER

GEM THE VICTIM

Gem Golding sat curled up on a white leather armchair wrapped in the fluffy blue dressing gown Drew had bought her for her birthday. She gripped a half-full mug of tea tightly in both hands, the bottom edge of the plaster cast on her broken wrist poking out of her right sleeve. The tea had gone cold a long time ago.

In the hallway, she could hear her mother speaking in hushed tones, explaining to the detectives that she'd traveled up from Wales by train as soon as she'd heard what had happened.

Day entered the room first, followed by Shields and then Gem's mother. Both detectives nodded sympathetically as they sat side by side on the sofa.

Gem's brain had started toying with her from the moment they'd telephoned to say they were on their way. Maybe they were coming to tell her that there had been a mistake, that Drew wasn't dead after all, that it had all been a terrible case of mistaken identity. Their eyes told her what she already knew. There had been no mistake.

Day cleared his throat and broke the awkward silence. "We are very sorry for your loss. We understand this is a difficult time for you."

Gem's mother, a tall, stylishly dressed woman, walked across the room and into the kitchen, announcing over her shoulder that she was going to put the kettle on and make them tea. *That's a good idea*, Gem told herself. *That'll solve everything, won't it? Why didn't I think of that?*

"We appreciate you agreeing to talk to us now," Day said. "We'll try to be as quick as possible."

Gem lifted her chin, opened her mouth to speak, but gave a slight nod instead.

Shields put her hands on her knees and leaned forward. "I know this is difficult for you, but is it all right if we ask you a few questions about Drew?"

Gem's red-rimmed eyes flicked from one detective to the other as if searching for an answer. Did they really believe that Drew had deliberately dived in front of the train? That was crazy. There was no reason on earth he'd want to want his life.

"Drew didn't kill himself. You know that, don't you?"

Day and Shields exchanged glances. "That's what we're trying to establish," Shields said. "We've been told by witnesses, including the train driver, that he jumped off the platform, but in a crowded situation like that, it's difficult for anyone to know what really happened."

Gem shook her head. "What reason would he have to take his own life? I don't care what your witnesses say. They've got it wrong. He wouldn't do that, to himself or to me. I know he wouldn't."

At that moment, her mother returned carrying mugs of tea and a plate of chocolate cookies on a tray. She placed the tray on the coffee table. "Help yourself to cookies, officers."

The detectives shook their heads in unison. "We're fine, thanks," Shields said.

Jan Golding stepped closer to her daughter, leaned over, and gently pried the empty mug from her fingers before going back into the kitchen.

"If you don't feel up to this right now, then maybe we could leave it a little longer," Day said.

Gem said nothing. She stared down at the space between her hands where the mug had been.

"Was Drew worried about anything?" Day asked. "Can you think of anything at all? Even something small."

Gem took a moment to think before nodding to herself. "He was worried about me. About what had happened to me. I think he was worried about how the attack would affect me in the long term. That's not a reason for someone to kill themselves, is it? It's more of a reason to stick around and look after the person you're concerned about."

Day gave Shields a sideways glance, and she took her cue. "Drew had no financial concerns? No problems at work?"

Gem shook her head. "He was so ambitious, and it was all going so well. He'd overcome so many difficulties to become a lawyer, and his career was taking off and he deserved it."

"What about your relationship, then? Had everything been going well? Sometimes becoming the victim of a crime can cause difficulties for a couple."

Gem sniffed, pulled a crumpled tissue from the pocket of her dressing gown, and buried her face in it. She waited for tears to come, but they didn't. She wondered if emotional numbness was her mind's way of protecting itself.

"Drew didn't kill himself. There is nothing you can say that will make me believe that. We are very…were very different characters. He was a quiet, thoughtful man, but we were happy. He talked a lot about our future together, about me having a baby and giving up work."

Day picked up his mug of tea and took a sip. "What about you? How did you feel about starting a family?"

Gem turned to Shields. Maybe she'd understand. "We were good together. Every couple has things they need to work on, don't they? He was happy. We both were."

Shields nodded. "We won't keep you much longer," she said. "But do you think you are up to looking at an image taken from CCTV footage filmed at the station where Drew died?"

Gem shrank back into the armchair. "No. I don't think I want to see. Don't make me look."

Shields stood up, walked over to the armchair, and knelt on the carpet facing Gem. "It's not Drew falling off the platform or anything like that. I promise. It's a still showing a side view of a man on an escalator."

"What man? Who is he?"

"We don't know who he is, but we'd like you to take a look and tell us if there's anything familiar about him. Do you think you could do that for us?" Shields pulled the printout from her jacket pocket and handed it over.

Gem cupped it in both her hands and took a long look. At first, she said nothing. She stared motionless at the image, her eyes unblinking, her face an alabaster mask.

A beard hid the man's jaw, but she scanned the sharp slant of his cheekbone, straight nose, and angle of his shoulders. Recognition hit her like a punch in the gut. First, her hands started shaking, then her whole body. Her breathing became raspy and rapid. "Him," she said. "It was him, wasn't it? He killed Drew, didn't he?"

23
FIGHT

GEM THE WARRIOR

Gem dropped her gym kit in the hallway, closed and double-locked the front door. Her shoulders and arms ached. Tuesday was an upper body day. Tomorrow, she'd focus on squats and leg presses.

In the kitchen, she made herself a coffee, sat down, and powered up her laptop. Most of the new emails in her inbox were from clients asking how she was and congratulating her on the *Daily News* coverage of her brush with crime.

She clicked on the top message. It had been sent by the owner of a new wine bar who'd hired Gem's company to arrange and publicize its opening night. She'd been working on the event for weeks. Cradling her head in her hands, she skimmed the text. *Hi, Gem. Can't believe what you've been up to. What an amazing story. You are incredible. I knew you were a feisty lady, but wow. What an example to us all. We women don't have to take this shit anymore. Can't wait to see you at the launch. Mia.*

Gem closed the email, moved to open another, but decided she couldn't face it. She switched the laptop off, picked up her coffee, and took a sip. This reaction to what had happened was one of the reasons she didn't feel ready to go back to work. No one knew what she was going through. Not even Drew. The thought of all the backslapping and the prospect of having to repeat the events of that night over and over again like a dinner party anecdote made her feel physically sick.

She'd done the newspaper interview because she'd believed it would help her process what had happened and make other women think carefully about what they would do if they found themselves in the same situation. She'd wanted to do something positive.

Now, she was starting to think Drew might have been right about keeping things low-key. People were treating her like some kind of superhero, the leader of a campaign against male-on-female violence. She didn't feel heroic. Far from it.

She didn't like leaving the house unless it was to go to the gym, and the sound of the home telephone ringing filled her with dread. When she'd told Drew about the silent telephone calls, he'd laughed them off. Most call centers used automated calling systems, he'd explained, and often, they'd cut off. It was, he'd assured her, a common glitch.

He'd wanted to put her mind at rest over the calls, and she didn't want him to think she was cracking up. So she'd smiled, feigned an expression of thankful relief, and hugged him, but she knew the truth.

She stood up, refilled her cup with coffee, and took another sip. Drew had been amazing since the attack. His patience had surprised her. Their relationship had been showing signs of strain, but now they were growing closer than ever.

Sighing, she picked up her coffee. As the rim of the cup touched her lips, her cell phone rang. The sound made her start, and a drop of the hot, brown liquid spilled down her sports vest. She flicked a finger over the stain and shook her head. Why the hell was she so jumpy? She picked up her phone off the kitchen table and checked the screen. It was her boss.

"Hi there, Melanie," she said, doing her best to sound upbeat.

"Hi there. How are you doing, honey?"

Gem hesitated. She knew what was coming and didn't feel ready to deal with it.

"I'm good, I suppose," she said. "I'm fine, thanks." She didn't expect her boss to detect the reluctance in her voice. Melanie usually only heard what she wanted to hear.

"Okay, that's great, really great, because I was wondering when you were thinking of coming back to the office. Soon hopefully. All our clients have been asking about you. The media coverage has been fantastic. We all think you're amazing, Gem. So brave. What you did, it's incredible. I don't think I could have done it. In fact, I'm pretty sure I couldn't. Haven't got the balls."

It wasn't bravery, Gem wanted to shout. It was desperation, an instinctive reaction. If she'd chosen not to resist her attacker because her gut instinct told her that was the best thing to do, would that have been wrong, cowardly? Of course not. What's the matter with everybody? Why don't they get it? She'd been terrified. She had thought she was going to die. She had made a split-second choice, and it had worked out for her. It could so easily have gone the other way. Nobody could imagine how that felt unless they had experienced it firsthand.

"The thing is, Melanie, I do feel I need a little more time off," she said. "Would you mind if I took another week or so, to get things together? I want to be able to focus on the job when I do go back. You understand, don't you? After everything that's happened, I still haven't quite got my head sorted out. Would that be okay?"

A sharp intake of breath at the end of the line gave Gem a strong clue as to her boss's true feelings about the request. The words that followed were spoken slowly and chosen carefully. "If you really think that you need more time, then take it, honey, but you know we are all dying to see you."

Gem imagined her boss shaking her head and gritting her perfectly whitened teeth. She was pretty sure that the main reason her colleagues and clients were asking when she'd be back was because they were itching for the chance to get a blow-by-blow account of the story. Simply thinking about their eager faces, their hunger for gossip, made it hard for her to breathe.

She wondered if all of them, including Melanie, would be so eager for her to come back to work if she hadn't fought off her attacker. How would they have judged her then? People want to believe that the world is fair, that you get what you deserve. Sometimes it's easier to blame the victim.

"That's wonderful," Gem said. "I really appreciate your understanding, and I'll definitely make it up to you when I'm back. Take you out to lunch. Treat you. I promise. So lucky I've got a boss like you. Thank you so much."

She ended the call before Melanie had a chance to change her mind and slammed the phone on the table. Sitting down, she wiped her sweaty palms on her gym leggings.

What the hell was happening to her? The Warrior for Women hiding indoors, too frightened to answer the telephone, too pathetic to go back to work. She'd always been scornful of people who let themselves be swept away by fear and self-doubt. She had to strike out, swim against the current, or drown.

She took a deep breath, pushed herself to her feet, and checked her watch. Drew wouldn't be back for a while, and she didn't feel like moping around at home all afternoon. Not anymore. Snatching her favorite hoodie from the banister post, she opened the front door and stepped outside.

The sky above Shoreditch was cloudless, but a strong breeze carried a memory of winter. Gem slipped on the hoodie and crossed the street. She and Drew were regular Sunday brunch customers at their local café, and the prospect of scrambled eggs and smoked salmon on toast made her mouth water. She had skipped breakfast because of a queasy stomach, not a good idea before going to the gym.

Smiling to herself, her chin held high, she headed briskly toward the northern end of the street. *Why is it taking me so long to shake off the trauma, pull myself together, and move on?* she wondered. She'd survived a vicious assault unscathed, she had a good career, and she had Drew. Life was good.

The streets in that part of the city were always hectic at lunchtime, and she found her way blocked by a group of students milling around outside a sandwich bar, engaged in a heated argument about the most effective cure for a hangover. As she stepped off the sidewalk to pass them, she glimpsed something out of the corner of her eye that made her stop dead.

She turned to take a longer look. The tall figure stood motionless outside a jewelry store on the other side of the street, about thirty yards away. The man's hands were tucked in his pockets as he peered intently at the items on display in the shop window.

He wore tight jeans, a short dark jacket, and a black baseball cap. Even though he had his back to her, the angle of his shoulders and the slight tilt of his head made her throat tighten. The man turned slowly until he was looking directly at her. The peak of the cap was pulled low, putting his face in shadow, but Gem could make out the slant of a lopsided smile.

Her heart drumming, she stepped back onto the sidewalk, pushed her way through the students, and ran.

THE DETECTIVE

Day pressed the doorbell, unsure of the warmth of the reception he'd get from his detective sergeant.

The rectangular security camera on the door flickered, and Day knew Shields was using her phone app to check the identity of an unexpected caller. He smoothed the front of his suit jacket and flashed her a toothy smile.

A moment later, the door opened. Shields wore a baggy blue sweater, a well-worn pair of jeans, and a puzzled expression.

"What the hell are you doing here, Boss?"

Day held up both hands, spreading his fingers wide. "This isn't a social call, don't worry. I'm not expecting to be wined and dined. I'm on my way to speak to Gem Golding. Thought you might want to come along."

Shields stepped back and invited Day in with a sweep of a hand. "You do know it's my day off?"

Day glanced around the apartment, taking in the bare walls and sparsity of furniture. "I do know that, but I thought if you get as bored as I do when I'm not hunting down some lowlife, then you might be interested in joining me. I could do with your help." He meant the last bit as a compliment and hoped Shields would take it that way. She knew he would have had his choice of the handful of detectives on duty.

She tilted her head and offered him a smile. "What's this all about? What's happened?"

"Golding has called in claiming that the man who attacked her has been harassing her. Stalking her. Making menacing telephone calls to her home and following her when she goes out."

"Shit," Shields said. "And she's certain that it's the same person?"

Day nodded. "She says she is. By all accounts, she's in a bad way. Says she's too terrified to pick up the phone or leave the house."

Day knew that didn't sound remotely like the woman who'd bitten her attacker's hand and taken him down by driving her car at him, but both detectives had been around long enough to know that coming face-to-face with a violent criminal, whatever the outcome, affected people in different ways.

"As you haven't kicked me out, can I assume you're coming with me?" Day asked.

"Give me five minutes to get changed."

"You look fine."

Shields glanced down at her faded jeans. "I can't wear these for work. I'll be a couple of minutes."

Day took a seat on the small leather sofa and took another look around the apartment. Rental agents would describe it as compact. With one bedroom off a single living room and an integral kitchen, he knew it was typical of the modern, low-level developments that had sprung up around the East End in recent years.

Shields emerged from the bedroom having swapped her jeans for a pair of dark-gray tailored trousers.

Day jumped to his feet. "Nice place," he said. "I take it you've not been moved in long?"

Shields smiled. "Only about fourteen months."

He scanned the apartment again. "There's not a lot of stuff in here for fourteen months."

Shields shrugged. "I detest clutter. It interferes with my thought processes."

Day nodded in the direction of the small television standing on the kitchen counter. "That's not even plugged in."

Shields walked to the door and pulled it open. "The only thing I hate more than clutter is daytime TV."

Day brought Shields up to speed as he drove. She listened attentively as he ran through the details of Golding's panicked telephone call, but she said little. He knew her well enough already to understand that she wouldn't comment until she had something useful to say. He wished he had more detectives who worked that way.

Golding had been praised in the media for fighting off her attacker, and no one could ever know what would have happened if she had chosen to be passive. *That's why it's not a black-and-white issue*, Day thought. It was never a case of fighting back is right and submitting is wrong. The *Daily News* had been right about the inconsistency of advice on what to do if you are attacked. If you can run away, then run. If the attacker wants your property, hand it over straightaway. After that, it gets complex.

Day had taken dozens of statements from victims of violence, and many who had the chance to run away didn't. They simply froze, a natural response to fear. It often happened in a flash and was beyond conscious control. No victim, male or female, should ever be blamed for freezing.

The drive from Mile End to Shoreditch was no more than three miles, but the traffic was heavy. Day glanced over at Shields, who appeared deep in thought as she stared out the passenger window as the bustling streets of east London slid by.

"What do you think, Cat?" he asked. "Was Golding right to fight back?"

Shields answered without hesitation. "Well, she came out of it unharmed, didn't she? Well, physically anyway. I'd like to think I'd do the same."

Day nodded. "Of course, but you're a special case. You're a detective. Trained to a high level in self-defense. For civilians, it's tricky."

He pulled up at a red light, and Shields waited until they were moving again before replying. "I agree, Boss. The only goal of anyone who finds themselves cornered by a violent attacker should be survival. If that means doing nothing, then you should do nothing. The problem is a victim would have to quickly assess the situation and the state of mind of the attacker to make an informed decision. How the hell can you expect an untrained woman or man to do that?"

Ten minutes later, Day pulled up outside the house. By the time they had climbed out of the car and walked up to the door, Golding was already waiting for them, her face pale and strained. She shut the door quickly, double-locked it, and ushered them into the large living room.

"Thank you for getting here so quickly," she said, sliding over to the window and peering out between the curtains. "He's definitely out there somewhere, you know. Waiting for his chance. I know it."

Day and Shields exchanged looks. This was a much less self-composed woman than the one they had interviewed after the carjacking. She wore gym leggings and sneakers, and her gray sports top was covered in sweat patches. The muscles around her shoulders and upper arms were thicker than Day remembered.

"Why don't you tell us exactly what happened?" he said.

Gem looked at Shields and then back at Day, her expression blank. "He was there, on the street, watching. I'm sure he must have been following me from the moment I left the house. When he realized I'd seen him, he didn't care at all. He stared across the road at me and smiled that scary smile of his."

Day took a step closer to the window. "I know you're still a bit shaken, but can you start at the beginning and tell us exactly where you saw him?"

Gem wrapped her arms around herself and hunched her shoulders. "I'd been to the gym and decided to go out for some brunch. I'd been spending too much time indoors, letting everything get to me, and wanted to start going out more. I was walking along Kingsland Road. About halfway up, I had to swerve off the sidewalk because a bunch of students were in the way. That's when I first spotted him. I couldn't believe what I was seeing. He just stood there, cool as you like."

The living room was uncomfortably warm and smelled of coffee. Day guessed that the central heating was probably still on its winter settings. He took his jacket off, draped it over the back of the sofa, and loosened the knot of his tie.

"Did he say anything to you, threaten you, do anything other than smile at you?"

Gem shot Shields a desperate look, a plea for help.

"Take your time," the detective sergeant said. "Why don't you sit down and try to relax. You've had a big shock."

Gem didn't answer. She paced restlessly across the room, passing between the two detectives, then back to the window. "He had a baseball cap on, with the peak pulled right down, but I knew who it was straightaway. The way he stood there, like he owned the street, like he owned the city. I'm certain it was the man who attacked me that night. I wish I could say it wasn't him, but it was."

Day didn't doubt that she believed what she was saying. As soon as they were back at the station, he'd get Detective Constable Bill Stock to check for CCTV footage in the area.

"What happened next?" he asked. "Did he approach you, try to speak to you?"

Gem shook her head and snorted. "What the hell do you think happened? I ran, didn't I? I ran and kept running until my heart felt like it was going to burst out of my chest. Then I made my way back here, avoiding Kingsland Road, of course, and telephoned the police."

Day crossed the room and nodded toward the armchair opposite the sofa. "DS Shields is right. I think you need to take a seat, try to calm yourself down."

Gem did as he suggested, dropping her head into her hands. "I'll calm down when that man has been arrested. Until then, I think calming down is out of the question."

"We understand that you've been getting menacing telephone calls as well," Shields said.

Gem looked up. Her eyes were dry, but the rims looked sore. "Every single day. Sometimes two or three times a day. He calls only after Drew has left for the office and never once he's home. That's how I know he must be watching the house. How else would he know?"

"What does the caller say? Does he threaten you?"

"The *caller* doesn't say anything," Gem said. "That's the whole point of silent calls, isn't it? Sometimes I can hear him breathing, sometimes I can't. He never speaks. Not a single word. But I swear it's him. It's not some random *caller*. It's him. Why don't you believe me? Drew doesn't believe me either."

Day stepped closer and sat down in the other armchair. "We're not saying we don't believe you," he said. "It's just the way we have to ask these questions."

He glanced over at Shields as they waited for Gem to compose herself. Neither of them spoke while she rubbed her eyes and took a couple of deep breaths.

"You did tell your boyfriend about these telephone calls then?" Day said.

Gem sniffed and nodded slowly. "I didn't want to at first. I knew he'd think I was being stupid. I thought they'd stop. Hoped they would. When I did tell him, he said I was worrying about nothing. That they were probably faulty calls from call centers."

"The calls were made to your home phone, not your cell?"

"That's right. Can't you trace the calls or something? That must be possible."

Day nodded. It made some sort of twisted sense that the carjacker would come after Gem. Her refusal to submit and the way she had fought him off would have been humiliating enough. If this suspect was the type of loaded weapon Day feared he was, then the *Daily News* interview could easily have pulled the trigger.

Gem let out a long breath. "You do believe me, don't you? Don't think I'm going crazy, because I know what I saw."

"We definitely don't think you're crazy," Day said. "We can access the telephone data, no problem. Whether we can trace the calls depends on where they were made from and what type of phone was used. We'll also pull in CCTV footage from Kingsland Road and surrounding streets. I assure you, we're taking this very seriously."

Gem's shoulders shook, and Day thought she was about to burst into tears. Instead, she managed a grateful smile.

"Have you told your boyfriend what happened today?" Shields asked.

Gem shook her head. "He's at work. He's always busy, in meetings with clients most of the time. Drew doesn't like me calling him at the office."

"When are you expecting him back home? Maybe you should call him, tell him what's gone on. I'm sure he'll come back early."

Gem paused to give the suggestion some thought. "Well, maybe I will. He's rarely home before eight or even nine. That's usually okay for us, because when I'm at work, I'm often even later."

Shields exchanged glances with Day. He gave her a quick nod. "How has your relationship been since the carjacking?" Shields asked. "Sometimes partners can find it difficult to come to terms with what has happened, especially when violence is involved."

Gem shook her head. With the exception of his criticism of her speaking out in the press, he'd been rock-solid in his support. He'd surprised her, because he hated her working late, and she'd been half expecting him to use what had happened as a good argument for giving up her job. "That's the one positive thing about all this," she said. "Drew has been fantastically understanding and caring. I'd say we're closer than we've been for a long time. This has definitely brought us together."

Day wanted to ask a question, but he stayed silent. Shields knew what she was doing. She'd gotten Golding talking freely, and he didn't want to break the flow.

"You were having problems before the carjacking then?"

Gem frowned at the suggestion. Day thought she was about to clam up, but Shields knew exactly how to nudge her along.

"Every relationship goes through tough times," she said. "I know all about that, believe me. If you come through them, then the bond is almost always going to be stronger."

Gem nodded and summoned a brave attempt at a smile. "We'd had one or two horrible arguments about Drew pressuring me to give up work. Only because he wants to spend more time with me, that's what he says. It's always caused a bit of friction between us. He says we don't need my salary. I couldn't get him to understand that it wasn't about money, that my career is so important to me. We argued every day for weeks, especially on the nights when I came home later than he did. It got to the point where I couldn't see a way forward, so I packed a case and went to stay with a friend."

"You actually walked out on him?"

"For a couple of weeks, yes. Drew was devastated. He called me every day, sent me texts saying sorry, promising to stop nagging me to give up my job. I figured we were both so miserable, it was worth giving it another try."

"And it's worked out for you?"

"Not at first. Drew kept his promise. He stopped going on about my work or about me coming home late, but I could tell he still wasn't happy. He didn't exactly sulk. It was more that he seemed subdued. Since the night of the carjacking, it's all changed. I thought that maybe he'd use the attack to insist that I shouldn't work late, but the opposite has happened. He's been caring and attentive and is encouraging me to go back to work. It's me who wants time off. I need to get my head together. I'm sure I will go back. When things return to normal. When I feel safe."

24
SURRENDER

THE MASTERMIND

Norton put his hands behind his head, stretched, groaned, and stared at the ceiling. Beneath him, the mattress springs creaked like an old man's bones.

Two of the room's four walls were still generously stained with the mold that had invaded during the damp winter months. Norton had gotten used to it. He definitely preferred the musty smell of the mold spores to the fatty aroma of reconstituted meat that wafted through the floorboards from Finch's kebab shop.

Not long to wait now, he told himself. Soon, he'd be out of this dump, living in comfort. He'd always known the time would come when he'd get the sort of life that was rightfully his. Bentley's death had brought that moment a step closer.

Some people found it hard to accept that bad things are fated to happen, but they are, and Norton was always happy to give fate a helping hand. Bentley had died a horrible death, his body crushed under the steel wheels of a Tube train. He had had it coming. Norton had understood that Bentley had to die if he and Gem were to have a chance.

Bentley thought he was something special; he thought he was cool. Norton grinned. He'd be super cool now, lying on his slab in the mortuary chiller. Underneath that smooth veneer, he'd been a nasty piece of work, a fake, and the world would undoubtedly be a better place without him. He had puffed himself up as a man of law, but he had had no respect for it.

Gem deserved more, and that's what she's going to get, Norton told himself. She just didn't know it. Not yet. When the time came, Norton would explain, and she'd have no choice but to understand and forgive.

Bentley had never loved her. That was obvious. He had wanted to make her something she wasn't. If she didn't shape up, he would have cast her off, wanted her gone, just like the other girl. The girl in the woods.

Once Gem finished grieving, when she'd thought things through, he would explain why he'd done what he'd done.

Since her display of disobedience at the carjacking, she'd shown her worth. She'd behaved perfectly, kept her head down. It wasn't love, whatever that was supposed to be. The simple fact was he wanted her. She played his game and won. Not only her right to live, but the right to live a new life. A special life. She didn't know it yet, but she already belonged to him. She'd understand. She had to.

He closed his eyes and dropped his arms to his sides. If he was going to watch over Gem, he needed plenty of rest. Bentley had been taken care of, but there were still people buzzing around her who would ruin everything if given the slightest chance. *That will not be allowed to happen*, Norton told himself.

Gem shouldn't be wasting her tears on a man like Bentley. He knew that right at that moment, shock, grief, fear, and confusion would almost certainly be taking an enormous toll on her. She'd be at her most vulnerable. All sorts of people would be whispering all sorts of things in her ear.

He'd make it his job, his mission, to protect her from the bad influences gathering around her, those who would do their utmost to keep them apart. Norton pictured himself standing in the shadows, watching over her like a guardian angel, unforgiving, steadfast, and all-powerful. The image made him shudder with pleasure.

His eyes snapped open, and he sat up quickly. There would be no rest now; he was too excited to sleep. But that wouldn't stop him. He had an assignment, a task to complete, and he'd do it, no matter what. Gem could depend on him to protect her, guide her, keep her safe from harm, as long as she followed the rules. His rules.

He'd do everything in his power to make sure that nothing and nobody posed a threat to her happiness. To her future. To their future.

THE DETECTIVE

Day summoned Shields and Stock into his office. He wanted to keep a lid on his belief that Bentley's death wasn't suicide or an accident. If that leaked, he'd have to report it to his detective chief inspector, and his old team would be called in.

Shields arrived to find Day standing behind his desk, his back to the window overlooking the station parking lot. "We need to move quickly on the Bentley case," he said. "It seemed clear to me on the CCTV footage that Bentley looked terrified when he saw the man in the baseball cap pushing his way through the crowd toward him. That suggests he knew him, knew him well enough to know what he might be capable of. He was clearly frightened of him."

Shields nodded. "It certainly looked that way to me. On top of that, Golding is positive that the image we showed her was the same man who attacked her. So somehow, Bentley knew the carjacker, or at least knew what he looked like."

Day shrugged and took a moment to think. "He knew his face, and he almost certainly was aware that he was a dangerous man, someone you wouldn't want moving toward you if you were standing on the edge of an overcrowded Tube train platform. The question is, did he find this out before the carjacking or after?"

Shields didn't respond. Day hadn't expected an answer. The question alone was enough for now. It meant that they had taken an important step toward catching Bentley's killer. Once they had the answer, he'd be in their sights.

"We need to pay a visit to Bentley's place of work," Day said. "Speak to his colleagues, get a list of his clients over the last few months. We're going to need to speak to Golding again, but we can leave that a day or so. Understandably, the woman's in a bad way. Cat, you're coming with me. Can you call Bentley's bosses and let them know we're on our way? Bill, I want you to stay here, go through the Liverpool Street CCTV footage again in case there is anything we missed. Don't forget, if anyone starts getting curious, we're simply trying to nail down whether this was a suicide or an accident. Once we've established that, we'll pass the case on to the coroner's office."

After Shields and Stock had left the room, Day sat down at his desk, took a deep breath, and let the air out of his lungs loudly and slowly. He wanted this man caught. Needed him caught. Day cared about the victims of violent crime and the families of those victims. He cared too much for his own good, according to his soon-to-be ex-wife. Getting too emotionally involved in his cases had been one of the many points on her why-I'm-leaving-you list.

————————

The offices of the Stone and Maddox law firm were situated above a coffee shop on the first floor of a red terracotta Victorian building in Chancery Lane. An immaculately groomed young man stood behind the reception desk, his eyes fixed on a computer monitor.

He looked up as Day and Shields approached and shot them a smile so broad, it must have made his jaw ache.

Day flashed his badge. "Detective Inspector Elliot Day," he said. "I'm making inquiries about a possible serious crime, and I need to speak to Mr. Stone or Mr. Maddox or whoever is in charge."

The smile vanished. "Is this to do with Drew Bentley's death?" A shiny badge on the receptionist's right lapel announced that he was called Miles.

"I'm not sure you understand, Miles," Day said. "We are here to speak to your boss, whoever he or she is. We will ask him or her questions. We're not here to answer your questions."

Miles turned back to his computer keyboard, his lips pursed like a sulking child. "Unfortunately, Mr. Stone doesn't exist," he said. "Not anymore. He died of a stroke a year ago. Give me a second, and I'll take a look at Mr. Maddox's schedule."

The detectives waited patiently as he typed. He tutted noisily and shook his head as he read the information on the screen. "I'm afraid Mr. Maddox is busy all afternoon. Would you like to make an appointment for later in the week?"

Day turned to his detective sergeant again. The corners of her lips twitched, but she kept a straight face. "This is trying my patience," Day said.

Miles spread his hands in a gesture of helplessness. "Mr. Maddox doesn't like being interrupted. In fact, he's made it very clear that he should never be interrupted when he's with a client. He is a stickler for routine and never deviates from his schedule. I'm afraid there is nothing I can do."

Day stepped closer to the counter and looked directly into the receptionist's eyes. "Miles, I'd like you to do something for me right now. Go and tell Mr. Maddox that the police want to speak to him. If you don't do that, then I will not be very happy."

Miles shook his head. "Sorry, sir, but I've already explained that's impossible."

Day slowed his breathing and kept his voice calm. "Please inform Mr. Maddox that the police want to speak to him about an urgent matter. I'm sure he will understand."

The receptionist opened his mouth, thought better of it, and closed it. Without another word, he turned and swiped his card over the security mechanism on the door behind the counter. It buzzed, and he pushed the door and slipped through.

Shields grinned at Day. "You made hard work of that, Boss. I hope you're not losing your touch."

Day didn't reply. He scanned the reception area, shaking his head. The building had an impressive Victorian façade, but inside, all the period features had been ripped out.

The door behind the counter opened with a click, and a red-cheeked Miles beckoned them in. They followed him along a brightly lit, white-walled corridor. As they walked, Day counted three doors, all with shiny brass nameplates. The third nameplate read *Drew Bentley*.

Ahead, at the end of the corridor, a fourth door was open, and Day guessed they were approaching the office of the boss man. Miles stepped aside to let the detectives enter and closed the door behind them.

The huge desk looked like it had been carved from a single block of oak; on it sat a green telephone, what looked like a large legal tome, and a brass plaque with *Edward Maddox* scripted in black enamel. *Why the hell are these lawyers fascinated with their own names?* Day wondered.

Behind the desk, in a throne-like upholstered chair, sat a man in his fifties wearing a silver-gray suit, a crisp, white shirt, and a silver tie. His hair was short and unnaturally black.

"Please take a seat," Edward Maddox said, his manner easy, unruffled by the unexpected arrival of a couple of detectives. "Tell me, how can I help you?"

Day sat on one of the chairs he guessed Miles had positioned at the request of his boss, and Shields followed suit. Maddox wore a neutral expression. He showed no sign that he was inconvenienced by the interruption.

"I am DI Elliot Day, and this is DS Shields. We want to ask you some questions about Drew Bentley."

Maddox's face remained impassive. Day got the impression it'd stay that way even if someone shot him in the groin with a fifty-thousand-volt stun gun.

"That was an incredibly sad business," Maddox said. "Drew was an excellent lawyer. One of our best. I had big plans for him."

"How long had he worked here?" Shields asked.

Maddox paused, a series of rapid blinks betraying his surprise that the female, lower-ranked detective had the nerve to jump in with a question. Day decided to sit back, watch, and see if Shields could unsettle him further.

"Drew joined us four years ago. Ambitious and a fast learner, he cottoned on to what our business is all about incredibly quickly. Over the past two years, he brought more money into the business than anyone else. We are really going to miss him."

Day caught his sergeant's eye, and he knew she was thinking the same thing. *Miss him or the money?* With people like Maddox, it always came down to the money.

The lawyer made a show of looking at the expensive gold watch decorating his left wrist. Before he had a chance to remark on how they were wasting his valuable time, Shields fired another question at him.

"Can you think of any reason why Mr. Bentley might have killed himself? Anything he said to you or other colleagues in recent weeks. Did he mention anything unusual that had happened to him?"

Maddox glanced at Day and raised his graying eyebrows. "We don't bring our personal lives to work with us at Stone and Maddox. I knew Drew lived with his girlfriend and that they were planning to get married and start a family. That was it. We don't gossip about our personal lives here. In fact, we actively discourage it. It's a distraction, not productive, and we want our staff to focus on our clients and their—"

"Yet you say Bentley told you he was planning to marry," Day cut in. Being lectured to always made him irritable.

Maddox leaned forward, rested his elbows on the desk, and steepled his fingers. "He did, and I was glad to hear it. He told me all about it after I called him into my office and asked him outright."

Day had no idea where this was going, but something told him it was important that he find out. "Why would you do that? Considering how you encourage your employees to keep their personal lives to themselves."

Maddox sat back in his chair, sighed, and folded his arms across his chest. "How much longer is this going to go on? I've put myself out to cooperate here, but I have an appointment soon, and I don't want to have to cancel it. Of course, I know that legally I don't have to speak to you at all, but I don't want to be deliberately obstructive."

Day didn't answer. He wanted to leave their response to Shields, because it would annoy Maddox more coming from her. She read her boss's silence perfectly and stepped in.

"We are, of course, extremely grateful for your cooperation," Shields said. "As you correctly point out, you are under no legal obligation to answer our questions, but if we have to apply to a judge for a warrant, we will, and that will result in us coming back with more questions and the authority to conduct a comprehensive search of your offices, including your computer network."

Maddox remained stone-faced. "I told you that Drew was performing incredibly well, so much so that I was considering making him a partner in the firm. He was delighted, naturally, but I pointed out that as a partner, he'd need to attend a lot more out-of-office events, networking functions, mix socially with some of our biggest clients and investors. You could describe it as old-fashioned, but I believe excelling in that kind of role is easier if you have a settled home life."

"And a wife on your elbow who can accompany you to these events?" Shields asked.

"Ideally," Maddox said. "We have no female partners right now, but if and when that happens, we will expect the same from them. We might be an old-fashioned law firm, but no one can accuse Stone and Maddox of being sexist."

Not without risking being sued, Day thought. "Doesn't it seem strange to you that somebody whose career was going so well and who was planning to get married would take his own life? It seems like he had everything to live for."

Maddox shrugged. The gesture looked unnatural, forced. "Who knows what's really going on in someone's mind?" he said. "People can be dealing with personal issues, such as mental health problems, and even those closest to them might be unaware. All I know is that at work, he was doing everything he needed to achieve his ambition of getting made a partner. He'd assured me that marriage was in the cards, and he had upped his pro bono work. That's something we like partners to do. It shows the firm has a social conscience."

"You deal exclusively with employment cases, don't you?" Day asked.

Maddox nodded. "Correct. Most of our clients are city

executives, bankers, etc., who have gotten or are about to get the ax. We negotiate settlements. The threat of legal action is an efficient way to push them higher. We also offer free advice to less fortunate members of society. People who believe they have been fired unfairly but don't have the resources to do anything about it."

"And Bentley did some of this pro bono work?"

"He certainly did. It's a requirement of becoming a partner."

A requirement, Day thought. *Not something you'd consider doing out of the goodness of your heart then.* "Okay, Mr. Maddox," he said. "We're going to need a list of all the clients Bentley saw in the last two months, including the pro bono ones."

The lawyer's thin lips stiffened. "That's impossible, I'm afraid. That's confidential information. Why is this necessary anyway? Are you suggesting that Drew didn't kill himself?"

Day glanced at Shields, again inviting her to deliver the bad news. "It's your right to refuse right now, of course," she said. "But if you do, we will return with a warrant giving us the power to search Mr. Bentley's office, and I have to warn you that we can't guarantee that the press won't get wind of what we're doing. Everyone knows they have their police sources."

Maddox took a moment to think. His gray eyes flicked from Day to Shields, then back again. Day had no doubt the veteran lawyer's legal brain was running through all his options and weighing up the damage a newspaper report about a police raid on his company's offices would do to the firm's reputation.

Day stood up to leave, and Shields did the same. At that moment, Maddox reached out, pressed a button on the telephone, and lifted the receiver to his ear. "I need you in my office now, Miles," he said. "I want you to compile a list for these detectives."

25
FIGHT

GEM THE WARRIOR

Gem drained her mug of tea, curled up in the armchair, and hugged her knees. Drew had jumped in a taxi and come straight home when she had called the office to tell him she was being stalked by the carjacker.

She'd burst into tears as soon as he walked through the door. He'd seen her cry plenty of times before, usually tears of anger and frustration when they'd argued about her job. He'd never seen her cry because she was frightened before.

Gem heard his footsteps on the stairs, lifted her head, and tried to muster a smile as he entered the room.

"Fancy another tea?" he said.

She shook her head. "No thanks. I think after the day I've had, I'd rather have a large vodka."

Drew walked to the sofa, brushed the seat with his fingertips, and examined them for dust before sitting down. "I'm not sure that's a great idea, darling. I didn't want to say anything before, but you've been drinking a lot more than usual lately. A good night's sleep is what you really need."

Gem felt a stab of embarrassment, and her cheeks burned. Maybe she had sought solace in alcohol, but who could blame her? What hurt the most was Drew suggesting that it was getting out of control.

She lifted the empty mug and waved it at him. "Actually, when you're ready, another tea will be perfect."

Drew tilted his head to one side and smiled benignly. "If you really want vodka, I'll make you one, no problem. I'm trying to think what's best for you, that's all. Still, if you want vodka…"

This is getting patronizing now, Gem thought, but she didn't want to start an argument. She didn't have the strength. "No, honestly, forget it. Forget the tea too."

Drew leaned forward and touched the back of her hand gently. "You know the police are going to arrest this man soon, don't you? He's made a big mistake confronting you in the street like that. If he'd kept his head down, he probably would have had a good chance of getting away. Not now."

Gem wasn't convinced. London was a place where you could disappear easily if you wanted to, especially if you were used to lurking in the shadows. Apart from that, there was something about this man, something she couldn't explain, but she'd looked into his eyes, and he was no ordinary carjacker.

"Do you really think the police will catch him soon?"

Drew nodded. "I do. Maybe then you can decide whether you want to go back to work or not. It's up to you, but I'd be happy if you took a less demanding job or didn't work at all. I'll never force you to do something you don't want to. I trust you to make the right decision. You've been through such a lot. The way you stood up to that carjacking was amazing, but now that he's stalking you, I don't want you taking risks."

Gem had heard him talk about her taking risks by working late so many times before, and it had almost always ended up with them shouting at each other. Eventually, she'd storm off threatening to pack her bags and leave, again, while he crossed his arms and shook his head in despair.

This time, there would be no argument. Instead of feeling that he was trying to stop her achieving what she had worked so hard to achieve, instead of dreading the thought of not being true to herself, Gem wondered if maybe he had a point.

"It's just so embarrassing feeling so scared," she said. "According to the newspapers, I'm the Warrior for Women, the woman who stood up and fought back. When I saw him in the street today, I felt terrified and helpless. I don't understand why he's doing this to me."

THE REPORTER

Subterfuge had never been Matt Revell's forte. Undercover journalism, setups, and stings were not for him. He liked to stick to what he was good at. The face-to-face stuff, the confrontations. His success in these situations wasn't down to aggression. Far from it. He'd discovered early in his career that he had the ability to avoid appearing to be accusing, judging, or condemning the person being ambushed.

Revell sat at a table opposite the bar, nursing a pint of beer and pretending to be reading something on the screen of his phone. The thrill of chasing a big story coursed through his system like a chemical stimulant. If he succeeded in finding the man who had attacked Gem Golding before the police did, it'd be the biggest success of his career so far. The mere possibility of seeing his name printed above such a sensational story gave him an adrenaline rush.

He'd chosen to sit next to the largest of the pub's two windows because he could see out onto the street and get a good view of everybody who walked through the door without having to turn his head. The lunchtime rush had ended, and the place was emptying fast.

Revell checked the time on his phone. He had no idea what the man he was waiting for looked like, but he'd bet a month's wages that he wasn't among the customers already lined up along the bar. They had all bought themselves a drink, and none of them showed any interest in what was going on around them.

At exactly five minutes past three, the door opened, and a lone man stepped inside, his narrow shoulders hunched, hands deep in his trouser pockets. Instead of approaching the bar, he stood in the middle of the room and looked around, checked his watch, and scowled.

Revell made a show of peering out the window, then returned to pretending to study the screen of his phone. He knew instinctively that it was the person who had identified himself during their telephone conversation as Finch.

Finch screwed up his narrow face and walked slowly to the bar. The lone barman, a floppy-haired surfer dude, grabbed an empty beer glass and smiled. Finch shook his head. After a final scan of the room, the man who'd been expecting to be bought several pints of beer and sell a story to a reporter made for the door.

Revell stood up and followed. This was the hard part. He hadn't a clue where Finch was heading, but he had to track him, preferably without being spotted. Finch had suggested meeting in the George in Stratford, and Revell hoped that meant it was his local pub. Out on the sidewalk, he spotted his target striding north along the bustling Broadway thoroughfare.

Finch moved at a surprisingly brisk pace. The street was bustling with shoppers, and Revell had to weave his way through the crowds to keep him in sight. He soon found himself uncomfortably close to his target and dropped back. The reporter had made it clear to Duffield that he believed the best way to handle the negotiations would be to keep it simple, but the news editor had been adamant. If they wanted to keep the price of the story down, they couldn't let the contact hold all the cards.

Revell slowed as he found himself stuck behind two women wearing colorful flowing robes and headscarves, both pushing strollers. It took him a second or two to squeeze past them, but that was long enough. Finch had disappeared.

Revell swore under his breath but kept walking. The only way Finch could have vanished so quickly would have been by darting into one of the stores. He pressed his face up against the window of a coffee shop. The place was busy, but there was no sign of Finch. He moved on, checking out a discount shoe store, followed by a betting shop. Then he struck lucky.

The shop sign, in bright yellow lettering, read Donna's Kebabs. A girl in her late teens stood behind the counter. She wore a dark-blue overall-style jacket and a sullen expression. Behind her, an inverted cone of brown meat glistened with fat as it turned slowly on a vertical rotisserie. On the other side of the counter, perched on a wooden stool, tapping away at his cell phone, sat Finch.

Revell stepped inside, smiling broadly at the girl. She yawned loudly. Without taking his eyes off his phone, Finch snapped, "For God's sake, Sharon, serve the man a kebab. He's hungry. Your customer service skills are nonexistent. I'm seriously considering sacking you for gross incompetence."

The girl opened her mouth to protest, but Revell silenced her with a raised hand. "It's okay. Don't worry, I'm not here for food," he said. "I'm from the *Daily News*. Here to see your boss."

Finch looked up, his eyes narrowing. "You were supposed to meet me in the pub. What's going on?"

"Yes, sorry about that. Something came up. Couldn't be helped."

The little man slid off the stool and tucked his phone in his jacket pocket. The top of his head was level with Revell's chin. He tilted his head back to look the reporter in the eye. "How did you know where to find me?" He didn't wait for an answer.

He worked it out himself. "You followed me here, didn't you? Sneaky fucker."

Revell laughed at the insult. The fact that he now knew about the kebab shop put the *Daily News* in a much stronger bargaining position. Finch was sharp enough to work out for himself that it'd be difficult to pull out of the deal and threaten to take the story elsewhere.

In those circumstances, Revell suspected that his bosses would almost certainly decide that the right thing to do, in the interests of public safety and justice, would be to inform the police that they knew someone who claimed they had information about the identity and whereabouts of a wanted man.

"Well, I'm here now, and we still need to talk, don't we? The paper is excited about your proposition, and I've got a lot of questions. And a lot of cash."

Finch shot a glance at Sharon, who had suddenly perked up. "All right, all right," he said. "I'm not talking about anything here though. Let's go back to the George. I'm dying for a beer."

Revell and Finch sat facing each other at the table by the window. To go with his pint of beer, the kebab shop owner had demanded a cheeseburger and double-cooked fries from the bar menu. He picked the burger up with his fingers and took a large bite, chewed it quickly, then washed it down with a mouthful of beer.

"Very tasty," he said. "But it's going to cost you more than this if you want what I've got to sell."

Finch still had bits of burger debris in his mouth, and Revell could see it swilling around when he spoke. The reporter picked up his pint and took a sip. "We're willing to pay a fair price for your information, but I can tell you now that you're living in a fantasy world if you think you're going to get ten thousand pounds or anywhere near it."

Finch lifted his beer to his lips and gulped it down until the glass was empty. "Get us another one, will you, mate? I find it hard to concentrate when I'm thirsty."

Revell stared across the table, thinking how much he'd like to tell the obnoxious weasel to go fuck himself. Instead, he smiled. "Of course," he said. "You have a good think about what you might consider a realistic payment. You've also got to understand that you won't see a penny until you convince me that you aren't bullshitting, that you really do know who this carjacker is and where we can find him."

Revell paid for the beer and slipped his wallet back into his jacket pocket. Over at the table, he could see Finch gnawing at the remains of the burger. He picked up the drinks and carried them over.

Finch grunted his satisfaction, took a long drink, and wiped his mouth with the back of his hand. "You took your time, mate," he said. "I thought I was going to be the first man ever to die of thirst in a pub."

Revell didn't bother to pretend to be amused. He pulled a newspaper cutting from his pocket, unfolded it carefully, and flattened it on the table. The security camera image of the man who'd attacked Gem Golding was grainy and dark. Next, the reporter produced a glossy version of the e-fit created by the police based on Golding's description of the attacker. He placed that on the table too.

"You say you can tell us who this man is? You know his name and where he lives?"

Finch looked at the images, his mouth twisting into a sneer. "I know exactly who that evil bastard is. He owes me money, so like I said, I'm going to need paying before I give you details. It'll be a bit like compensation, won't it? To show you I'm not a greedy man, I'll drop the price to five thousand pounds."

Revell shook his head slowly. "What part of London does he live in?"

"Around here. Not far from here at all. That's all I'm saying until I see the color of your money."

Finch was about as trustworthy as a snake in a sleeping bag, but Revell sensed he was telling the truth. The thought made his heart beat harder. "The most I'm allowed to agree to is one thousand pounds."

Finch snorted and swept his right hand across the table, knocking the e-fit onto the floor. "That's nowhere near enough, no way," he said. "Are you kidding me? You must think I'm an idiot. I'll tell you something for nothing. This man you're after is a nasty piece of work, an animal. No, worse than that, he's a fucking psycho. I'm putting myself in danger just sitting here with you."

Revell bent over, picked up the e-fit, and placed it back down next to the newspaper cutting. He knew Finch would try anything to push the price up.

"I'll go to fourteen hundred pounds, but that's my limit," he said. "You get seven hundred of that up front and the rest once we've got our story and this so-called psycho is in police custody. You can take it or leave it, but I have to warn you that if you decide to back out, I'd have to seriously consider telling the police what I know anyway. It'd be the right thing to do, in the public interest."

Finch screwed up his face as if he'd just detected a bad smell, a combination of desperation and calculation in his bloodshot eyes.

"I get half the money right now, you say? It'd have to be in cash, no checks or bank transfers, if you want me to even consider dropping that low."

Revell kept his face straight, but that was the moment he knew he had Finch hooked. He lifted a hand to his chest and tapped the pocket where he kept his wallet. "I can make that happen for you, no problem. But I'm going to need something more to convince me that this is going to be worth my while and that you're not pulling some kind of scam."

Finch picked up a leftover piece of burger bun, studied it for a few seconds, rolled it between his grubby little fingers, and let the crumbs drop to his plate. "I know it's the man you want," he said. "I'd recognize that bastard anywhere. He lives in the apartment above the kebab shop, and he owes me a month's rent. He's taken too many liberties with me, taken advantage of my generosity too many times."

Revell wanted to jump up and punch the air. For a split second, he considered running around the pub whooping like a madman. Instead, he nodded sagely and pulled out his wallet.

26

SURRENDER

GEM THE VICTIM

Gem Golding was already sitting at her desk catching up with her emails when her boss arrived and walked into her office. Before she could speak, Melanie stepped close, bent over, and hugged her tight.

"You know, I think you're doing brilliantly," Melanie said. "I really don't know how you are being so brave."

"I'm fine as long as I keep busy," Gem said. "Just fine."

After Drew's death, Gem had taken a few days off before insisting on returning to work. There'd be no funeral until the police released the body, and she dreaded the idea of spending long days at home, surrounded by reminders of what she'd lost.

Melanie dropped her expensive handbag on the desk and placed her hands on her hips. "I've got meetings all day today, but like I said before, if you need to talk, then don't hesitate to call my cell, and I'll do my best to make some room in my schedule. Ignoring grief doesn't do anyone any good. When you're feeling up to it, maybe a night on the town would be a good idea. We haven't done that for a while."

Gem allowed herself a half smile. Melanie's solution to most problems was a night out and more than a few glasses of wine. "I'll think about it. At the moment, keeping my head down and working hard is definitely helping me cope. It's giving me focus and structure, and that's just what I need."

Melanie picked up her bag. "That's all well and good," she said. "But please don't overdo it. There is no need. And by the way, honey, everyone loves the new hairdo. You know what they say. A new look, a new you."

When her boss closed the office door behind her, Gem went back to the task of clearing her emails. *Thank God for Melanie*, she thought. She was the only one of her colleagues who spoke to her about what had happened to Drew. She assumed the others found the subject too uncomfortable.

Since returning to the office, she had regularly been the first one in and the last one to leave, often still busy at her desk when the cleaners turned up. Her mother had instilled a strong work ethic in her from a young age. After school, when all her homework had been done, she'd been encouraged to study a little longer. Gem remembered sulking as a thirteen-year-old after being told to put her phone down and read an extra chapter of her history textbook. "You may be close to the bottom of the pile right now, Gem," her mother told her, wagging a finger to drive her point home, "but you're worth so much more. It means you've got to work harder than everyone else to get where you want to be. It's as simple as that."

Jan Golding had been right. She'd raised her daughter on her own and had done a pretty good job of it. After Gem and Drew had gotten together, her mother had sold her two-bedroom west London home and moved to a village in north Wales, close to where she'd spent her childhood. Gem loved the fact that her mother enjoyed telling her new friends that her daughter worked in the big city in the glamorous world of public relations.

Gem closed her emails and leaned back in her chair. Drew was gone. He was never coming back. Life had promised so much before they were both touched by evil.

The police had warned her that they wouldn't be releasing the body in the near future. She didn't know how she was supposed to react, but the last thing she expected was to feel relieved. She wasn't ready to think about funeral arrangements. When the time came, the responsibility would fall on her because Drew had no family.

He'd never spoken in detail about his time in foster care, but he'd used it to tease her whenever she tried to talk to him about growing up as the only child of a single mother. *At least you had a parent*, he'd say. *You were part of a family. Consider yourself lucky.*

Gem checked her watch. She had an appointment with a prospective client in half an hour. Focusing on work had been the right thing to do. *Drew would want me to be strong and move on, wouldn't he?* She'd been terrified, confused, and passive during the attack, but it would be the aftermath, her reaction to Drew's death that counted. She wasn't going to crumble. That would mean that the killer had won. Drew had always talked about the law of the land. How it applied to everyone. She'd often mocked him for being pompous when he went on one of his rants. *The law isn't funny*, he'd say. *It's sacred. The law must be upheld, and those who break it must be punished.*

THE DETECTIVE

Day leaned back in his chair, stretched, and yawned. He'd worked late the previous night helping Shields check out the list of Bentley's recent clients. It was basic police work, something a detective inspector would normally delegate to junior officers, but he'd been happy to get his hands dirty.

Between them, they'd been able to contact all six of the paying clients Bentley had advised in the two weeks before his death. They were all banking executives, earning big bucks and huge bonuses. Two had been out of the country at the time of Bentley's murder, and the others had all provided alibis that he expected to check out.

Of course, their wealth didn't mean they weren't capable of committing criminal acts. Day knew the reverse was true. Most of them would probably sell their grannies into the sex trade and have no qualms about it if they thought it made financial sense. You needed a ruthless mind-set to make the sort of money they pulled in.

Shields had promised to make an early start on the four pro bono names on the list. The man they were hunting was cunning. Day doubted he'd give his real name and address when filling in the appointment form, but he'd been arrogant enough to commit his crimes on camera, and arrogance could bring downfall.

The door of the office swung open, and Shields entered carrying a cardboard tray with two large coffees. She placed one on Day's desk, tossed the tray in the trash can in the corner, and took a long swig of her drink.

Day eyed her suspiciously. She'd never bought him a coffee before. "What's this for?"

"I thought you might need a caffeine boost after last night."

Day nodded, picked up the cup, sniffed the aroma, and took a sip. The coffee was exactly how he liked it: black, strong, and hot.

"Also," Shields said, "you're not going to have time to get your own, because we're heading out."

Day picked up on the excitement in her voice, put the coffee down, and stood up. "The pro bono list, you got something?"

Shields nodded. "They all check out except for one. We have a name. Connor Norton. It could be false—the address he gave certainly is—but I called the warehouse where he said he'd been working. They confirmed they had a Connor Norton there briefly, and the description fits."

Thirty-five minutes later, the detectives turned in to a run-down east London industrial area and pulled up outside a detached, single-story, redbrick warehouse.

They headed for a door to one side of the loading bay, helpfully marked with a sign reading *Reception*. Before they could knock, the door was opened by a rotund woman wearing a voluminous floral dress.

"No, no, no," she said, jabbing a plump forefinger accusingly at the unmarked police car. "Yer can't park there. No way. Yer got to move it. Right now. Come on."

Day showed her his badge. "We're investigating a serious crime and need to speak to the boss about a former employee."

The woman stood her ground, her frame filling the doorway, her hands resting defiantly on her ample hips. "Yer talking to the boss, and the boss says yer need to move that pile of rust away from the loading bay. We got a delivery due, and we're going to need to get it unloaded."

Day took a half step back and assessed the woman. It was a cool spring day, but her face was red, her forehead glistening with sweat. The colorful dress flowed down to her bare shins, and on her feet, she wore black work boots. He looked at his sergeant and shrugged. Shields sighed, pulled the ignition keys from her pocket, and trudged back to the car.

The woman grinned and waved at Day to follow her into the office. She sat on the only chair behind a small desk cluttered with paperwork, three empty cans of diet cola, and an ashtray overflowing with cigarette butts. The room smelled of sweat and cigarette smoke.

The woman pointed at the door. "Shut that, will yer? Then tell me what this fuss is all about."

"Why don't we keep the door open for now?" Day said. "It's pretty stuffy in here. Let's start with you telling us your name. When you say you're the boss, do you mean manager or owner?"

The woman glared up at him and wiped her broad forehead with the back of her hand. "Me name's Kath Brook, and I mean what I say. I'm the boss. Inherited the place a few years back, and it's doing fine, thanks very much. Better than when me dad was in charge. Can we get to the point here? I've got things to do."

"We have some questions about a former employee, a Connor Norton."

Brook's gaze flicked to Shields, who by now was standing in the doorway, then back to Day. She screwed up her eyes, and her nose twitched as if she'd just detected a bad smell. "Oh, yeah, him. Only here a few days. Well, definitely no more than a couple of weeks."

Shields stepped forward and placed the e-fit and CCTV still of the suspect on the desk. "Is this him?"

Brook leaned over and squinted at the pictures. "I think so," she said. "He wasn't too bad to look at, but we have different men working in the warehouse every day, and I'm terrible at putting names to faces."

Day waited, letting the silence weigh heavy in the air, before picking up the images and handing them back to Shields. "We're going to a need a list of your employees, going back at least a month," he said.

Brook pulled open a drawer and grabbed an already opened packet of cigarettes. She pulled one out, slipped it between her lips, but didn't light it. After a few seconds, she took the cigarette out and held it delicately between her thumb and forefinger.

"I ain't got a list that's going to do you any good," she said. "I run this place on casual labor. Buy up bankrupt stock. Footwear, lamps, chairs, all sorts. When it's busy, they come in. When it's quiet, they don't. Mostly Poles and Romanians. It's all legal like, but flexible."

Day wasn't convinced, and he could see Shields wasn't either. It didn't sound very legal. "To tell you the truth, we're not really interested in how you staff this place and how legal or illegal it is. We need you to help us out with an investigation. We know this Connor Norton worked here because it appears he sought legal advice about suing you for unfair dismissal. Claimed he was falsely accused of starting a fight and fired on the spot."

Brook snorted, throwing her head back so violently, she almost fell off the chair. "Yer got to be joking," she said. "He lasted two weeks, that's all. He seemed all right at first. Pretty smart, you know, efficient and quiet, kept his head down. Then one night, he lost it. Didn't like being told what to do. That was his problem."

Brook put the cigarette back in the packet, opened the drawer, dropped it in, and slammed it shut. "Trying to give up," she said. "It's not going well."

"So, tell us what happened," Shields said.

Brook sighed and wiped her forehead again. "It was Karol, one of our Polish regulars. Very reliable. We paid him a bit more than the others to act as a sort of unofficial foreman. Help the new ones settle in, yer know. One day, we had a delivery of wooden dining chairs, and he asked this Norton to stack them at the back of the warehouse. When he went and checked an hour later, Norton had only shifted a handful of them, and Karol wasn't happy. Told him to get his ass into gear. He was a bit blunt, I heard. Big mistake. Norton knocked him down and started throttling him. According to witnesses, he seemed strangely calm all the time he had his hands around Karol's throat and stopped just before the man passed out. At first, Karol wanted to call the police, but I was told Norton had a quiet word with him and managed to change his mind. Don't know what he said, but it must have been persuasive."

Day and Shields exchanged looks. "We're going to need to speak to this Karol as soon as possible," Day said.

Brook shook her head. "Yer'll have a hard job. He's gone. Quit the day after the attack. Went back to Poland. Crying shame that. One of our best workers, Karol was."

It was inconvenient, but Day knew the Polish authorities would cooperate and track the man down if his evidence was required. "We're going to need all the paperwork you've got on Norton," he said. "Address, bank account, national insurance number, the lot."

Brook shrugged. "Ain't got nothing like that. No details at all. He wasn't here long enough to warrant it. I paid him cash, didn't I? We would've sorted out the necessary documents, done it all correct and proper if he'd stayed longer, but like I said, these people come and go."

"You're saying you haven't got his address?"

"Not his address exactly," Brook said.

"What does that mean?"

"Well, some of the guys had an idea where he lived, I think. Well, they knew he had a place not far from here in Stratford. They used to laugh about it. Not to his face, obviously."

"Laugh about what?"

"About him living in an apartment above a takeout. About him coming to work stinking of cooking oil and kebab meat. There can't be that many kebab shops around, can there?"

27

FIGHT

THE MASTERMIND

Norton looked at the pound coin in the palm of his hand and closed his fingers around it until he'd made a fist. Excitement fluttered in the pit of his stomach.

Simplicity gives the game its power, he told himself. *There must be no room for ambiguity.* A flip of a coin was the perfect way to start. The player would have only two options, heads or tails. The coin decides. The game master executes.

Norton slid the coin onto his thumbnail and flipped it high into the air. He held his breath as he watched it rise, then fall even faster, a spinning blur of light, until it hit the threadbare carpet, bouncing once before rolling to a standstill.

He squatted down and stared at it. *Tails it is*, he thought. *Life is a game of lies, and death is the only truth. Time to play.*

THE REPORTER

Revell paid for the coffees and carried the tray to the corner table where Duffield sat checking the news headlines on her phone. He slid the cup over to his news editor. She put her phone down and nodded her thanks.

"I suppose you're going to put these down on your next lot of expenses?" she said.

"You bet your life I am. That's what expenses are for, isn't it? I'm even thinking about treating myself to a chocolate muffin when we've finished our little chat."

Duffield scowled across the table. "Let's make this quick and painless, shall we? I want to get back to the newsroom soon as possible. I've an editorial conference to prepare for."

Revell would have been happy meeting in the room they had used before, but this time, Duffield had insisted on a rendezvous outside the office. Convinced that traitors lurked in her newsroom, she didn't want to risk the story being leaked to rival papers.

When Revell had dared to suggest that maybe she was being paranoid, she'd glared at him and declared, "You can't trust journalists to keep their mouths shut, believe me."

Duffield picked up a plastic spoon and stirred her coffee slowly. "I think you should go for it first thing tomorrow," she said. "Do it like the police do, you know, surprise the nasty Mr. Norton before he's had a chance to properly wake up. Take a snapper along with you, knock on the door, job done. I'll tip off the police before you go in for the kill, and they'll have him in handcuffs before you can say 'broken nose.'"

Revell sipped his coffee and shook his head. She made it sound easy, risk-free, but this kind of job was never simple. There was so much potential for things to go wrong.

"I don't know if that's the best way to go about it," he said. "Confronting someone like Norton on his doorstep might not be a sensible idea. I think I'd prefer to ambush him on the street when he leaves the apartment. He'll be less likely to take a swing at me if there are witnesses around."

Duffield lifted the spoon again and tapped the side of the cup while she took a moment to think. A tightness in her jaw suggested to Revell that she'd already made up her mind and nothing he could say would sway her.

"It'll be so much better for us if it's a doorstep job," she said. "Then we can announce to the world that the *Daily News* tracked the beast down and led the hapless police right to his lair. We don't want it to look like we accidentally stumbled on him in the street, do we? Obviously, I don't expect you to try to get an in-depth interview, get him to describe how his traumatic childhood is the reason he turned into a full-blown scumbag. Catch him off guard, let the snapper snap away while you challenge Norton about the attack on Gem Golding. When he tells you to fuck off, then do exactly that."

She knows better than anybody that it's never that simple, Revell thought. *It never is.* An alternative news angle flashed through his mind. The *Daily News* finds the attacker and the paper's brave reporter is beaten to a pulp before the police arrive. Photographs of the previously fresh-faced journalist lying battered, bandaged, and semiconscious in a hospital bed would enhance the story no end. It was a win-win situation for Duffield.

"This Norton character is clearly dangerous. On that basis, I think there's a good chance that when we knock on his door, I could end up with a lot worse than a broken nose."

Duffield grabbed her phone off the table and studied the screen. "I've got to get back to the newsroom, pronto," she said, standing up. "Take my advice and don't overthink it. It'll be fine. I have complete faith in your determination to do whatever is needed to get this story. You've done a surprisingly great job so far."

Revell studied her face for a hint of humor. He found none. "Are they supposed to be words of encouragement? If so, then I think you'd better start brushing up on your motivational skills. They definitely need some work."

Duffield dragged her chair to the side and stepped away from the table. "Remember this is an incredible opportunity for you to enhance your reputation as an investigative reporter," she said. "Think of the byline, the kudos you're going to earn. This is award-winning journalism, mark my words. I tell you what, just to be on the safe side, we'll pair you up with the biggest, toughest, ugliest photographer we can find. The two of you can look after each other. Enjoy your cake."

Revell watched her walk away, her eyes fixed firmly on the screen of her phone. He wasn't happy, but he knew that he had no choice. This was his story, potentially the biggest of his career so far, and there was no way he was going to hand it to anyone else. Even if it meant taking a beating.

THE DETECTIVE

Day held his phone to his ear, his heart thumping. He couldn't remember the last time the prospect of talking to his wife had raised his pulse. It wasn't having to speak to her that worried him; it was what he had to tell her.

She answered on the sixth ring. One word. "Elliot."

"Hello, Amy. Sorry to ring you so late. How are things with you?" Day knew he sounded lame and suspiciously friendly.

This time, she responded with two words. "I'm good."

Day knew there was no point wasting time on small talk. He squeezed his eyes shut and went for it. "I'm phoning about tomorrow. I'm not going to be able to pick Tom up. I'm going to have to cancel, but I'll have him next Saturday as usual."

He braced himself for the explosion of anger. It never came. Not a sound. The silence damned him more effectively than any words could.

"Please tell Tom I'm sorry for the short notice and that I'll make it up to him. I promise. I can't take the weekend off because there's too much going on at work right now. A big case, and I'm needed. Please tell Tom that it can't be helped and that I'll miss him."

More silence. Day wondered if his wife had simply put the phone down and walked away in disgust. *Maybe she's gone to fetch Tom*, he thought. Having to break the news personally to his son would be humiliating. Maybe he deserved a bit of humiliation.

He tried again. "Are you still there? Could you tell Tom that for me? I'll apologize and spoil him a bit when I see him next week."

Amy let out a long, loud breath. *Here it comes*, Day told himself. But he was wrong. His wife's response was matter-of-fact, measured even.

"I'll tell him," she said. "He'll be disappointed, but he'll get over it. He can spend the day with me and Rob instead. It'll be nice. We'll make sure he has a good time."

Day clenched his jaw at the mention of Rob. The mere thought of the three of them enjoying a day out together burned like bile in his throat.

"Don't forget to tell him I'm sorry, will you?"

"I'll tell him," Amy said, ending the call without saying goodbye.

Day took a beer from the fridge, walked over to the window, and took a long swig from the bottle. He stared out into the night. The streetlights were on, spraying their haze of sodium yellow. Day had come to hate this time of day. He desperately needed sleep, needed to keep his brain sharp, but going to bed this early would be futile.

Before he'd left the station, he'd asked Shields to pay Gem Golding another visit. He wanted to reassure the poor woman that they were taking the case seriously. He checked his watch and considered calling his sergeant to say he'd meet her at Golding's home. Instead, he downed the last of the beer and thought about getting another bottle.

He pressed his face close to the windowpane and gazed up above the city. It was a cloudless night, but east London's electric glow blurred the stars. Somewhere out there, Day told himself, under the same light-polluted sky, the man who had attacked Golding prowled the streets. They had some useful CCTV stills of him and a decent e-fit image, but so far, the few calls they'd had from members of the public had led nowhere.

Day had dealt with a lot of violent, evil people over the years, but something about this suspect scared him. The sensible thing to do after the failed carjacking would have been for him to keep his head down, lie low, and stay out of trouble until the police gave up, then find a new victim to vent his rage on. It seemed clear to Day that the man they were hunting was doing exactly the opposite.

THE MASTERMIND

Norton tugged the hood of his top down over his forehead, leaned against the bus shelter, and watched the car pull up outside the house. A tall, athletic woman climbed out from behind the steering wheel and strode up to the front door. It opened before she reached it. Norton recognized the silhouette framed in the rectangle of light, remembered the pain as her teeth tore into his flesh, and smiled to himself.

He dug a hand into his pocket, found the coin, and caressed it with his fingers. He'd been watching the house for a couple of hours and was confident that he hadn't been seen. When Bentley had returned home from his plush office in the city, Norton had deliberately brushed past him on the sidewalk. The lawyer had been too preoccupied to notice.

Why, Norton wondered, *are the police making a house call so late in the evening?* Perhaps the woman hailed by the *Daily News* as a warrior for women, the victim praised for bravely fighting off an attacker twice her size, was running scared? Maybe it had dawned on her that all her talk, her blatant self-promotion, her disgusting allegations, had been a huge mistake? The possibility widened his smile.

GEM THE WARRIOR

Gem Golding led Shields along the hallway into the living room where Drew stood with his back to the window, expertly swirling a glass of whiskey in his right hand. He acknowledged the detective with a curt nod and sniffed the amber liquid.

"I assume you're here to tell us that you've made an arrest," he said, unbuttoning the collar of his shirt with his free hand and tugging the knot of his tie loose. "I must say it's about time."

Gem looked at Shields, shrugged an embarrassed apology, and sat down on the sofa. She was beginning to find Drew's attitude toward the police unsettling. She understood his impatience, but sniping at detectives who were doing their best was not going to help.

"I'm afraid not, not yet," Shields said. "But Detective Inspector Day asked me to call in to reassure you, both of you, that we're doing everything we can to track the suspect down and get him off the streets."

Drew took a small sip of his drink, rolling it around his mouth before swallowing. A smirk tugged at the corners of his mouth.

"With all due respect, Detective, wouldn't your time be better spent getting on with solving this case rather than making house calls just to let us know how hard you're working?"

Gem's head snapped up, her eyes blazing. "There's no need to be like that, Drew. What's the matter with you tonight? I'm sure Detective Shields and her colleagues are doing their best, and I, for one, appreciate that she's made the effort to keep us informed."

Shields joined Gem on the sofa and offered her a grateful smile.

"This is bound to be a stressful time for you both," she said. "I understand that, believe me. Another reason for this visit was to check how you are doing. I know you fought the carjacker off, but that doesn't mean the experience wasn't traumatic for you. Sometimes shock can creep up on people. There is plenty of support and expert counseling available for the victims of violent crime, and I can put you in touch with the right people if you feel you need it. If you want, we can arrange for you and Drew to talk to someone together. This kind of situation can put big pressure on relationships, especially if they are already under strain."

Gem looked across the room at her boyfriend, as if half expecting him to object. He met her gaze briefly before he turned away and took another sip of his drink. She knew he'd picked up the reference and she'd have to explain why she'd opened up to the detective about their relationship troubles.

"It's good to know that the help is there if I want it," she said. "I'll think about it. Can I think about it? Drew has been supportive, but maybe it would be a good idea for me to talk to an expert."

Drew put his drink down on the coffee table, walked around behind the sofa, and started to gently massage Gem's shoulders. "The worst thing is that you're not getting any decent sleep," he said. "I think being so tired is making everything worse. Maybe something simple like a trip to the doctor for some sleeping pills would sort you out."

Gem didn't like the idea of taking pills to sleep, but Drew sounded so sure of himself, she didn't know how to respond. Uncertainty and doubt were alien to Gem. Her childhood had been tough, but her mother had stressed that not having a father simply meant she had to be strong and determined to get what she wanted, and she'd been right. Gem had worked in bars to pay her way through university and landed her dream job in publicity. Maybe she just needed to pull herself together.

"Thanks for the offer of counseling," she said. "I promise I'll think about it, but I'm not really a victim, am I?"

Shields nodded slowly and stood up. "I'll leave you to enjoy your evening, but remember that the help is available. Don't be afraid to ask for it. Physically, you certainly got the better of your attacker, but you may have suffered psychological trauma."

"We'll keep that in mind, Detective," Bentley said. "Personally, I think Gem will be absolutely fine. She's had an ordeal, but she's an incredibly accomplished and determined woman. She won't let these anxieties get the better of her. I'll make sure of that." He threw his head back and drained his glass. "I would offer you a drink, but I assume you're on duty. Gem will see you out. I've promised to cook dinner, and if I don't get going soon, we won't be eating until midnight."

Once he'd disappeared into the kitchen, Gem got to her feet and led Shields to the front door. "Please take no notice of Drew," she said. "He can seem prickly sometimes, but he's just being a bit overprotective. This business has hit him harder than he's letting on. I think he feels guilty about what happened, that he wasn't on hand to help me. It's illogical, I know, but it's probably a guy thing."

Shields smiled and stepped out into the crisp evening air.

THE MASTERMIND

Norton stepped away from the bus shelter as the detective emerged from the house. Dusk had fallen, the streetlights stretching shadows across the sidewalks. He crossed the street, darting between the traffic, and walked swiftly toward her car.

It's all about timing, he told himself. *Timing and confidence.* He tugged at his hood, pulling it further over his forehead, and dropped a hand to his pocket, caressing the blade through the material of his jeans.

The policewoman yanked the driver's door open and glanced briefly in his direction. Thirty yards from the car now, he bowed his head a little but kept striding. He would have one chance, one split second to act. If he timed it wrong, he'd have to keep walking. He'd get another opportunity, but he hated having to adapt.

The detective ducked her head to climb into the driving seat, then flicked him another glance. She hesitated for a moment but turned away, distracted by the sound of raised voices approaching from the other direction.

Norton lengthened his stride to make sure that he reached the trunk of the car at the same time as the young couple arguing about whether to go home or find another pub and carry on drinking stepped off the sidewalk in front of the vehicle as they staggered across the road.

Close enough now to see the detective shake her head and glare at the couple as she slipped behind the wheel, Norton pulled the passenger door open and slid into the seat.

The detective's eyes widened, and she started to swing her left elbow at Norton's face. *She's quick*, he thought, *but not quick enough*. She felt the hard, cold pressure on the inside of her upper left thigh and froze. She turned her head to try to look at the figure beside her but jerked it back when Norton increased the pressure on her leg.

"That's right, you've got it," he said. "Keep your eyes looking straight ahead. Do exactly as I say unless you want to bleed to death. I guess you're smart enough to know that the blade of this extremely sharp knife is pressing on an artery. The femoral artery to be exact. Isn't it amazing what you can learn from TV crime and medical dramas? You're pretty slim, so there won't be much flesh between the edge of the blade and certain death."

The policewoman didn't answer. Norton could see she was doing her best to keep calm, struggling to keep her breathing steady. *Why was she bothering?* he wondered. He knew that right now, her heart would be trying to jump out of her chest.

"I'm a police officer," she said. "You're making a big mistake. The best thing you can do is give up your weapon."

The fear in her voice made Norton smile. Taking a detective like this was even more satisfying than he'd expected. He'd prove to Gem Golding, to the police, to the newspapers, that the carjacking fiasco was a one-off. He'd been careless, too soft. Everything was as it should be again.

He shifted in the seat, pulled the seat belt across his chest, and looked across at the detective. Her breathing was ragged, and her eyes were busy as if her brain was desperately searching for a way to escape.

"If you want the chance to live, then do as I ask, without question," Norton said. "If I slice the artery, and I will if you disobey me, it'll take two minutes, max, for you to bleed out. There's no way an ambulance would get to you on time. Do you understand?"

She said nothing. Instead, she reached for her seat belt, pulled it across her body, and clicked it in.

Norton chuckled, the sound low in his throat. "You're pretty smart for a cop. Now start this thing up and get driving. Straight on to the end of the road, then take a right."

The detective did as he ordered, the blood draining from her fingers as she gripped the steering wheel tightly to stop her hands from shaking. She put her foot down on the accelerator, and the car surged. The knife bit deeper, cutting through the material of her trousers. She braked hard.

"Don't even think about crashing," Norton growled. "That would be incredibly dangerous for you. This knife is super sharp."

At the end of the street, the policewoman turned right as instructed, into a narrow, unlit lane. Norton had checked it out earlier and found the perfect spot to play. The car headlights lanced through the darkness, and they soon arrived at a small industrial estate. The place was deserted, most of the units dilapidated wooden structures.

Norton pointed ahead to the entrance of what appeared to be a tire-fitting workshop, the only unit with a working security light. "Park right there, in front of the gates."

As the car pulled up, he opened the glove compartment and laughed out loud. "This is just perfect," he said. "I know you detectives haven't got the belts the uniforms use to carry around equipment, so I was hoping there would be something like this in the car." He rattled the handcuffs and offered them to the detective.

"Don't worry," he said. "There's a key here too."

She hesitated, her eyes flicking down to the hand holding the knife against her thigh. "You really don't need to handcuff me," she said. "I'll do whatever you want, I swear, but I don't want to be cuffed. I'm not doing it. That's final."

Norton knew what she was thinking. Being handcuffed would mean giving up control, total surrender. She'd be helpless, at his mercy. He had to explain to her that she had no choice.

"Now, Detective, tell me your name."

She opened her mouth, paused, then nodded. "Cat Shields. Detective Sergeant Cat Shields."

The blade pierced her skin, and she cried out. Warm blood trickled down her thigh, pooling on the seat between her legs.

"Take a moment to think carefully about the situation you're in," Norton said. "Take as long as you like; there's no rush. Then ask yourself this question, Detective Sergeant Cat Shields: Are you really going to make me do it?"

She reached out, took the handcuffs, and slipped them onto her wrists, clicking them into place.

Norton got out of the car and dashed around to the driver's door. He opened it, waving her to her feet. He pressed the hunting knife against her ribs.

"Don't try anything stupid, or, at the very least, you'll lose your right kidney. Remember what I said. If you do what you're told, you won't get hurt. I guarantee it."

He slid the blade around to the small of her back, gripped her shoulder with his other hand, and guided her toward the iron gates at the entrance to the tire fitters. The security light was attached to a pole to one side of the gate, with a camera fixed to a bracket below it. As they walked, Norton crouched, using Shields as a barrier to hide his face.

When they were roughly ten feet from the gates, he swiveled her around until they both had their backs to the light and the camera. Norton stood motionless and silent for a few seconds before releasing his grip on the detective's shoulder and stepping back.

"You can turn around now," he said. "Turn around and hold your arms out in front of you. Don't try to be brave or clever, and don't speak unless I ask you a question."

She did as he asked, and he grinned at her confusion when he unlocked the handcuffs, twisting the key with the same hand that held the bloodied knife, and slipped them into his pocket. He'd simply wanted to see if he could get her to put them on, to see if even a police officer could be made to decide to make themselves helpless if it meant they might survive. That had worked perfectly, but the real test was yet to come.

Shields flexed her wrists and raised a hand to protect her eyes from the glare of the security light. Norton stood no more than an arm's length away. He lifted the knife until the point almost touched the hollow of her throat.

"You are doing very well. Keep it up, and maybe you'll be able to walk away from this in one piece. Who knows?"

The detective's left leg trembled, and Norton noticed the muscles of her jaw tighten. *She's fighting to stay composed*, he thought, *trying to draw on her training, waiting for that all-important opening.*

"Whatever you think you're doing, it's not too late to stop," she said. "Please listen to me. If you give yourself up, the court will take it into consideration, and you could end up with a lighter sentence."

Although she looked far from calm, her voice was steady, and Norton was almost impressed. He moved the knife closer to her throat until the point pricked her skin, drawing a tiny droplet of blood.

"You were doing so well. Now you've gone and spoiled it. I told you not to say a word."

Her leg trembled again, and this time, she couldn't stop it. A smile slanted across Norton's face. "Do you know what, Detective? I'm in a generous mood. I think I can give you one more chance."

He pulled the knife back and dropped his arm to his side. With his left hand, he pulled the handcuffs from his pocket and rattled them in her face. Shields stared at them as if hypnotized. At that moment, he let the knife slip from his grasp and fall to the ground, instantly squatting to retrieve it.

Norton was on his haunches, turned slightly away from the detective for less than a second. In that moment of truth, he felt her eyes on his back, imagined her heart hammering at her rib cage, sensed her brain weighing up her options, assessing the risk should she fail to overpower him.

Rising swiftly to his feet, he turned to face her. She looked confused, panicky, and disappointed. He stepped forward, snapped one of the handcuffs over her right wrist, and dragged her to the gates, locking the other cuff to a vertical bar.

Norton watched the detective drop her chin to her chest and slump to the ground in despair. She had spurned an opportunity to fight back, and now she was helpless and at his mercy.

He turned and walked slowly away into the darkness.

28
SURRENDER

GEM THE VICTIM

Gem stepped carefully through the revolving doors and strode up to reception. A heavily made-up blond wearing a red jacket with a matching knee-length skirt stood behind the counter, talking animatedly on the telephone. When she saw Gem waiting, she lowered her voice and turned away.

Hanging on the wall behind the receptionist were twelve life-size tabloid front pages displayed in black frames. Above them, giant chrome letters spelled out the slogan *Always First with the Daily News*.

After a couple of minutes, the blond put the telephone down, turned to Gem, and flashed an impressive set of recently bleached teeth. "What can I do for you?"

Gem stepped closer and placed both her hands flat on the counter. The sleeves of her jacket rode up, exposing the cast on her right wrist, the once pristine white plaster now a dirty gray.

"I'd like to speak to one of your reporters if that's possible," she said. "I think I have a news story your paper would be interested in."

The receptionist looked her up and down, pursing her lips as if she found the suggestion hard to believe. "Would you mind telling me what this so-called news story is about?"

Gem frowned. "You are a receptionist, correct?"

"That's right."

"Then yes, I do mind. I mind quite a lot actually. I'm here to talk to a reporter."

The receptionist glared back at her and snatched up the telephone, her smile now more like a sneer. "If you'd like to take a seat, I'll call the news desk, but I can't guarantee that they'll have anybody available. Our reporters are constantly working to deadlines, you know. You're likely to have a long wait. I can take your name and telephone number and get someone to call you if you'd prefer."

"I'm happy to wait."

Gem walked over to the seating area and made herself comfortable on the faux leather sofa. She watched the receptionist glance toward her as she spoke into the receiver and suspected that she wouldn't be doing her best to encourage a journalist to make an appearance.

After ten minutes and several smug looks from the receptionist, Gem reached the conclusion that she was wasting her time. She was about to leave when the elevator doors slid open with a ping and a man in a light-blue linen suit stepped out. As he approached the sofa, he grinned and held out a hand. "Hi there, I'm Matt Revell, a reporter on the *Daily News*. I hear you might have something interesting for us," he said.

Gem stood and shook the reporter's hand, his grip warm and firm. His clear blue eyes flicked down at the cast on her wrist, but he made no comment.

"I hope you will find what I've got to say worth writing about. I've thought long and hard about whether to go public on this and now feel it is the right thing."

Revell nodded. "Let's take a seat, shall we? Then you can tell me your name and explain why you're here."

Gem sat beside him on the sofa, took a deep breath, and sighed, relieved that on first impression, he seemed to be a genuine and down to earth guy. More than a few of the journalists she'd had to deal with for work had been too impressed with their own importance.

"My name is Gem Golding, and I was recently the victim of a carjacking. I was assaulted and mown down with my own car."

Revell cut in before she could go on. "Of course, that's it. I remember that," he said. "I thought the name sounded familiar. The bastard broke your arm." He paused for a moment, brushing his floppy bangs to one side with a sweep of his hand. "What happened to your boyfriend, that was tragic. I can't imagine how you must be feeling."

Gem could tell he'd had plenty of experience talking to people gripped by grief and read the look in his eyes as genuine compassion. Compassion she could handle. Pity was her weak point. It hollowed her out every time.

She sat up straight, stiffening her back. "I want the man who attacked me caught and am prepared to talk to you about what happened. Nothing is off-limits in the hope that someone might come forward with information."

Revell squirmed uncomfortably in his seat. "The problem is that we have already covered the carjacking. I'm sure you know they happen fairly regularly in this city. I don't think my news editor is going to want to go over the same ground again. Of course, if and when someone is arrested and charged, we'd report that, and after the court case and sentencing, an interview with you would certainly add a bit of color."

Gem didn't even attempt to hide her disappointment. She dropped her chin to her chest and shook her head slowly. She needed to do something positive to fill the gaping hole in her heart.

"The last thing I want to do is make a tragic situation worse for you," Revell said. "But maybe there is a way we could move the story forward. If you were willing to talk to me about your boyfriend's death, then..."

Gem lifted her head. The pain behind her eyes made the reporter falter.

"I'm so sorry," he said. "I was only trying to think of a way that we could do this. Forget I even mentioned it."

Gem blinked hard and held his gaze. "That's all right. It's not that," she said. "The thing is I don't think...in fact, I'm pretty sure that Drew didn't jump in front of the Tube train. He was pushed by the same man who attacked me and stole my car."

Revell's eyebrows disappeared under his bangs. "You're telling me that your boyfriend was murdered?"

"That's what I believe."

"But what about the police? What do they think? I'm sure the last press release I saw said that the death wasn't being treated as suspicious."

Gem hesitated. She wondered why Detective Inspector Day hadn't gone public with the CCTV image of the carjacker on the escalator. It had been obvious that he and Shields had serious doubts about Drew's death being suicide. The last thing she wanted to do was jeopardize the investigation, but she'd gone too far to back down now.

"If they truly believe that Drew's death wasn't suspicious, then they're making a huge mistake. He had no reason to kill himself. Everything was going so well for him career wise, and he often talked about our future, about me giving up work to have a baby. Does that sound like someone who was contemplating suicide?"

Revell shrugged. "I'm no expert, but I don't think there always has to be a reason for someone to be depressed, and many people are good at concealing the way they're really feeling."

"I wouldn't be here if I thought there was the tiniest of chances that Drew killed himself. If you are not interested in what I am telling you, then maybe I should speak to another newspaper."

Revell put up both hands. "I haven't said I'm not interested, have I? I'm just trying to think this whole thing through."

Gem realized she'd hit a nerve and decided to press harder. "I do understand that, but maybe I need a reporter who isn't so busy." She stood up, and Revell did the same.

"I tell you what," he said. "Give me a couple of minutes to nip back up to the newsroom, would you? I'll put in a call to the Metropolitan Police Service's press office to double-check what the official line is on your boyfriend's death. After that, we can walk around the corner to my favorite coffee shop, and you can tell me in detail why you think he was killed by the man who attacked you."

Gem gave a curt nod and sat back down on the sofa. She took a long, slow breath as she watched the reporter dash to the elevator. Drew would have been impressed with the way she'd handled that.

THE DETECTIVE

Day drained his coffee and tossed the empty paper cup into the trash can next to his desk. It was his second shot of caffeine since arriving at the station at 6:00 a.m., and he'd need several more to keep him going as the day wore on. The thought that they were so close to hauling Connor Norton into an interview room had kept him awake most of the night.

They'd have no trouble nailing him for the carjacking. Getting enough evidence to charge him with the murder of Drew Bentley was another matter. The CCTV proved that he was on the escalator at Liverpool Street Tube station shortly after the lawyer's death, but the platform footage was less conclusive.

They needed evidence to connect the cases. They were clearly linked because of the pro bono appointment Norton had with

Bentley before attacking the lawyer's girlfriend. But they needed facts that would stand up in court.

Day stood up, pulled his jacket off the back of the chair, and slipped it on before striding out of his office into the noisy squad room. He nodded at Shields, who was standing by a large whiteboard on which was written a list of addresses including postal codes. Spread around the room, some on chairs, others perched on desks, were eight detective constables. Half of them had been brought in from other east London stations for the operation.

"Right then," Shields said, raising a hand. "Listen up, everybody." The room hushed, and all heads turned to face the detective sergeant. "It turns out there are nineteen takeouts that sell kebabs in the Stratford area, but only seven of those have apartments above them. You all know where you are going, and each team has been assigned three uniforms. It's still pretty early, so hopefully we'll catch the suspect in bed. I know I don't need to tell you this, but I will anyway. Whichever team hits the jackpot and makes the arrest needs to seal the property off until the crime scene investigators arrive. We don't want contamination of evidence to wreck the case."

A stocky, middle-aged detective standing at the back of the room, his arms folded across his barrel chest, grunted loudly. Dan Bridger had been seconded from Mile End station and clearly resented having to give up sleeping in. Shields had worked with him before her promotion to detective sergeant and regarded him as a smart operator.

"You got a question for me, Dan?"

He grunted again. "Yeah, I do. We're going to all this effort to arrest a suspected carjacker, right? Or is there something you're not telling us?"

Shields opened her mouth, but Day jumped in before she could answer. "Since when has carjacking been considered a minor crime?

Don't forget this man viciously assaulted the victim, throttled her, then ran her down before driving off."

Bridger uncrossed his arms and hitched the waistband of his trousers over his sizeable gut. He wasn't convinced but was wise enough not to argue further.

Day stepped across to join Shields in front of the whiteboard. "You've all been fully briefed, so let's get going. Don't forget what I said. This suspect is potentially extremely dangerous, so don't take any risks. Get him handcuffed, read him his rights, and get him back here for an interview as soon as possible."

29

FIGHT

THE DETECTIVE

Day shunted forward to the edge of his chair as Shields's eyelids flickered open. He looked down at her and smiled.

"You're in the hospital," he said. "You're going to be fine."

"How long have you been watching me?" she asked.

"Not long. You've just come out of surgery. Apparently, the wound in your thigh is small but dangerously deep. They needed to put you under to stitch it up securely."

Day stood up, picked up a glass of water from the bedside table, and offered it to her. When she didn't react, he put it back down.

"Fortunately, the guy who runs the tire-fitting outfit likes an early start. He found you handcuffed to the gate and rang for an ambulance. You were semiconscious by then. Probably a combination of blood loss from the thigh wound and shock."

Shields looked away and stared at the ceiling. "I'm so sorry, Boss," she said.

Day stepped closer and rested his fingertips on the crisp bedsheet. "You've nothing to be sorry for, Cat. You'll need to be interviewed in detail about what happened, but not right now. Maybe in a day or so."

Shields blinked several times. For a moment, Day thought she was on the brink of tears, but her eyes stayed dry.

"I could have taken him," she said. "At least I should have tried. The opportunity was there. I can't explain what happened. I can't believe I didn't go for it when I had the chance."

Day backed away from the bed and sat down. "You don't need to think about this right now," he said. "You got a good look at him anyway. You'd have no trouble identifying him, would you?"

Shields frowned and rolled her head from side to side on the pillow as if struggling to retrieve a memory. "I did get a good look at his face, and the scary thing is he didn't look evil. I think most people would describe him as good looking. A good-looking monster." Her frown deepened, and she pushed herself up onto her elbows.

Day jumped to his feet. "What's the matter?" he said. "Are you in pain?"

"The camera," Shields said, struggling to catch her breath. "There was a security camera near the light by the gate. If it was working, then everything will be on there."

Day lifted a hand and waved in an effort to get her to calm down. "Don't worry, we know all about the camera. It was working, and we've got the footage. We'll go through it together in a day or so when you're out of here. Now lie down and rest, will you?"

He'd already seen it several times and wasn't looking forward to watching it with his sergeant. It made disturbing viewing.

"You've already had a look at it, haven't you?" Shields asked.

Day chose not to answer the question, aware that her humiliation would take longer to heal than the wound on her leg.

"We'll analyze it together when you're feeling better. Right now, I want you to rest so you can get out of here as soon as possible. I need my best investigator back on the job."

Shields went back to staring at the ceiling. "Your best investigator? What a joke. Why didn't I fight back when I had the chance, Boss? I'm a detective. A bloody good one, or so I thought. I was always so confident that I'd be strong in that situation, but I did nothing. When he dropped the knife, I froze. Compared to Gem Golding, I…well, I…I did nothing. She took the bastard on and won, while I, despite years of service as a police officer, reacted like a frightened child."

"You're being too hard on yourself," Day said. "He had a knife, he's a dangerous individual, and he'd already come close to slicing through your thigh. You're alive, and maybe that shows that your decision not to take him on was the right one. Maybe instinct kicked in and saved your life."

Shields shook her head. "I didn't make a decision. That's what I'm trying to say. I froze. You know, if I'm honest, I've always felt a tiny bit of contempt for victims of violent crime who meekly raise their hands and give their attacker total control. I've got no reason to feel smug now."

Day walked around to the end of the bed to give himself time to think about his response. "Nobody's judging you, Cat. Certainly not me. He obviously carefully planned this thing out in great detail. We've got good-quality CCTV film of the incident, and when we catch the bastard, he will be going down for a very long time."

Shields sighed. "He knew exactly where he wanted to take me," she said. "He must have checked the spot out, so he'd have known all about the security camera, yet he made no attempt to put it out of action. He's not stupid, far from it. I can vouch for that. He knew exactly what he was doing. He'd clearly planned the whole thing in meticulous detail. Looking back, I'm sure the handcuffs thing, getting me to put them on, then take them off, was to firmly establish that he was in control, part of a mind game designed to demoralize and disempower me. What I don't get is why on earth he would take me to a place he knew was covered by a working security camera?"

Day said nothing, although he knew the answer. Shields would work it out once the fog had cleared from her mind. The suspect took her to that particular spot precisely because the camera was there. He wanted the whole thing captured on film. He was toying with Shields, taunting the police, and he wanted everyone to see.

30
SURRENDER

THE MASTERMIND

It took Norton one hour and twenty minutes to walk east from Shoreditch through Bethnal Green and across the Queen Elizabeth Olympic Park. Yesterday had started with a shock so big, it had almost made him lose faith in his mission. Almost.

He'd followed Gem to the offices of the *Daily News* and watched her emerge with a young man in a linen suit. You didn't need to be a genius to work out that he was a reporter. Norton had used the hour they'd spent in a coffee shop trying to understand what was going on.

At first, he couldn't believe that his Gem would betray him. Then he realized the press would be sniffing around for one reason only. An interview about the carjacking and the death of her scumbag boyfriend.

He had to admit, he'd almost lost it. The bond he had with Gem, though unspoken, was so special. He knew it, and so did she. That's why it had been almost impossible to come up with a reason why she would ruin everything.

It had come to him before the hour was up, five minutes before

Gem and the snake of a reporter had walked out of the coffee shop and parted ways. Another one of those moments of revelation. The answer was so simple, it made him laugh out loud.

Her head had been turned. The reporter and the police had joined forces to talk her into going public. He was sure of it. She'd resisted the pressures to speak out, to speak ill of him for so long, but in the end, the whisperers, the truth twisters had done their job.

She was going along with this charade, but Norton knew that she was really fooling them, not betraying him. The best thing was, she would know full well that he would have worked this out.

Satisfied that he'd solved the mystery, he'd followed her home and watched over her until morning. It had been a long, cold night, but far from being tired, he was feeling energized.

Norton strode briskly past Stratford Underground station toward High Street, then turned left, heading north onto Broadway. The sun hadn't been up long, but the center of Stratford was already clogged with traffic, and the sidewalks were crowded with commuters.

He was about one hundred yards away from the narrow passage-way leading to the rear of the kebab shop and the stairway to the entrance to his apartment when a car pulled up at the curb.

He stopped, dodged into the doorway of a greeting card store, and watched. One man and a younger woman in plain clothes got out of the car, followed by two uniformed police officers. One of the police constables carried what looked like a metal battering ram.

All four officers ran down the passageway. Norton stepped out onto the sidewalk, turned back the way he'd come, and started walking. He'd taken a few steps when he heard the sound of splin-tering wood.

That had been close, he told himself, wondering how they'd found his apartment. He allowed himself a smile at the thought of the police kicking themselves when they discovered the place was empty. He needed to find somewhere else to shelter, but that wouldn't be a problem. Fortunately, he always carried his money with him, and he still had plenty left.

As he approached the Underground station, he had to slow down because the sidewalk was jammed with commuters funneling toward the entrance, walking three or four abreast. All around him, London buzzed with life. Car engines revved, doors banged, and on the other side of the street, raised voices shouted insults. In the distance, a siren wailed.

This was what Norton loved about the city: its vastness. He suddenly stopped walking, causing pedestrians behind him to swear and swerve. He savored the chaos, the belief that everybody except him led pointless lives, spinning around and around like hamsters running in wheels. He stood as still as he could, holding his breath to emphasize his motionlessness. *This is the best feeling in the world*, he thought. *Absolute control.*

He filled his lungs and started walking again. For Norton, control was the key to everything. As a young child, he'd been under the control of a mother who didn't want him. At the children's home, he was controlled by rules and regulations. He had no say, was allowed no opinion. He was dehumanized. Cared for without care.

The trip to the woods. That was the day that had changed everything. It was the day he had discovered the thrill of gaining and exerting power over another human being. Of course, he knew long before he started killing that he was going to end up killing. Murder was the ultimate form of control.

THE DETECTIVE

Day looked across at the little man and shook his head in frustration. Kev Finch had refused the offer of having a public defender present, but he'd obviously watched a lot of TV crime shows.

"How long had Connor Norton been a tenant in your apartment?"

Finch folded his arms tight across his chest and sat back in the chair. "No comment."

"Did you know he had left the property?"

"No comment."

"Did he tell you where he was going?"

Finch's sly eyes slid to the right to look directly at Day. "No comment."

They had already run through their list of questions twice, and every time Finch parroted the words *No comment*, Day found the urge to punch his smug face a little harder to resist. He decided that enough was enough. Finch was enjoying himself far too much.

Day clenched his right fist and brought it down hard on the table. "Norton is wanted in connection with serious crimes, including assault and possibly murder, and you're in danger of being charged with harboring a violent criminal."

Finch sat up straight in an unconvincing show of defiance. "No comment," he said, the smirk wiped from his face for the first time since the interview had begun.

Day felt a stab of satisfaction. "This is wasting everyone's time. I know you think you're being clever, but all you are doing is digging yourself into a deeper hole. It's starting to make me wonder why you are so keen to protect a fugitive like Norton. Maybe the two of you were in on these crimes together? Now he's run off and left his pal to face the music."

Finch studied the room's whitewashed walls, then raised his eyes to the ceiling. "He's definitely not my pal. Never was. I wouldn't spit on him if he were on fire. The evil bastard owes me money."

Day nodded, stifling a smile at the breakthrough. "Norton paid you rent for the apartment then?"

The lines around Finch's thin lips tightened. "No comment," he said.

The apartment above the kebab shop had been barely habitable. It had no heating, the walls were riddled with damp and covered in black mold, and the crime scene investigators had discovered signs of rodent infestation. Apart from a few clothes and a couple of illegible notes scribbled on scrap paper, they hadn't found any personal belongings.

An unofficial arrangement would have suited both men. Norton would stay unrecorded on any documents, and Finch would be able to pocket rent without having to spend money upgrading the accommodation or declaring the extra income to the tax man.

Day placed his hands on the table and clasped them tightly.

"I want you to think very carefully about what I am about to say. I really don't give a shit if you have managed to avoid paying a few hundred pounds in tax. What I do care about is catching violent criminals like Norton. If I think that you are deliberately obstructing my investigation, I'm not going to be happy, am I? Understandably, I'm almost certainly going to be less laid-back about you dodging a bit of tax. One brief but satisfying telephone call to Her Majesty's Revenue and Customs is all it'd take. I guarantee they'll sink their teeth into you faster than you can say doner kebab."

Finch's scrawny body sagged, his narrow shoulders slumping in defeat. "Norton moved into the apartment about three months ago," he said. "Someone told him I had a place to rent, but he didn't want anything official. Nothing on paper. He liked to keep everything under the radar, you know. That's what he told me. Didn't want anybody knowing where he was or what he was doing. I would have been happy with a proper tenancy agreement. I really would've. But he insisted, and he's a scary son of a bitch."

"He scares you, does he?"

Finch nodded. "I've not actually seen him hurt anyone and he can be a smooth talker when he wants to, but he can turn in a second. You know, like that Jekyll and Hyde character, or whatever he's called. Then he looks at you, stares at you like you're a snack and he's hungry. There's something about him that frightens the shit out of me. I wouldn't advise anyone to mess with him, if you know what I'm saying."

Day knew exactly what he was saying. Norton had tried to throttle Gem Golding and had almost certainly murdered her boyfriend. "Where does Norton get his money to live on, to eat, to pay rent? If he's living under the radar, he wouldn't be able to claim benefits."

Finch shrugged. "There are always plenty of opportunities to get your hold of cash in a city like this if you are comfortable breaking the law, if you're prepared to intimidate, threaten."

"Not like you then," Day said. "What a fine, upstanding, clean-living, tax-paying citizen of the world you are. An example to us all."

Finch tried his best to appear insulted, but instead, the way he screwed up his face made him look as if he was suffering from a serious case of trapped gas.

"Didn't you see the news coverage about the carjacking of that public relations executive?" Day asked. "The woman was assaulted, then run over with her own vehicle. I'm surprised you didn't recognize Norton from the CCTV footage or the police e-fit."

Finch shook his head for several seconds. "No, didn't see them," he said. "Don't watch the news. Can't bear all that doom and gloom. Too depressing. Norton doing that stuff don't surprise me at all though. If I'd known, I would've sold him out to you lot, no question about it."

Day didn't believe a word of it. He thought it more likely that Finch hadn't wanted to lose a tenant who didn't give a damn about

living in a rat-infested hovel. Or maybe he didn't want him hauled
off by the police before he'd coughed up the rent he'd owed.

"Have you any idea where Norton could have gone? Did he
ever mention any old haunts, any parts of the city he preferred, any
places where he might have friends or family?"

Finch laughed, a snickering, wheezing sound. "You've never
met him, have you? The man's got no friends, and I reckon any
family would have disowned him years ago. Shortly after he was
born probably."

Day reached across to the recording device and turned it off.
"You're not taking this seriously or being as helpful as I had hoped,"
he said. "Perhaps I should do my duty and inform the tax man about
your little arrangement after all. They'll probably want to check
your little kebab shop business out too."

Finch blanched. "All right, calm down," he said. "I know that
before coming to me, Norton was staying at some cheap bed-and-
breakfast place in Stepney. I'm not saying he'd go back there, but if he
needed to find somewhere quickly, it'd be convenient, wouldn't it?"

There were thousands of places across the city offering bed-and-
breakfast at various price ranges. Day was pretty sure that Norton
wouldn't stray far. The streets of east London were his territory, his
hunting ground.

"What did you say was the name of the place in Stepney?" he
asked.

"I didn't say, but I think it was Roman Villa, or Roman Villa
Rooms. Sounds grand, don't it? It's probably just a tarted-up
Victorian terrace."

Day sat back in his chair. He was about to take a coffee break
when Finch raised a hand and snickered. "Yeah, I remember now.
The woman who ran the place, she had a thing for Norton, apparently. The gossip at the pub was that they were sleeping together.

Of course, nobody dared mention it when he was around, but I reckon he was doing it so he didn't have to pay for his room."

Day slipped his right hand under the table, made a fist, and thumped his thigh. A few days ago, they had nothing on Norton. Not even his name. Now they had an ex-girlfriend.

31
FIGHT

THE MASTERMIND

Norton sat on the edge of the bed and rubbed the coin between his fingers. Last night's bit of fun with the detective couldn't have gone better. The coin had chosen surrender, and then she had obliged. She might not have realized it yet, but by following her instinct not to resist him, she had come out of the game with her life.

In that sense, she'd won, but Norton knew that the victory would be hollow. She'd bowed to his will. He'd exercised such total control over her, she'd ignored her police training and failed to do her duty. For one precious moment, the detective had belonged to him. She would have to live with that knowledge forever.

There had been only one real victor. The game master had triumphed. He lay back on the bed, put his hands behind his head, and wallowed in the memory. The rules of the game meant he had to spare her. The simple act of letting her live had thrilled him to the core. It had been almost as empowering as depriving someone of their life. Almost. He was already impatient to play the game again.

A flip of the coin would decide, fight or surrender, and the victim's choice would seal their fate.

Norton rolled off the bed, walked out into the living area and over to the cluttered kitchen counter. He picked up a loaf of bread, pulled out two slices, and studied them for mold before dropping them into the toaster. He hadn't eaten for more than twelve hours, and his stomach was letting him know it. Hidden under a pile of dirty plates and empty soup tins, he found a half-empty can of tuna. When the toast was done, he laid the chunks of fish between the two slices and took a large bite.

His mouth was still full when he heard a knock on the door. It was early for Finch to come calling. The greedy little rodent had probably come to whine about the rent. Norton was in the mood to teach him a lesson.

He was still chewing when he opened the door to be confronted by a slender man in a crumpled linen suit and an older, taller, greasy-haired man holding an expensive camera. The younger man attempted a smile, and Norton remembered why his smug face was so familiar.

"My name is Matt Revell, and I'm a reporter from the *Daily News*. I'm here to ask you about—"

Before he could utter another word, Norton took a long stride forward, forcing the two men backward. The photographer raised the camera. That was his first mistake. Norton grabbed at it, wrenched it out of his hands, and smashed it with as much force as he could muster onto the bridge of his nose.

The photographer staggered back and fell to his knees. He cupped his hands over his face as blood streamed into his beard. He looked up at Norton and yelled, "I'm suing you for assault, you fucker!"

That was his second mistake. Norton's right foot connected with the center of the man's chest, rocking him off his knees and sending him crashing onto the floor. He writhed on his back, making horrible choking sounds as the blood from his nose streamed down his throat. Norton turned to Revell, who was standing with his back to the wall, his eyes wide, the color draining from his face.

"The *Daily News*... I mean, we...believe you are the suspect," the reporter stuttered, holding the portable digital recorder in his right hand. "Believe you are the person wanted for the crime...in connection with...the attack...the violent assault on Gem... The police are on the way. Would you like to comment?"

Norton stared at the reporter, his dark eyes narrowing to slits. After a few seconds, he reached out and took the recorder from Revell's hand, then turned and walked back into the apartment.

Keep calm, Norton told himself, dropping the camera and the recorder on the food-stained sofa. Walking across the room to his bed, he smiled. What the hell was he thinking? He'd never had a problem keeping calm, even when the rage burned inside. On the outside, he always stayed in control, always knew exactly what to do and when to do it.

He'd been thinking about leaving Finch's rathole anyway. He walked over to his unmade bed and picked up his jacket. Lifting the mattress, he poked a hand underneath it and rummaged around until his fingers closed around the hilt of the hunting knife. He slid it into his pocket, then swept up a handful of coins scattered on the bedside table.

He had to move swiftly. They had been telling the truth about the police, he knew that. The reporter didn't have the guts to come knocking on his door without backup.

Norton thought about the pile of clothes he'd stashed under the bed and decided to leave them. He'd be able to buy a whole wardrobe of new gear soon. He strode over to the sofa, picked up a cushion, unzipped the cover, and pulled it off. Picking up the camera and the reporter's recorder, he put them inside the cushion cover and headed for the door.

Stepping outside, he saw Revell kneeling beside his semiconscious colleague, trying but failing miserably to stem the flow of blood. Norton considered using his knife to make the reporter reveal the name of the person who'd betrayed him. The wail of a siren stopped him. Instead, he placed the sole of his boot on Revell's back and pushed hard, sending him crashing on top of his bloodied colleague.

Norton ran down the stairs, slipped out the back door, and sprinted along the passageway. Emerging onto Broadway, he casually stepped onto the sidewalk to join the stream of commuters heading for Stratford's Underground station.

Dozens of heads turned as a police car passed, its siren screaming and blue lights flashing as it wove its way through the rush-hour traffic. Norton kept his eyes forward and his pace steady as his mind replayed the morning's events.

By the time he reached the entrance to the Tube station, the answer had come to him. As far as Norton was aware, only one person knew where he lived. Only one person was such a slave to greed that he'd sell that information to a newspaper and risk the consequences.

THE REPORTER

Revell accepted the cup of coffee from the uniformed constable and took a sip. It was lukewarm, but he desperately needed a shot of caffeine. He'd already given a detailed witness statement describing the assault on the *Daily News* photographer and had expected to be allowed to go home.

Instead, the fair-haired constable, who Revell guessed was about his age, had advised him there would be more questions and explained that the interview would be led by a senior officer. The use of the word *interview* had set alarm bells ringing. It was too close to *interrogation*.

The door opened, and a detective entered. He took a seat but said nothing. Revell sensed that he was being weighed up, and the feeling was unnerving.

The older detective looked to be in his midthirties. He was the tallest in the room and lean with it. His dark-brown hair showed no sign of graying, but faint lines around his eyes suggested a lack of restful sleep.

Revell lifted the paper cup and took another sip. The movement spurred the senior detective into action.

"I am Detective Inspector Elliot Day," he said. "This interview will be recorded, and it may be used as evidence if your case is brought before a court."

Revell choked on the coffee, coughing and spluttering until his eyes watered. "Hey, wait a minute," he said, still struggling for breath. "What's going on? If my case goes to court? What the hell are you talking about?"

Day put his hands flat on the table and drummed his fingers. "I'm talking about using the tape of this interview as evidence if we decide to charge you."

Revell looked at the constable, hoping for some sign that they were joking, but all he got in return was a stony glare. "You're kidding me, right? All I'm guilty of is trying to do my job, witnessing a colleague being brutally assaulted, and having my digital recorder stolen. I'm a victim, not an offender."

Day smiled and drummed his fingers again. "What about withholding evidence?" he said. "How long have you known where a possible suspect in the Gem Golding case, the man you have identified as Connor Norton, was living? He's an extremely dangerous man, and if you'd told us earlier, we'd almost certainly have him locked up by now."

Revell lifted his hands to his face and massaged the bridge of his nose. The action made him think about the *Daily News* photographer lying in a hospital bed. Day was right. A violent man was still prowling around the city because he wanted his name above the crime story of the year. He still had a story to write once he got out of there, of course. A pretty hot one. But not the one he wanted.

"I'm genuinely sorry about Norton getting away," he said. "But you know a charge of withholding evidence is never going to stick. I was doing my job, that's all, and the paper did call you to report the suspect's whereabouts before I went in."

Day put his elbows on the table and leaned forward, pushing his face close to Revell's. "Tell that to Gem Golding," he said. "How do you think she's feeling about all this?" Day sat back and gave the uniformed officer a nod. "Let's switch the recorder on and get started with the interview, shall we?"

Revell took a deep breath and thought about asking for a lawyer. The *Daily News* would willingly provide one. He discarded the idea, because it would only lengthen his stay at the station. The last thing he wanted was to spend a night in a holding cell because a hotshot lawyer wasn't immediately available.

He wanted to get out of there as soon as possible to get working on the story. He was already thinking about a follow-up interview with Gem Golding.

32
SURRENDER

THE DETECTIVE

Shields pressed the doorbell and waited. She caught Day's eye and pressed it again, holding the button down longer this time. "I don't think it's working," she said. "I can't hear it chiming."

Day stepped forward and knocked three times on the flaking paintwork.

Above the door, a hand-painted sign attached to the Victorian brickwork by four rusty screws read *Roman Villa*. Day wondered if the interior of the guesthouse was in a better state of repair than the outside.

The door cracked open, and a pair of dark-green eyes below deep-red bangs peered through the gap. "No vacancies," the woman said. "Both rooms are rented out long term."

She moved to close the door, but Day slid his foot over the threshold, making it impossible. He showed her his badge but could tell by the wariness in her eyes that she'd already worked out that they were police officers.

"We'd like to come inside if it's not too much trouble," he said.

"We need to talk to you about someone we believe stayed here three or four months ago."

The woman opened the door wider. "What's this all about?" she said. "I haven't got time to waste, you know. I've got rooms to clean. My place has a reputation for being spotless."

She was an inch or so shorter than Shields, slim and smartly dressed in black slacks and a tight-fitting maroon sweater.

Day gave up waiting to be invited inside and brushed past her, striding swiftly down the narrow hallway. The woman scurried after him, high heels scraping the tiled floor. Shields followed, closing the door behind her.

Day paused at the end of the hall where he found himself with a choice of three doors. One straight ahead, one to his left, and one to his right. The woman caught up to him, pushed past, and led both detectives into the back room. It was surprisingly large and stylishly furnished. Day could see that double doors in the back wall led to an extension housing a modern kitchen.

"Nice place you've got here," he said, smiling broadly.

She responded with a frown, her furrowed brow mostly hidden beneath her bangs.

"The Roman Villa guesthouse is registered as being owned by Alice Shelton. I take it that is you?"

"That's right. This is my business. You can call me Ms. Shelton. Now what is it you want? I do have a record of all my guests somewhere on my laptop, but so many people have stayed here over the years, it would be impossible for me to remember them all."

"You'll remember this one," Shields said. "Trust me."

Shelton's eyes flashed at the detective, but she turned her attention to Day. "Who are we talking about?"

"Maybe we should sit down," he said. "This could take a while."

Shelton sighed long and hard, making no attempt to hide her

exasperation. "You can take a seat if you want to. I haven't got the time."

Day shrugged and stayed where he was. "The guest I want to ask you about is a man called Connor Norton." As he said the name, he studied Shelton's face carefully. Her expression didn't change, but he thought he glimpsed an involuntary tightening of her jaw.

Shelton looked up and then to the right, adopting an expression of intense concentration. Day exchanged glances with Shields. They both knew she was playacting.

"You claim you haven't got time to waste, so it's best if we don't play games," he said. "We have information that Norton stayed here for several weeks, and not simply as a paying guest."

Shelton didn't flinch. "When you say 'information,' you really mean 'gossip,' don't you? What have people been saying?"

"That's not important. We know Norton stayed here, and we know you were in a relationship with him."

Shelton closed her eyes for several seconds. When she opened them, they were full of humiliation, and she started to sob softly. "I don't want to talk about him. I can't." Shields pulled a wad of tissue from her jacket pocket and held it out. Shelton took it and dabbed her eyes.

"I'm sorry if this is upsetting for you, but we do need to ask you some questions about Norton's stay here," Day said. "He is wanted in connection with a serious assault on a woman."

If the news surprised Shelton, she didn't show it. "What exactly do you want to know?"

"Were you two very close?"

Shelton had pulled herself together, and the tears had stopped flowing, but she gripped the damp tissues tightly in both hands. "I thought we were, but the truth was he was playing me. He wanted a warm bed, that's all, and he didn't want to have to pay for it. That's what he told me before he left. Those were his exact words. Why would you say something like that unless you really wanted to hurt…" She faltered, blinked several times in succession, then bowed her head.

Day didn't want to give her time to start crying again. "Did you have a sexual relationship?"

Shelton didn't bother answering, but she twisted the wad of tissues so hard, they began to shred, the tiny white flakes falling onto the carpet. Shields flashed her boss a look that made him feel uncomfortable.

"Can you remember how long Norton stayed here?" he asked.

"Three months, I think. Yes, that's right."

"And for exactly how long were you sleeping together?"

Shelton lifted the tissues to her nose and sniffed. "We were together for about two months. He moved into my room so we could get another paying guest in. I thought it made financial sense. Con was lovely, at first. He even started to help me run the place. A bit of cleaning and cooking. He said he wanted to help because I wouldn't let him pay rent once we were…you know. It didn't seem right. He protested, but eventually, I persuaded him." She walked unsteadily over to one of the three armchairs in the room and sat down.

Day looked at Shields and tilted his head to the right. She accepted the invitation and asked, "Was there a particular reason he walked out when he did? Did you have an argument?"

Shelton shook her head. "He woke up one day and out of the blue told me he was bored out of his skull. That was how he put it. Laughed in my face and said I was a dull bitch. That was it. Nothing else. He was gone before breakfast."

Shields took a step closer to where Shelton was sitting. "Didn't you have it out with him? Get angry? Demand a proper explanation? I know I would have done."

Shelton stared into space, her eyes wide and unfocused. Day sat down in the armchair closest to her, rested his elbows on his thighs, and leaned forward.

"During the weeks you were sleeping with Norton, did he ever assault or threaten you?" he asked. "Men like him are skilled at using violence or the threat of violence to control people, especially women."

Shelton glanced up at Shields, then shifted her gaze to Day. "I never saw him lose his temper once. He's not a patient man, and I noticed that some men—no, most men—are intimidated by him. But I honestly never saw him lose it."

That doesn't mean a lot, Day thought. Some of the most violent men he'd put behind bars were cold-blooded, emotionless.

Shelton jumped to her feet, hands flapping. "I really haven't got time for this," she said. "I've got to get my guests' rooms ready, and I'm already behind schedule."

She walked briskly into the hallway, expecting the detectives to follow so she could see them out. When it became clear they were staying put, she walked back and stood in the doorway, fists on her hips.

"Bear with us a little bit longer," Day said. "This is a major investigation, and the sooner you answer our questions, the sooner we'll leave you in peace."

Shelton let her hands drop from her hips but kept her fists clenched tight.

"Think carefully about this, please," Day said. "When you were with Norton, I mean after he moved into your room, did he ever talk about his past, his family background?"

Shelton raised a hand to her forehead. "I told you I don't want to think about him. I want to put this behind me. I'm trying to get the bastard out of my head."

Shields stepped toward her and offered her a smile. "Then help us catch him and lock him up. Take your time. This is important.

There must have been some moments, intimate moments, when you talked about your lives."

Day could tell Shelton was struggling, torn between her desire to airbrush Norton out of her life and her desperation to get him and Shields to leave the house. Her eyes flicked around the room, searching for an answer.

"He never was much of a talker," she said, her voice so soft, Day stood up and joined Shields so he could hear what was coming next. "But he did once mention a children's home in south London, or maybe Surrey. He was there for years and hated every minute of it. I don't think he ever told me the name of the place."

Day glanced at Shields, who raised an eyebrow. It wasn't a lot to go on, but it was a new lead. "Is that it?" he said. "Nothing else that might help us?"

"Yes, that's it," Shelton snapped. "I told you I'm busy. I've done my best to help you, but if you want to waste more of my time, then I'm afraid you'll have to arrest me." She turned around, walked down the hall, and opened the front door.

This time, Day and Shields followed her.

Shields walked straight to the car, but Day lingered on the threshold. "Thanks for your cooperation, but there is one last thing," he said. "Did you say your guest rooms are occupied at the moment?"

Shelton half closed the door. Day didn't move.

"That's right, both of the rooms upstairs," she said. "Both long stays and prompt payers. I don't want to give them any reason to leave."

Day nodded, smiled, and stepped out. He turned to thank Shelton again, but she slammed the door in his face.

33

FIGHT

GEM THE WARRIOR

Gem stood in her bedroom and studied her reflection in the full-length mirror. She found herself looking at a person she didn't know. A person she never thought she'd become. Where had the self-confident, ambitious, young woman gone?

Drew had nagged her again that morning about skipping breakfast. Over the last few days, she'd been feeling queasy, but her appetite usually returned by lunchtime. Nervous energy had always unsettled her stomach. She'd never been able to eat before presentations to clients. That's why she had preferred to arrange them for early in the working day. Once they were over, she'd feel ravenous and fill up at lunch.

She'd been so lethargic recently, she'd even cut short her last couple of workouts at the gym. She walked out of the bedroom and went downstairs, determined to keep her promise to Drew that she'd at least venture out of the house for a walk.

Sitting on a wooden stool in the hall, she pulled on her lilac sneakers. Tying up the laces, her arms felt leaden. Her fingers were so stiff and clumsy, it took her three attempts to complete a task a seven-year-old could manage with their eyes shut.

She stood up, flexed her knees, and touched her toes. Panic rose in her chest at the thought of stepping outside. She sat back on the stool and buried her head in her hands. Why the hell was she letting this happen? She'd always prided herself on being adventurous, always up for a challenge. Not long ago, she'd stood up to and fought off a man who got his kicks out of terrifying women, and now the thought of him walking the streets turned her legs to jelly.

During the carjacking, she'd stayed strong, physically and mentally, but now it felt as if her life was crumbling around her, and she couldn't understand why. He was winning. She felt she was morphing slowly from a warrior into a victim. She closed her eyes and tried to shake away that thought. *How has it come to this?* she wondered.

Gem wanted to cry. She thought that maybe it would make her feel better, but no matter how hard she tried, the tears wouldn't come. She took that as a good sign. *You can beat this*, she told herself.

She stood up and walked to the door. A gentle jog around London Fields in the spring sunshine would do her a world of good. Lift her spirits. She'd promised Drew she'd do it, and she wanted to prove to him that she had turned a corner.

She stretched out a hand and grasped the handle. Her brain urged her to turn it, but her arm refused to obey the instruction. She sank to her knees and pressed her head against the central door panel.

THE DETECTIVE

Day sat in the unmarked police pool car outside the main entrance to Newham General Hospital. In the five minutes he'd been there, he'd been approached by two different parking wardens ordering him to move on or be towed away. Each time, he'd seen them off with a wave of his badge.

When his detective sergeant finally emerged from the building, he felt it had been worth the wait. The sight of her in a wheelchair being pushed by a male nurse made him smile. The expression of fury on Shields's face was the funniest thing he'd seen for months.

He climbed out from behind the driver's seat and ran around the car to open the nearside back door. Shield waved an angry hand at him.

"In the front. I'll sit in the front."

"You'll have more leg room in the back," Day said. "It'll be more comfortable for you."

Shields glared at him until he stopped grinning. He slammed the back door shut and helped her into the front passenger seat as the nurse hurried back into the hospital with the wheelchair.

Day slipped back behind the steering wheel. "Have you been causing trouble in there? The nurse looked relieved to see the back of you."

Shields adjusted her position in the seat and winced, turning her head to try to hide the fact that she was in pain. "We had a difference of opinion about whether I needed to leave the hospital in a wheelchair. I'm quite capable of walking, but he claimed that the stitches could tear and if I didn't let him push me out to the car, then I'd have to stay in another night. One night in that place was more than enough for me."

Day had decided to pick her up from the hospital himself because he wanted to assess if she was up to viewing the CCTV footage of the attack. Watching the video would certainly put her resilience to the test.

"I assume they've given you something for the pain," Day said, starting the engine and pulling away. "If not, we can stop at a pharmacy on the way back."

"Thanks for the thought, but I'm good. Fully medicated."

The traffic on the A12 was flowing smoothly for a change, and the drive to Hackney Central took them twenty minutes. Apart from a bit of complaining about how the hospital ward smelled of bleach, blood, and decay, Shields didn't say a lot. Day guessed she was gearing herself up for what was to come, and he couldn't blame her.

He parked and hurried around to the front passenger door to help Shields get out, but she waved him away. "I can do this myself," she insisted. "I'm not an invalid, you know."

Day walked slowly to the station entrance to give his limping detective sergeant the chance to keep pace, and they took the elevator to his second-floor office. CCTV footage was usually viewed on one of the larger screens in the detectives' squad room, but Day didn't want Shields to have to cope with an audience.

He sat behind his desk, and Shields took the seat opposite. After adjusting the position of his computer monitor until they could both see it clearly, he opened the CCTV file.

"Are you sure you're ready for this?" he said. "If not, it can wait a day or two."

"For God's sake, just do it. Play the video."

Day did as she asked. Both of them edged their chairs a fraction closer to the screen and leaned forward eagerly. Day had watched the footage several times the previous day and had formed his own opinion about what was going on, but he was interested in the victim's take on what had happened that night.

They watched the car pull up outside the gates of the tire-fitting unit and Norton walk around to the driver's door, a hunting knife in his right hand. When he yanked the door open, the glare of the security light lit up Shields's pale but remarkably composed face.

A sharp intake of breath from across the desk prompted Day to offer reassurance. "You did well to stay so calm," he said. "It must have been difficult."

"I might have looked calm, but the truth is I was anything but. I should never have let myself be handcuffed like that."

"You didn't have a choice."

They fell silent again as the action unfolded. Before they reached the point where the knife fell from Norton's hand and he turned his back on Shields, Day paused the footage.

"Watch this carefully," he said. "I'd be interested to know what you think."

"About what?"

"Watch and tell me what you see."

Norton pulled the handcuffs from his pocket and held them up. The knife dropped from his other hand onto the ground with a clang. He turned and squatted to pick it up. Day felt Shields stiffen. He knew she was reliving that fraction of a second when Norton had his back to her, that moment when consciously or subconsciously, she decided not to fight back.

He paused the video again and clicked on rewind. He hated putting Shields through this, but it was necessary. "This time, I'm going to zoom in on the hand holding the knife."

After a few seconds, Shields sat back. "Oh shit," she said.

"You see it too then?"

Shields nodded. "The knife doesn't slip accidently from his fingers, does it? He lets it fall to the ground."

"That's exactly what I thought," Day said. "Then he deliberately turns his back on you while unarmed."

Shields thought for a moment. "The son of a bitch gave me an opening. A chance to resist. He was testing me, and I failed."

"I don't see it that way," Day said. "I think it might be more of a case that somehow you followed some set of warped rules. Maybe, in his twisted mind, you did the right thing by not resisting when you had the chance, so he let you live."

Shields stood up and limped over to the window behind Day. "But if I'd gone for it and managed to overpower him, then we'd have him locked up and this nightmare would be over."

Day spun his chair around until he faced her. "That's right, but what if you'd tried to take him on and come off worse?"

He looked Shields in the eye and knew that they were both thinking the same thing. "If you had fought back and failed to overpower him, then I believe he would have killed you."

Shields went back to the chair and sat down. "Maybe this should make me feel better about standing there like an idiot doing nothing, but it doesn't."

Day restarted the video, and they watched the rest of the footage, which ended with Norton tucking his hands into his jacket pockets before sauntering off into the darkness.

Shields took a deep breath. Day had taken the view that his detective sergeant was strong enough mentally to cope with watching the footage, and he'd been proved right.

"Do you think it's that simple?" she asked. "His sick rules. Submit and you live, resist and you die?"

Day shook his head. "Things are rarely that simple where psychopaths are concerned. This individual hasn't suddenly turned bad. It's likely he was born bad. The Gem Golding incident was probably a trigger event for him. He has drawn up his own set of rules, how he decides whether to take a life or spare a life. We'll know more when he chooses his next victim, because he will strike again, and I'm certain his ego will make sure we get another good look at him in action. Unless, of course, we catch him first."

34

SURRENDER

GEM THE VICTIM

Gem stood patiently by the police station counter, having been told that she'd be seen by someone from the Criminal Investigation Department as soon as possible. Having spent twenty-five minutes lined up to speak to the police constable manning the front desk, she was surprised how promptly a door to the right of the counter opened. A fresh-faced young man wearing black trousers and a gray jacket with black elbow patches beckoned her in. He looked much too young to be a detective, she thought. Surely CID didn't do work experience placements?

"If you'd like to come upstairs with me, my boss will be with you in a minute or two," the detective said.

Gem nodded and followed him up a flight of steps to the first floor. He led her into a room furnished with a worn but comfortable-looking sofa, a small table, and two plastic chairs.

The detective smiled nervously. The fine lines that appeared around the corners of his mouth and eyes reassured Gem that he was probably old enough to arrest real criminals. "How's the injured arm doing?" he said, pointing at the cast on her right wrist. "How much longer have you got to have that thing on for?"

Gem hiked up the sleeve of her jacket, revealing a few more inches of the graying plaster. "I think it's healing pretty well, thanks. No pain now, but it itches like crazy under the cast. It has to stay on for a week or so yet."

The detective gave her a sympathetic nod. "Would you like me to fetch you a cup of tea or coffee? I'd recommend tea, because the coffee here tastes like pond water. If you're lucky."

"Tea would be perfect, thank you. Two sugars."

Once he'd left the room, Gem sat on the sofa and let out a long, loud sigh. She hoped the sweet tea would settle her stomach down in time for lunch. When the police had first told her that Drew had died, she'd almost thrown up on the spot, and the nausea had never completely gone away.

She took a deep breath and exhaled slowly through her nose. She could cope with a queasy stomach. There were more important things to worry about.

Things like finding out when Drew's body would be released for his funeral, like making sure the police would do everything possible to find the man who killed him, like not letting herself panic that her whole life was unravelling.

Her attacker had assaulted her, humiliated her, snuffed out her boyfriend's life. Now she was doing her best to take ownership of everything that had happened. Facing up, fighting back, it was the only way she could keep everything together.

The door swung open, and she looked up, surprised to see Detective Inspector Day enter the room carrying a tea. He was smartly dressed in a dark suit and tie and appeared taller than she remembered.

"Two sugars for you," he said, handing her the cup. He pulled one of the plastic chairs away from the table and placed it so he could sit facing her. "So tell me," he said. "What can we do for you?"

As far as Gem could judge, Day was a respected detective and a decent man, but she no longer had space in her head to worry about offending people. Even people she liked.

"You can arrest the man who took Drew away from me, who destroyed my life, that's what you can do. Find the man who deliberately shoved him under the wheels of a Tube train. It would be really great if you could do that for me, Detective Inspector."

Day responded with a rueful smile. "I promise you we are trying our best to do exactly that. In fact, we have recently made some interesting progress in the investigation into both the attack on you and your boyfriend's death."

Gem guessed that the detective had dealt with plenty of grieving loved ones over the years. He showed no sign of taking her outburst personally. She also gave him credit for not claiming that he understood how she must be feeling. "What do you mean by progress?"

Day edged his chair a fraction closer. "We are confident that we now know the identity of your attacker. I'm afraid I can't release his name right now. But we have also established that he had an appointment with Drew Bentley at Stone and Maddox. He was after free advice about losing his casual job at a warehouse in south London."

Gem sat up straight and perched on the edge of the sofa, wondering if she'd misheard. "He was one of Drew's clients?"

Day nodded. "A nonpaying client, a pro bono case. It's not clear why he thought he had grounds to complain about being fired. He was never officially an employee at the warehouse and had to leave after seriously assaulting a coworker."

The skin on the back of Gem's neck prickled. "This doesn't make any sense. Are you sure about this?"

"We're sure."

"Was this appointment with Drew before or after he attacked me?"

"It was definitely before the carjacking. Two weeks before to be exact. We have a copy of Mr. Bentley's appointment records. Did he ever mention having had a disagreement or being threatened by one of his pro bono clients?"

Gem took a sip of the tea and made a face. She stood up, put the almost full cup on the table, and sat down again. "We never really talked much about Drew's work or mine," she said. "We both did long hours, so when we'd have some time together, it was the last thing we wanted to discuss. I did know that he was close to making partner, which was why he had to increase his charity work. It was expected. He would have been the youngest ever partner at Stone and Maddox."

"Did you have any plans to get married?"

"We had talked about it, but that's all. Drew was keener than I was, and it did cause some friction. As far as I was concerned, it wasn't something we needed to think about."

"I take it he didn't mention that Stone and Maddox encourage partners to have a settled home life and wives to show off at functions?"

Gem frowned. Drew had never mentioned that, and she found it hard to believe that he would approve. "Please tell me you're joking," she said. "We are living in the twenty-first century, aren't we?"

Day shrugged one shoulder. "I know, I know, but it seems some of the people at these old City firms either don't know that or don't care. You'd think a lawyer smart enough to make partner wouldn't put up with it, but the rewards of towing the line are pretty tempting. Detective Constable Stock checked out the figures, and some partners in law firms the size of Stone and Maddox made more than 1.5 million pounds last year."

Gem tried to think back to the few conversations she'd had with

Drew about him becoming a partner. She was fairly sure that he'd never once mentioned what the promotion would mean to him financially. He'd certainly never said he'd been pressured to get a wife.

"Are you really saying Drew was expected to marry before he could be made a partner?"

"We interviewed his boss, Edward Maddox, and while he didn't actually say you had to have a wife, or a husband for that matter, he did tell us that his firm preferred potential partners to have a settled home life, and that Drew had assured him that he would be getting married soon."

Gem shook her head. "We had no plans to get married. I think I would have known about it if we had, don't you?"

Day shrugged. "I'm not trying to upset you," he said. "I'm just trying to catch a killer."

Gem took a long, slow breath. She knew none of this was the detective's fault. She didn't want to believe that Drew would go along with that kind of sexist crap, but most of the friction in their relationship had been caused by her dedication to her job.

"So, can you explain to me," she said, "what all this has got to do with the investigation?"

Day stood up and paced across the room and back again. "We don't know yet," he said. "But it can't be a coincidence that your boyfriend gave legal advice to the man who later attacked you and then killed him."

Gem watched the detective inspector walk across the room again. "You say you know the suspect's name. Why can't you just pick him up?"

"Because it's not that simple. If you don't want someone to find you, the metropolis of London is a perfect place for a fugitive to hide, especially if you move from address to address, don't use smartphones, and make sure you pay for everything with cash."

Gem had been wondering whether to tell Day that she'd offered to do an interview with the *Daily News* and decided this would be a good time to bring it up.

"What about using the press to flush the suspect out? The *Daily News* is interested in doing a story on the fact that the man who attacked me is suspected of killing my boyfriend."

Day stopped pacing and sat back down on the plastic chair. "Officially, Drew Bentley's death was either suicide or an accident. We're not yet in a position to release the news that we now suspect he was deliberately pushed onto the track."

Gem waited for an explanation but didn't get one. She took a deep breath and asked the one question she'd been dreading. "When is Drew's body likely to be released? There are a lot of arrangements to make." Grief rose in her throat, but she swallowed it down.

Day raised a hand and reached out to offer comfort but pulled back at the last second. "Unfortunately, it's going to be a while before we can release the body," he said.

THE MASTERMIND

Norton wiped a smear of tomato sauce from his lips with the back of his hand. Alice had offered to cook him a meal, but he'd sent her out for a pizza instead. He'd never liked her culinary skills. She was much better in the bedroom than she was in the kitchen.

He screwed up the greasy pizza box and dropped it on the carpet beside the bed. *That'll drive her crazy*, he thought. Serves her right. Since her slip of the tongue, she'd been desperate to make it up to him, constantly apologizing and begging for forgiveness. She claimed she'd panicked under pressure.

She wasn't really sorry. He knew that. She knew him as well as anybody. Knew what he was capable of. The bitch was right to be scared. He strongly suspected that her telling the police about the children's home hadn't been an accident at all.

He wondered whether returning to his old stomping ground in Stepney had been a mistake. He'd needed somewhere to bed down, and this place had been an easy short-term solution. Once everything was sorted out, he'd be where he belonged. With Gem Golding. For the moment, he had to keep a tight rein on Alice. He'd always believed himself a good judge of people, especially women. There was a slight risk that she'd eventually summon up the courage to turn him in, but he planned to be long gone before she reached that point.

He swung his feet off the bed, swiveled, and sat on the edge of the mattress. The door opened, and Alice poked her head into the room. "Can I get you a beer, Con?" she asked. "I've a few in the fridge."

Norton beckoned her in, flicking his head toward the space on the bed beside him. She obeyed, closed the door behind her, and sat down. He draped an arm around her shoulders and pulled her close, digging his fingers hard into her flesh until she winced.

"Not right now," he said. "I'm going out soon and will probably be back late. Very late. Got some important business to attend to, so I wouldn't bother waiting up."

He released his hold on her, and Alice edged away but stayed sitting on the bed. Norton looked down at her black pencil skirt and smiled broadly. "I'm glad to see you've got your legs out at last. You look much better."

Alice stood up, smoothing the front of the skirt down with both hands. "I decided you were right about me wearing trousers."

"Of course I was right. I always know what's best for you. You should know that by now."

"They don't suit my shape. I'm going to stick to skirts and dresses from now on."

Alice's eyes flicked down to the crumpled pizza box on the carpet. She bent down and picked it up without comment.

Norton grinned and shook his head slowly. He'd learned about the power of fear early in life. It was the first thing he could remember feeling, and he had soon come to understand two crucial things. First, fear doesn't exist except in people's minds, and second, it's a potent weapon of manipulation and control.

He maneuvered himself onto his back on the bed, stretched, and tucked his hands behind his head. "I'll be needing a front door key so I can come and go without disturbing you. You see, I'm still as thoughtful as ever. I remember that was always one of the things you liked about me. I've probably still got my old key somewhere, but I imagine you've had the locks changed."

Alice didn't respond and moved toward the door.

Norton stopped her in her tracks with one word. "Key," he said softly.

She reached out and grabbed the handle. Norton watched her knuckles turn white.

"I've got a spare one," she said. "I'll leave it in the kitchen for you on the hook next to the microwave."

When she'd gone, Norton laughed and stared up at the ceiling. After a while, he closed his eyes and began planning the night ahead. The desire for revenge was prehistoric. The thought of it warmed his blood.

He'd grown sick and tired of living in Finch's dump in Stratford and had been thinking about moving on for a while. But that didn't mean he could accept being forced out. Betrayal was unforgivable. In Norton's mind, he had an obligation to exact retribution. Someone must have tipped off the police. Someone must pay.

———

Norton pressed his back against the wall, slid his hand into his pocket, and pulled out a coin. He flipped it, caught it, and slapped it down on the back of his other hand. He'd carefully chosen the spot because it was dark and out of range of the nearest streetlight, but when he revealed the coin, its surface still glinted in the gloom. Tails. Surrender. Norton smiled. *This could go either way*, he thought. *He's a cowardly little rat, but cornered rats can bite.*

He put the coin away and edged along the wall to get closer to the door as Finch stepped out onto the street, turned, and rummaged in his pockets for the key. He could tell from the smug look on the little slimeball's face that it had been a profitable night.

Norton waited until the key was in the lock, then pounced. Sliding swiftly out of the shadows, he slipped an arm around Finch's neck in a choke hold, rammed his head into the door like a battering ram, and dragged him into the shop.

Kicking the door shut, Norton used all his strength to increase the pressure on Finch's throat. In a few seconds, he felt him go limp and let him drop to the floor.

Gasping for breath, Finch rolled onto his back, raised a hand to his forehead, and stared at the blood on his fingers. Only then did he look up at the face of his attacker. "Oh God, no," he said. "Please, no."

Finch's pleading filled Norton with disgust. He grabbed his arms, pulled him into the storeroom next to the counter, switched on the light, and closed the door.

Finch tried to lever himself up into a sitting position, but Norton placed a foot on his chest and pushed him down onto his back. Rivulets of blood ran down the side of his face from the cut in the middle of his forehead.

"That looks nasty," Norton said. "You should get it seen to. We don't want those good looks ruined, do we?"

"What do you want from me?" Finch asked.

"I want what I'm due. Compensation."

"For what?"

Norton squatted down to look Finch in the eyes. "For being forced to leave that rathole upstairs. No notice. No nothing. Did you think it'd be an easy way to get rid of me?"

"I don't know what you're talking about," Finch said, frowning. "Honestly, I don't understand."

Norton tilted his head, then shook it slowly. "Tipping off the police was a big mistake. The biggest you'll ever make. I can't actually believe you had the guts to do it."

"I didn't tell anyone about you. That's the truth. Please. Why would I do that? I wouldn't. I didn't. You've got to believe me."

Norton stood up. "I haven't got to do anything," he said. "I thought you'd have learned that by now. I also always make sure that anybody who betrays me pays the price."

"I didn't do anything," Finch said. "I swear it. I don't know how the police knew about you living upstairs, but I didn't tell them. I wouldn't snitch, honest."

"Don't lie to me," Norton hissed. "Just do as I say. Don't give me any trouble and maybe I will show you mercy. Even though it goes against my nature." He placed the heel of his right boot on Finch's forehead and ground down on the wound. Finch cried out, grabbed Norton's ankle with both hands, and wrenched it hard to the right. Norton wobbled, almost lost balance, then pressed his heel down harder on Finch's head until he released his grip.

Norton took his foot away. "You're such a pathetic loser, aren't you?"

Finch said nothing. He slipped a hand inside his coat and pulled the money bag from his pocket. "You're right," he said, his voice weak with pain. "Here, it's only fair. There is more than three hundred pounds in there. Take it."

Norton crouched down, reached for the bag, then toppled onto his right side. Finch took the bait, twisted to his left, and aimed a vicious kick at Norton's groin. The kick never hit its target. Before Finch could even think about his next move, Norton's right knee slammed into his stomach. The little man doubled up in agony, rolling from side to side, groaning and gasping for air.

Norton jumped up and checked the contents of the bag. The cash would come in useful, but he felt nothing but contempt for Finch's belief that this was about money. He stood up and put the bag on top of three cardboard boxes that had been stacked against the wall. Pulling what looked like a large plastic bottle of mineral water from his pocket, he unscrewed the top. A strong smell of gasoline filled the room.

"What's going on?" Finch asked, wriggling up into a sitting position. "What the hell are you doing?"

The panic spreading across his face made Norton smile. "You've paid me for having to find somewhere else to live. Now you've got to pay for your betrayal. You had your chances, I gave you chances, but you failed. You lost. Rules are rules. I have no choice now."

"What are you talking about? Are you crazy? I told you I didn't tell the police anything."

Norton started pouring the gasoline liberally around the room, spraying the walls, cardboard boxes, and furniture. Finch attempted to scramble to his feet, but Norton placed the sole of his boot on his chest and stamped hard, forcing him onto his back again. Finch whimpered like a wounded dog as Norton poured the last third of the gasoline over his face, shoulders, arms, and legs.

When he'd finished, he dropped the empty bottle and walked out, switching off the light as he went. He turned and stood silently in the darkness for a few seconds. He could see Finch lying perfectly still, waiting meekly until he was sure that he was safe.

Norton took a box of matches from his pocket, struck one, tossed it into the storeroom, and ran for the door. Outside, he stopped running and walked calmly away, heat on his back and Finch's screams ringing in his ears.

35
FIGHT

THE BOYFRIEND

Drew Bentley sat back, stretched his legs, and rubbed the soft leather arms of his chair. He loosened his tie and surveyed his office, recalling how excited he'd felt on his first day at Stone and Maddox. He'd made it. A big-city lawyer, with a big desk and a salary to match.

He smiled at the memory. Through a combination of hard work and talent, things had gone well for him, and now he was on the brink of achieving heights he had believed were out of his reach. Considering where he'd come from, he had a lot to be proud of.

Along with being made a partner would come a bigger, grander office and what some people might describe as an obscene salary. To him, obscene was good. The annual partners' bonus would be the icing on the cake.

Everything was falling into place, even Gem. Initially, he'd been worried that after the carjacking and the hysterical news coverage of her bravery, it would be even harder to get her to come around to his way of thinking.

Things had turned out differently. She'd become more and more affected by what had happened to her that night, to the point where she thought she was being stalked every time she left the house. Each day that passed, she showed less and less interest in climbing back onto the career ladder.

She'd become nervous and a little feeble. Not a good image. The last thing he wanted was for her to lose the spark that had attracted him in the first place, but that didn't mean he couldn't try to take advantage of her anxiety while it lasted. He picked up the telephone and dialed Gem's cell phone. She answered on the third ring.

"Hi, Drew, are you on your way home?"

He found himself wanting to smile but knew she'd be able to detect it in his voice. "I'm so sorry, darling, but I'm going to be busy here for a while yet. You'll be all right, won't you?" The line fell silent, but he could hear her breathing become louder and faster.

"Are you still there, Gem? Look, I've got a pile of case files I really need to go through, but I'll only do half of them tonight so I can get back sooner. What about that?"

"If you really need to stay, then I'm fine with that," Gem said, sounding anything but fine. "It's just that I've been at home on my own all day, and I'm feeling a bit miserable. You know I can't even think about going to bed and trying to sleep until you get back."

Bentley sighed, unnaturally loudly. "You've not been out of the house at all? You didn't go for that walk we talked about then? I thought you were determined to get out, to start getting on top of this thing?" Gem sniffed twice, and he wondered if she'd started to cry.

"I know I promised," she said. "It's hard to explain. I really wanted to, but I just couldn't do it. Not on my own. I will though, soon. Maybe tomorrow, or the day after. I'm determined to sort myself out. I need a little bit more time, that's all. I've been thinking that perhaps it would be a good idea to do what that detective suggested and have some counseling."

Bentley thought for a moment. "Maybe we should have a serious talk about it," he said. "I tell you what I'll do tonight. If I set myself a lower target, aim to work through only a third of these case files, then I should be able to get back home by 10:30, 11:00 at the latest. If I get in early tomorrow and work through my lunch, I should be able to catch up. What do you think? If you really can't cope on your own for a couple of hours more, then I'll drop everything and come straight home, of course. The problem is that will only create a backlog, which will mean I'll have to stay even later another day."

Gem stayed silent. Bentley imagined her holding the telephone in one hand and nervously twirling a lock of her hair with the other. When she did speak, it was short and to the point. "Do whatever you want," she said, terminating the call.

36
SURRENDER

THE DETECTIVE

Day smiled at his son and pulled away from the curb into the slow-moving traffic. The boy didn't smile back, and he couldn't blame him. Pressure of work meant their outing was going to have to be cut short.

Day had tried to explain that he shouldn't even be taking the morning off, but his estranged wife and Tom hadn't been impressed. The Gem Golding carjacking and the death of her boyfriend had become all-consuming. The investigation was finally starting to get somewhere, making it increasingly difficult to keep the Bentley case from being taken out of his hands and passed to his old squad.

Day flicked a sideways glance at Tom in the front passenger seat. The boy's head was bowed, his dark bangs falling away from his forehead. You didn't need to be a detective to work out that he was sulking.

"I thought we might spend a few hours visiting the London Dungeon," Day said. "We haven't been there for a while, and I know you love all that gory stuff. What do you think?"

"If you want."

Day was wondering whether it would be worth splashing out for a ride on the London Eye or even a short Thames cruise when his cell phone rang. He let it ring out and drove on for a couple of hundred meters until he could pull up on the forecourt of a gas station.

Shields knew he had taken the morning off, but he'd said she could contact him if it was urgent. He checked his phone's screen, hoping that the caller had been someone he could safely ignore. It wasn't.

"Damn," he said.

His son lifted his head and gave him a curious look.

"Sorry about this, Tom, but I have to make a quick telephone call about work. It won't take a minute."

Day climbed out of the driver's seat, slammed the door shut, and phoned Shields. She answered straightaway.

"I know this isn't good timing, but it couldn't wait," she said. "I think you need to see this, Boss."

"See what?"

"We've got another body."

Day knew that if he ever caught any of his detectives bringing a child along to a crime scene, he wouldn't hesitate to tear a strip off them and suspend them from duty for at least a week. Somehow, he'd convinced himself that his situation was different. He couldn't face driving Tom back and explaining to his wife that their outing had been canceled.

At the end of Stratford High Street, the entrance to Broadway was blocked by two uniformed police constables standing in the road. One of them recognized Day and waved the car through. A fire engine was parked outside the kebab shop, and Day pulled up beside it. Tom had perked up and was gazing intently at the flame-blackened brickwork and the shattered glass shopfront. Naturally, a bit of real-life gore was more interesting than a trip to a tourist attraction.

"Sit tight here for a while," Day said. "I need to take a look, but I promise I'll be as quick as I can."

Tom nodded but said nothing. He was more interested in the devastation caused by the fire than anything his father had to say.

Day climbed out of the car and spotted Shields deep in conversation with a tall, gray-haired firefighter, his bright-yellow helmet tucked under his arm. The detective sergeant beckoned her boss over.

"The blaze was extinguished in the early hours," she said. "But the body was only discovered recently when the firefighters went in to clean up. They'd assumed that the place was empty. There was no reason to believe there was anybody in there."

Day turned to the firefighter. "Does it look like the fire was started deliberately?"

"Officially, our investigation isn't yet complete, but from what I've seen, there is no doubt about it. There is evidence that an accelerant was used, probably gasoline or some kind of oil."

"Is it safe to go in and take a look at the body?"

"It is, but we used a lot of water, so watch your step." The firefighter raised a hand and signaled to a younger colleague who jogged over carrying yellow hard hats for the detectives.

Shields led the way into the building. The floor was blackened, the walls were charred, and the service counter had been partially melted by the intense heat. Shields covered her mouth and nose with a hand, walked cautiously over to the doorway of what looked like a storeroom, and gestured for Day to do the same. He stepped closer and gagged. He'd experienced the smell of roasted human flesh once before and had suffered nightmares for several weeks after.

His eyes rested on a pile of charred debris on the floor. It took him a few seconds to realize it was human shaped. "I take it we don't know for sure who this is yet?"

Shields reluctantly removed her hand from her face. "The pathologist and crime scene investigators are on their way, but it will take a while before we can formally identify the body. It'll probably come down to dental records, but I don't think there's any great mystery here."

Day didn't say anything. He raised an eyebrow and waited for Shields to explain herself.

"We sent a couple of uniforms around to inform the owner about the fire, and his wife said he didn't come home last night. She had no idea where he might be. She said she was worried about him because he'd never stayed out all night before."

Day took a long look at the black, twisted corpse. "So that's probably Kevin Finch. The man who swore that he'd no idea that our suspect was living in the apartment above his business. He's obviously upset someone, and I think we both have a good idea who that person is. He's moved from carjacking to pushing someone under a train to burning a man alive."

"We don't know that for sure," Shields said. "It's not going to be easy to prove. The body's well on its way to being cremated, and the heat is likely to have destroyed any forensic evidence. Maybe Finch started the fire himself, or a faulty electrical device burst into flames and he happened to find himself trapped."

Day knew she was right to be cautious, to wait for the pathologist and fire incident reports before jumping to conclusions. He also knew he was right about who'd done this to Finch. This was Norton's work. He had to be stopped, and Day wanted to be the man to do it.

"Take a good look, Cat," Day said, pointing at the body. "We know that Norton has been living in the apartment above this room, and despite what Finch claimed, the two men would have known each other. We're starting to get an idea what Norton is capable of. Do you really think it possible that this fire was an accident?"

Shields let her gaze linger on Finch's scorched remains for a few seconds. She didn't say anything. She didn't have to. Instead, she turned and walked away.

Day joined her on the sidewalk outside. He took a deep breath and exhaled loudly, trying to clear the smell of barbecued flesh from his nostrils. "When you get back to the station, I want you to check on how Stock is doing chasing up those children's home records. I'll be there in an hour or so."

Shields nodded, but he could see that her eyes and attention were focused on something behind him.

"Tell me something, Boss," she said. "I assume you know that there's a child in the passenger seat of your car?"

Day took off his hard hat and handed it to Shields. "That's Tom. I'll see you back at the station as soon as I can."

37
FIGHT

THE MASTERMIND

Norton stepped out of the bathroom, wrapped a towel around his waist, and sat on the double bed. He was still sore about being forced to abandon Finch's hovel when the meddling reporter had come calling. The budget hotel room was even smaller than the kebab shop apartment, but at least it was clean. It was as good a place as any to hole up until he could find something cheaper and long term.

He reached over to the bedside table and picked up the camera he'd taken off the newspaper photographer. Norton didn't know much about the technology, but it was clear it could be used for shooting video footage as well as still images.

He placed it back on the table, switched it on, and pressed Record. He lifted his jacket from the bed and fished a pound coin from a pocket. Crouching, he positioned his hands in front of the camera lens and flipped the coin. Heads. Fight this time. The coin had decided. The game master will execute.

Twenty minutes later, he was dressed and walking along Mile

End Road toward the Underground station. Every few hundred meters, Norton passed a neon sign advertising fried chicken, and all the takeouts were packed with ravenous, drunken customers.

It was a clear spring night, and in the distance to the south, he could see Canary Wharf's forest of illuminated towers.

He rode the Central line to St. Paul's, and as the train slowed on its approach to the station, he scanned the miserable faces of the other passengers in the rattling car. The contempt he felt made him smile and shake his head. How would these people react if they knew who he was, what he'd done, and what he was about to do? Their ignorance of his power over life and death thrilled him to the marrow of his bones.

Riding the escalator up to the ticket hall, he patted his pockets. Satisfied that he had everything he needed, he walked through the barrier and out of the station. Turning onto Paternoster Row, he headed west toward the floodlit dome of the cathedral.

GEM THE WARRIOR

Gem stood by her bedroom window and squinted through a chink in the curtains. Two women deep in conversation stood near the bus shelter at the top of the road, one with a muscular, brindle-colored dog straining on its leash. The rest of the street seemed quiet, but that didn't make her feel safer.

In the past hour, she'd checked the front and back doors three times, making sure they were double-locked and that the extra bolts Drew had fitted for her were in place. A cyclist without lights on his bike slowed as he rode past the front of the house on the sidewalk. Gem tracked him carefully until he was out of sight.

Fear and anger burned high in her chest. Turning away from the window, she walked into the bathroom, bent over the sink, and splashed cold water on her cheeks. Catching a glimpse of herself in Drew's shaving mirror, she paused to stare at her reflection. She took a short, sharp breath and sent the mirror flying with a swipe of her hand. It landed in the bath with a loud clang and slid toward the taps, the chrome frame scraping the white enamel.

Gem picked it up and placed it back on the tiled shelf, relieved to see the surface of the mirror hadn't cracked. She despised the way she was behaving. It was almost as if she'd been the loser in her struggle with the carjacker, as if he still had his fingers around her throat and was slowly squeezing the life out of her. She knew she couldn't allow things to slide any further. There would be no coming back from self-hatred.

Gem went downstairs, sat on the sofa, and picked her book off the coffee table. She was a third of the way through the story, a mystery set during the reign of Queen Elizabeth I, but she hadn't read a line since the night of the carjacking.

She started to read but found it impossible to concentrate, her trembling hands causing the text to blur. Closing the book, she put it down on the arm of the sofa, stood up, and walked into the kitchen. She poured herself a large glass of white wine, drank half of it, then topped it up.

She hated the person she was becoming. Things had to change and soon. Drew was due home in an hour, and they would talk, draw up a plan, work out the best way to get her life back on track. Thank God she had someone she could depend on to help her through this living nightmare.

THE BOYFRIEND

Bentley put the last file in his desk drawer and locked it. If he left in the next few minutes, he'd be home earlier than Gem would be expecting. He let himself imagine the look of relief on her face and smiled.

He stood up, pushed the chair closer to the desk, and bent down to pick up his briefcase. As he straightened up, the office door opened, and a tall, hooded figure stepped into the room. Bentley froze. He couldn't believe what he was seeing.

The man half turned, closed the door, and pulled the hood of his jacket back onto his shoulders. "Good evening, Andrew," he said.

Bentley dropped the briefcase and gaped. He hadn't prepared himself for this. He'd assumed that Norton would never be stupid enough to confront him again.

"What the fuck are you doing in my office?" he said.

Norton took a couple of steps closer. "Now, that's not a very nice welcome. I've been here before, remember? I'm back because we have unfinished business and you know it. You didn't think I was going to let it go, did you? You know me better than that."

Bentley pulled his chair back. He'd been caught by surprise, but the shock was starting to wear off, and he felt that psychologically, he'd a better chance of controlling the situation from behind his desk. He sat down and gestured for his unwelcome visitor to do the same.

Norton stayed where he was, his lips curling into a sneer. "I'm not one of your self-important, puffed-up clients. I'm not here to sit down and listen to you spouting bullshit. You owe me, and I'm here to collect."

Bentley put his hands on the desk and clasped them tightly. His heart had stopped hammering, and he was feeling confident again. There was no reason for him to worry, he told himself. He was skilled at this. He'd always been a talented negotiator.

"I'm not aware that I owe you anything. Not a single penny. Why don't you enlighten me?"

Norton threw his head back and laughed. "I'm not going to spell it out for you. I shouldn't need to do that. But it's typical of you to think that this is all about money. Do you really think you'd be here if I hadn't saved your skin?"

Bentley shook his head slowly. He didn't want to go there. "How did you get inside the building?"

"I forced the back door. It wasn't a problem. You know, it's surprisingly easy to creep up on somebody when the place is decked out with plush carpets. I knew the alarm would be off because you were still here, working late like a good little office boy."

"How did you know I'd be here at this time?"

A familiar smile slanted across Norton's face. "I've been watching you for a while. It might surprise you, but I'm very methodical. I've always been much more organized than I let on. I know what sort of hours you've been putting in. I'm not sure whether you're trying to impress the boss or simply desperate to avoid going home to that bitch of yours. Knowing you, it's probably both."

Heat flushed Bentley's cheeks. "What's to stop me calling the police right now? They'd be here in a few minutes. You know, for the life of me, I can't understand why you've been making such a nuisance of yourself. The clever thing to do would have been to go to ground, keep your head down for a while."

Norton lifted the hood back over his head, pulling the top down low over his forehead. "I'm done with keeping a low profile. It doesn't suit my personality. Go ahead, pick up the telephone, and call the police if that's what you really want. Or maybe you're scared. Frightened about what I might tell them? I wouldn't blame you. You've good reason to be frightened. Now, are you going to give me what I'm owed, or am I going to have to take it from you?"

Bentley licked dry lips. Nobody liked being threatened. He wasn't going to accept it. He hadn't been talked to like that for a long time. He had to make it clear to Norton that he wasn't in a position to get away with anything.

"There are cameras in all the common areas of this building, the stairs, the lobby areas, every corridor on every floor. They are the best security cameras money can buy, and the quality of the footage is exceptional. You've been captured on film getting to this office, and you'll be captured on your way out."

Norton shrugged. "I've been caught on CCTV cameras plenty of times, and I'm still walking around this city, doing as I please. The truth is I don't mind being filmed. I like people seeing exactly what I do. I'd hate to be accused of something I hadn't done. Actually, because I knew there wouldn't be a camera in your office, I've brought my own along."

Unzipping his jacket, he reached inside it and pulled out an expensive-looking digital camera. He walked across the room, positioned it on the top of an oak-and-glass filing cabinet standing against the wall, making sure that the lens pointed at the desk.

"I've switched it on, and it's recording now," he said, striding back and checking over his shoulder to make sure he was in shot. "This baby shoots good-quality video too. I've tested it out."

Bentley jumped up, balled his hands into fists, and stalked around to the front of the desk. "What the hell are you playing at? I haven't got time for this."

Norton whipped his right hand around to the waistband of his trousers at the small of his back, pulled out a black-handled hunting knife, and jabbed the blade in Bentley's direction.

"That's where you're wrong," he said. "Whether you like it or not, you've got all the time in the world."

Bentley's brain raced with possibilities. He knew what Norton was capable of. He held up his hands in a placatory gesture. "There's no need for that. If you feel so strongly about this, I'm willing to pay you something, even though you messed up." He reached inside his jacket and produced a black leather wallet. "Here you go then," he said, slapping a wad of notes on the desk. "Two hundred and fifty pounds in cash. You can take that, then make yourself scarce. Leave the city for a while. That'll be the best thing for the both of us."

Norton stepped closer, holding the knife in front of him. Bentley winced as the point of the blade pierced his shirt, nicking the skin above his navel. A blood rose bloomed on the crisp white material. He tried to back away but found himself trapped against the desk.

He unclenched his fists, then clenched them again, weighing up whether he had the strength and speed to grab Norton's hand and wrench the knife away.

Norton sneered. "You're dying to have a go, aren't you? I can see it in your eyes. Go on then. Show me what you can do. Have you got the guts? Not if I remember correctly."

Bentley had always considered himself the stronger of the two. *Now's not the moment*, he told himself. *Too risky. Keep him talking and bide your time.*

"Listen to me," Bentley said. "There's no need for any of this. Consider that cash a first installment, a down payment. Take it for now, and I'll get you more, no problem."

Norton pulled the knife back a couple of inches. Bentley groaned with relief.

"How do I know I can trust you?" Norton said. "Forget that. Stupid question, because I know I can't. You've always been as slippery as a fucking eel and twice as slimy."

Bentley pressed the palm of his right hand tentatively against the patch of blood on his shirt. The wound was sore but superficial.

"I'll get you more money, I swear. I've got plenty of it. Think about it. You're going to need a lot more than two hundred and fifty pounds if you're going to leave London and set yourself up somewhere else."

Norton stayed silent, but Bentley thought he was getting through to him. He'd always been unpredictable, but you could usually get him to come around to your way of thinking if you were smart enough.

"Take that cash now, then give me a couple of days, and I'll get the rest of what I owe you. More if you want."

Norton lifted the knife and wiped a smear of bright-red blood off the point of the blade with his thumb and forefinger. Bentley took that as a good sign.

"Don't even think about moving," Norton said. He picked up the money with his left hand and stuffed it into his jacket pocket. A couple of notes came loose and fluttered to the floor. He bent down to scoop them up, placing the hand gripping the knife on the edge of the table for support.

Bentley tensed every muscle in his body, ready to launch himself at Norton. His heart hammered as adrenaline surged through his body, but he didn't move. The moment seemed to stretch out in slow motion. Bentley's gut urging him to attack. His head telling him to hold back. There was no need to take a risk. He could talk Norton around, have him eating out of his hand within the hour.

Norton stood up and flexed his shoulders, his eyes like ice.

"That's it then," he said, moving closer.

"What are you…"

Before the words were out of his mouth, a muscular forearm slammed into the side of his neck. The force of the blow sent him crashing to the floor, dazed and writhing in pain. Before his head cleared, a hand grasped his throat. Norton's speed and power had surprised him. The man was so much stronger than the boy.

The grip on his throat loosened, and he coughed and spluttered as he tried to suck in air. He closed his eyes and let his breathing settle. When he opened them, Norton was staring down at him, shaking his head. Bentley opened his mouth, but before he could speak, Norton jammed a forearm hard across his windpipe. Bentley flailed his arms and kicked his legs in panic, his lungs crying out for air. *This can't be it*, he thought. *There's no way this is it.*

Norton shifted his weight until he was in a position to bear down harder. Bentley stopped kicking. His skull felt like it was about to split open. His vision blurred, then dimmed. He tried to focus on Norton's face, but it faded to nothing.

The last words he ever heard were whispered in his ear.

"Game over. I win."

38

SURRENDER

THE DETECTIVE

Day flicked through Kev Finch's postmortem report while he waited for Shields to arrive. As he'd expected, there were no surprises. It was murder. He'd been beaten then set alight.

Likely cause of death: multiple organ failure brought on by agonizing pain and massive shock to the system. The presence of ash and soot in his trachea showed the poor bastard was alive when engulfed by flames.

Shields entered the office, closed the door behind her, and took a seat. Day thought she looked tired.

"How are the children's home checks going?" he said.

"Nothing so far."

Day picked up the pathologist's report, waved it at Shields, and let it drop back onto the desk. "Definitely murder," he said. "Not that there was ever much doubt about it. It seems that Finch was very alive when he was set alight. Alive and probably conscious."

Shields winced. "To burn someone alive like that. That's pure evil."

"It's worse than that," said Day. "According to the pathologist and the fire brigade, the seat of the blaze was actually the body. Finch was doused in gasoline, then Norton tossed a lighted match on him. In other words, he used Finch to start the fire, turned him into a gasoline-soaked pile of human kindling."

Shields raised a hand to her face and rubbed her eyes. "There's no way we can keep this one to ourselves."

"I've no intention of doing that. It would be impossible. Finch's death is being passed on to the murder investigation team immediately."

"With the name of the suspect?"

"We'll give them everything we know about Norton. Why wouldn't we? In fact, I've already set the process in motion. The Gem Golding carjacking is technically still our case though, so I don't see any reason we should stop going after Norton. With a bit of luck, we'll get to him first."

Shields tilted her head to one side and frowned. "What about Drew Bentley? We're pretty sure he was pushed under the train by Norton. Surely Scotland Yard needs to know the man they're hunting has killed at least two people so far."

Day thought for a moment, then nodded. "I agree. Let the coroner's office know Bentley's death is no longer thought to be suicide and notify the murder team of the link to Finch's death. I'm sure they'll be grateful that we've already done a lot of their work for them."

At that moment, they were interrupted by a knock on the door. Shields stood up and opened it to find a sheepish-looking Stock holding a cup of coffee.

Day looked at Shields and rolled his eyes. "For God's sake, I take it you're knocking on my door for a reason, so quit messing around, get in here, and tell us what it is."

The young detective hurried into the room, put his coffee on Day's desk, and slipped both hands into his pockets. He slid Shields a flustered glance and shifted his weight from one foot to the other.

"The thing is, Boss," he said, "we just received an email from Scotland Yard letting us know the name of the DCI who'll be leading the investigation into the Finch murder."

"Right, that was quick," Day said. "Is this a guessing game, because if it is, then you've got to give us some kind of clue."

"It's...er...apparently, it's Detective Chief Inspector Rob Hardy, Boss."

Day sat back in his chair and crossed his arms, the reason for Stock's awkwardness clear to him. Everyone in the station knew by now that his wife had packed her bags and left him for Hardy. They'd been having an affair for months.

The one positive thing was that when he felt low, he could always conjure up the memory of Hardy stretched out on the floor, the smile wiped off his smug, fat face, blood dripping from his mouth onto the squad room carpet. That always cheered him up.

"Well, I'll tell you both something for nothing," Day said. "It's a good job that we're still going to be doing our best to hunt this psychopath down, because Rob Hardy is one of the worst senior investigating officers I've ever worked with. To make matters worse, the irritating little shit actually thinks he's some kind of hotshot."

Shields gave him a half smile. "Right, Bill, now that's dealt with," she said. "What's the latest on Norton's children's home history?"

Stock rummaged in his jacket pocket, dug out a crumpled notebook, and flipped it open. "Well, I think we've hit the jackpot there. I was going through the records of children who were resident at a home called Greenhills in Croydon in 2008, and on the list is a Connor Norton. It's not a common name. It must be him."

"What age was he then?" Day asked.

Stock consulted his notes again. "It says here that he was sixteen, so that sounds about right, doesn't it?"

Both Day and Shields nodded. Encouraged, Stock carried on.

"Greenhills closed down four years ago, something to do with local government funding cuts, but I have got some names and addresses of staff who were working there at the time Norton was a resident."

Day stood up quickly, took his jacket off the back of his chair, and slipped it on. "Good work," he said. "We need to interview those home workers as soon as possible. You stay here and see what else you can dig up about Norton in the foster care system."

Stock smiled and squared his shoulders. "That's not all, Boss. There's more. There was another name on the Greenhills list that jumped out me. A resident called Andrew. Andrew Bentley, aged seventeen and a half."

39
FIGHT

GEM THE WARRIOR

Gem sat on her bed hugging her knees, wiped her bloodshot eyes, and wondered if she was going crazy. Drew was dead. Murdered in his office. Her initial reaction to the news had surprised the detectives. She'd laughed. Not because she thought it was funny but because it had to be a sick joke and breaking down and crying would make it normal. Make it true.

Everything changed, the true horror hit, when the tall, female detective asked if she wanted her to contact a family member or a close friend and promised to arrange for a liaison officer to stay with her for a few days. Those simple words had crushed her heart like a vice, set her whole body shaking, and released a flood of tears.

When Drew hadn't come home and wasn't answering his cell phone, she'd known deep inside that something was seriously wrong. It was out of character for him not to let her know if he'd had to change his plans. He'd always insisted that she do the same. Even so, she'd waited another hour before calling the police.

A rap on the door made her start. "It's Carol. Are you all right in there, Gem? I'm putting the kettle on. Would you like me to make you a tea or coffee?"

The family liaison officer was only doing her job, but Gem found her irritating, especially the shrillness of her voice. She didn't want tea or coffee. She didn't want anything or anybody, except Drew. If she couldn't have him, she wanted to be alone.

"No thank you, Carol," she said. "Nothing for me. I'm tired and am going to try to get some rest."

"Are you sure I can't get you anything for breakfast? A bowl of cereal or some toast?"

Gem didn't answer. She didn't want a conversation. She wanted silence. After a minute or so, she heard Carol retreat on the landing, then her footsteps heavy on the stairs.

Gem looked across the room at the silver photograph frame on the dressing table. It contained a picture of her and Drew sipping cocktails on the beach in Barbados during their first holiday abroad. They both looked tanned and deliriously happy. It was their favorite holiday snap.

She slid off the bed, picked up the photograph, and stared at it for several seconds, her eyes fixed on Drew's smiling face. Draped over the back of a chair beside the wardrobe, she noticed one of his black cotton T-shirts. She lifted it up to her face and smelled it, smelled him. She folded the shirt carefully around the photo frame, lay back down on the bed, and curled into a ball.

The thin morning light slid through the blinds, throwing angled stripes on the wall. In the distance, Gem could hear the constant rumble of traffic. She'd been awake all night and desperately needed the refuge of sleep. The last thing she wanted to do was lie there awake, imagining Drew stretched out cold and lifeless on his office floor, but she knew she would.

The detectives would be back in a few hours to ask her more

questions. They hadn't yet told her who they suspected had murdered Drew. As if she needed telling.

She squeezed her eyes shut as tears slid down her cheeks. Drew's life had been snuffed out like the flame of a candle. If she hadn't stopped at the store on her way home that night, if she'd been more passive when attacked, done what she'd been told, let Norton grope her and take the car, none of this would have happened. If she could go back and do it differently, be a meek little victim, she would.

Why had she gone to the press and humiliated her attacker, provoked him? Drew had been unhappy about her decision to go public. He'd urged her to be cautious, but she'd pushed his concerns aside.

She hugged the T-shirt and photograph closer to her stomach. Drew had gone. Nothing would bring him back. But part of him would always be with her.

THE DETECTIVE

Day and Shields sat through the video footage of Drew Bentley having the life choked out of him in silence. Both of them had dealt with dead bodies before, but this was the first time they'd watched someone being murdered.

When the recording finished, Day raised a hand to his face and rubbed his eyes. A mixture of anger and despair filled his chest. *Who or what shaped this cold-blooded killer?* he wondered.

"Do you want a replay?" Shields asked.

Day shook his head. "No, shut it down for now. I think we've seen more than enough for the moment."

Shields closed the video file, stood up, and limped slowly over to the window. The thigh wound was obviously taking its toll on her physically, and seeing Norton choke Bentley to death would have reminded her how close she'd come to a similar fate. He considered suggesting that she take some time off but dismissed the thought straightaway. He needed her on this case.

"Why is Norton so keen for us to see him in action?" Shields asked. "He set up the camera he stole from the *Daily News* photographer to film everything and left it there for us to find. The footage starts with him flipping a coin. What the hell does that mean? It must be important."

"He wants us to see because he's proud of what he's doing," Day said. "He's an exhibitionist. The sicko is showing off and mocking us at the same time. He gave you a moment when you could have resisted him, you didn't, and that turned out to be the right decision, because he let you live. It looks to me like he deliberately gave Bentley a similar opportunity to have a go. When he dropped the money and reached down to pick it up, it looked to me as if he was tempting Bentley to fight back. The way Bentley held himself, leaned forward, at that moment suggests to me that he was poised to go for it but decided not to. They seemed to be having a long discussion prior to that, but the sound was off, so I guess the conversation wasn't important as far as Norton was concerned. But I'd bet money that he was goading him to fight for his life."

Shields sat up straight in her seat. "You flip a coin to settle something, decide something. Heads or tails. Everyone knows that. Maybe that's what Norton's doing here. Deciding whether his victim lives or dies."

Day locked eyes with his sergeant. Something told him she was on the right track. "I don't think it's going to be quite as simple as that," he said. "But it's possible Norton has come up with some kind of twisted game and is using the coin to set the parameters. Everything seems to hinge on whether his victim fights back or caves in. What if that split-second decision Bentley made not to risk resisting cost him everything? If he'd fought for his life, then maybe Norton would have allowed him to live."

Day paused and tried to put himself inside the head of a psychopath, a person with no conscience, devoid of empathy. He thought about putting his needs, his desires, above all else, about controlling people for fun, about hurting people for the sheer thrill of it and not giving a shit. It was surprisingly easy to think that way if you tried hard enough.

"Well, I don't think he's using the coin to decide who his victims are. He clearly has other motives that seem to be linked to Gem Golding. Maybe he's flipping the coin to decide how they will die."

"I think that could be right," Shields said. "I also think it's unbelievably twisted. It's full of risk though. How could Norton be sure that he would be able to get the better of Bentley if he needed to? It could have gone the other way. If I'd taken the fight to him, maybe he'd be behind bars already."

Day shook his head and slapped the desk. "That's just it. Real hard-core psychopaths love taking risks. I've met a few, and believe me, the excitement of risk-taking, the thrill of the kill, is one of the few emotions they're capable of feeling. Apart from that, their egos cannot let them even envisage defeat. They come to believe they are invincible, especially after they have killed. The more people they kill, the more they think they are untouchable. That's usually their downfall, how they end up getting caught. They eventually push the risk-taking too far."

"Hang on a minute," Shields said. "Let's run the Bentley video again. Just the start though. The bit where he flips the coin."

She limped back to her chair, grabbed the mouse, and clicked Play. They watched the pound coin spin, land in Norton's palm, and then be flipped onto the back of his other hand. Day leaned closer to get a better look.

"The coin landed on heads," Day said. "Bentley scorned the opportunity to fight for his life and was killed. If he had gone for it when Norton bent down to pick up the cash he clearly deliberately dropped, would he have been allowed to live? Think about what's happening to Gem Golding. She fought back. What if he'd flipped tails and she needed to surrender to survive. Instead, she got away, and that means he still has to apply the rules. Why he won't let it go."

Shields shrugged, but a surge of adrenaline quickened Day's pulse. They were finally getting under the killer's skin, delving into his thought processes. His time on the murder squad had taught him that was a good thing. He'd arrange for a police psychologist to study all the footage they had to draw up an offender profile and, at the same time, give her opinion on the flipping of the coin. These people knew more than anybody how the minds of killers like Norton worked.

"Of course, the murder investigation team will take on the Bentley murder, which is obviously linked to the Gem Golding carjacking. However, the carjacking is still technically our case."

"The Yard may not see it like that," Shields said. "In fact, I'm pretty sure that they'll see it as unnecessary interference with the potential to obstruct their murder inquiry. They won't want us stepping on their toes."

"I don't care what they might think," Day said. "We're still investigating the carjacking, and as long as we move quickly, we could pick up Norton before the MIT even get rolling. That can only be a bonus. I don't see how Scotland Yard can complain about that. I want a thorough check on Bentley's background. His family, all that stuff. Remember, officially, this is part of the carjacking investigation, not his murder."

Shields opened her mouth to protest but changed her mind.

Day knew what she was thinking, why she was concerned about bending the rules.

"There's no reason for you to worry about any comebacks on this. It's my decision. If we catch Norton before the murder squad get close, then all's good. No one in their right mind is going to complain about us catching a killer. On the other hand, if it all goes to shit, then you were only following orders. My orders."

40

SURRENDER

GEM THE VICTIM

Gem stood under the showerhead, letting the hot spray sting her face until she stopped crying. She stepped out of the cubicle, placing her feet carefully on the white rubber mat, and dried herself slowly and methodically.

Her mother had taken the train back to Wales but had promised to return to London before Drew's funeral. When that would be was anybody's guess. So far, the police had been unable to say when the body might be released, especially now that his death was being treated as murder.

Gem was secretly content to push the finality of a funeral service to the back of her mind. For now, she wanted to focus her mind on the hunt for the killer.

She'd finished drying off when the hall telephone rang. She needed to get dressed for work and was tempted to ignore it. Instead, she wrapped the towel around her body, walked out onto the landing, and headed down the staircase.

She hitched the towel a fraction higher and picked up the

receiver, anticipating a call from the police or the *Daily News* reporter she'd spoken to a couple of days ago.

"Hello," she said.

Silence.

"Hello."

"How are you?"

The voice was deep, smooth, and familiar. A shiver played down Gem's spine.

"Who is this? What do you want?"

"I'm sure you know who I am, Gem."

The casual use of her first name made her stomach churn, and she fought the urge to slam the telephone down. Instead, she took a long, deep breath.

"You killed Drew," she yelled. "You murdered him."

The line fell silent again, but Gem could hear his breathing, faint and steady. She didn't wait for him to respond.

"Why are you doing this? I don't understand."

"Oh, but I think you do understand," he said, a smile in his voice. "Deep down, you know, but you won't accept it, not yet. Drew Bentley wasn't the man for you. He would have destroyed your life. I know it's difficult for you right now, but there is no need to worry. I'll look after you. You can depend on that."

Gem's head swam. He wasn't making any sense. "Why did you kill Drew? Why are you coming after me? Haven't you done enough?"

She could hear her own breathing, loud and ragged. A single bead of sweat trickled down her forehead. She didn't know whether she should keep him talking or end the call.

"You're confused, of course, but it will all make sense to you soon. I promise you. You're wrong about one thing though. I'm not coming after you, Gem. Not at all. I'm coming for you. We're going to be so good together."

Gem wiped her moist brow with the back of her hand. "You must be a madman, totally insane."

He laughed loudly. The sound scared her more than anything he'd said. "My sanity has been questioned before, but in a crazy world like this, I think it helps if you're a little bit unhinged."

Gem leaned against the wall to stop her legs giving way. "Why me? What is it you want?"

"Isn't it obvious? I want you, Gem. Right now, I want you to go upstairs and put some clothes on. You must be getting cold standing there in nothing but a towel."

Gem let the telephone fall to the floor and dropped into a crouch, pulling the towel higher to her shoulders and tugging it down over her knees.

THE DETECTIVE

The woman who opened the door looked younger than Day had expected. Amanda Turner had been employed at the Greenhills children's home for ten years, and by the time it closed, she'd worked her way up to the position of assistant manager. Tall and stick-thin, with straight, gray-streaked brown hair, she peered at the two detectives from under blunt bangs.

Day held up his ID. "Good afternoon, Mrs. Turner. You're looking a bit confused, but Detective Shields here did speak to you earlier on the phone to ask if we could talk to you about Greenhills."

Turner stepped back nodding, holding the door open wide for them to enter. "Of course," she said. "Forgive me. I don't know why, but I was expecting someone in a police uniform."

She led them into a tiny, cluttered living room. Extra shelves had been put up in the alcoves on either side of the fireplace to display porcelain figurines of every type of animal you could think of. Next to the ancient-looking television stood a glass display case full of miniature crystal ornaments.

There was just enough room for the detectives to sit side by side on a tiny sofa, their shoulders and elbows touching, while Turner disappeared into the kitchen. She promptly reappeared carrying three milky teas in delicate china cups on a floral-patterned plastic tray.

Day would have preferred a large mug of coffee, but he smiled his thanks and took a sip. Shields took her cup and drained it in one gulp.

"Interesting collection you've got here," Shields said, nodding at the animal figurines. "Must have taken you years to amass this lot."

Day slid her a sideways glance, wondering whether she was simply being polite or had extremely poor taste.

Turner put the tray on the reproduction coffee table and sat down. "They were all collected by Charlie, my late husband. He died of a heart attack a year ago. I don't like them actually. Never have done, but I can't bring myself to get rid of them. Not yet. It doesn't seem right."

Day put his cup on the table. He understood that the woman was making the most of the company, but he was eager to get straight to the point.

"We want to ask you some questions about your time at Greenhills," he said. "In particular about a couple of the residents. Connor Norton and Andrew Bentley. Do you remember them?"

"Connor and Andrew? Yes, I remember them, of course. Greenhills was small, and we had no more than fifteen residents at a time. Boys between the ages of fourteen and seventeen. With the older ones, we'd be focused on preparing them to cope on their own once they'd left the home."

"How old were Norton and Bentley when you started working at the home?"

Turner took a moment to think, crinkling her brow in

concentration. "It was a long time ago, but I think they must have both have been around fifteen or sixteen."

"Did they get along? Were they friends?"

Turner picked up her tea and raised it to her lips. Shields noticed her hand trembling as she put the cup down, a smear of dark-red lipstick on its rim.

"As far as I can remember, they got on like a house on fire. They shared a room at one point, I think, and I don't recall them ever falling out, which is unusual for kids of that age. I think they'd both been in the foster care system since they were very young. Toddlers even. Never knew anything different. They were both excited about reaching the age when they could leave Greenhills and had even talked about getting a place together."

"Were they difficult teenagers?" Shields asked. "How would you describe their personalities?"

Turner put her hands on her stomach and clasped them tightly. "Every child at Greenhills had their own issues," she said. "As a young boy, Connor would regularly get in fights with locals, but he started therapy with a child psychologist, and it seemed to work. He learned to control himself most of the time, but he could still be extremely intimidating when he wanted to."

"What about Bentley?" Day asked.

"Like I said before, all these children had problems. Remember they would have either been orphaned, abandoned, neglected, or abused. The thing about Andrew was he was very focused and very ambitious. That's why I found it strange that he and Connor were so close. Naturally, it all changed when…"

"When what?" Day prompted.

Turner blinked and lifted a hand to her throat. "Oh God, don't tell me Connor has turned up? After all these years. Is that what this is all about?"

Shields breathed in sharply and leaned forward in her seat as if she was unsure whether she'd heard right. "What do you mean turned up?"

"You're not saying he's dead? That you've found his body?"

"No, we haven't found his body. What did you mean about him turning up?"

Turner looked quickly at Day, then back at Shields. "Oh, right," she said. "I assumed you knew about Connor running off. He had only a year or so before he would have been old enough to leave us anyway, but he disappeared. Ran off and was declared missing."

Day couldn't make sense of what he was hearing. "You're saying Connor Norton was officially a missing person?"

Turner nodded. "That's right. He was and, as far as I know, still is. Hundreds if not thousands of children in care homes go missing every year. A lot of them turn up eventually, but some don't. Connor never did. And it wasn't because the police didn't try to find him. It was a big story around here. His disappearance coincided with the disappearance of a local girl. Mary Freeman, she was fifteen I think, vanished from her parents' home on one of Croydon's biggest estates. The police thought the disappearances could have been connected, that they might have run off together, but couldn't find anything to link them. The girl's poor parents even made a television appeal for information, but she was never found."

Day shot a look at Shields. They were both thinking the same thing. "What about Bentley? How did he take losing his best friend?"

"Surprisingly well, actually. Andrew always was the sensible one. When he left Greenhills, he went on to further education, and we heard that he eventually qualified as a lawyer. We were all very proud of him. Andrew was definitely Greenhills' biggest success story."

Day stood up. "Thanks for the tea," he said. "You've been extremely helpful."

Turner put her hands on the arms of her chair and pushed herself up with a groan. "You didn't answer my question about Connor earlier. I've wondered what happened to him a lot over the years. Has he turned up?"

"He's turned up all right," Shields said.

Turner smiled as she led the detectives to the front door. "After all these years. How strange."

———————

A blanket of gray cloud had settled over south London, dumping its rain on Croydon's tower blocks and skyscrapers. Day stared out the passenger window, watching the raindrops bouncing in the gutter.

The windshield wipers swished loudly, fighting a losing battle with the downpour. Shields squinted through the rain-blurred glass and pulled up at a red traffic light.

"Norton didn't show up on the databases because I didn't check the missing persons records," she said. "We only looked for information on past offenders or people who'd been arrested, charged, or cautioned." The traffic light changed to green, and she moved off slowly.

"No point worrying about it now," Day said. "How were you supposed to know that he was in the records as a missing person? No one's going to blame you, so don't blame yourself."

"I don't."

"Good. The important thing is that we now know a lot more about Norton's background. He ran away from Greenhills seven years ago, and all that time, he's been lurking in the backstreets of London. Now, it seems, for some reason, he's had enough of lying low. Maybe he simply got fed up of crawling around in the shadows."

The heavy rain had reduced the flow of traffic to a crawl. Day estimated that the drive to the station was going to take them at least an hour.

"As soon as we get back, I want you to pull everything available on the Mary Freeman inquiry. I'm sure she'll be on the missing persons list too, but because of her age, there's no doubt the Croydon police would have considered her disappearance suspicious."

"Do you think it could have had anything to do with Norton going missing from the home? Now that we know what we know about him?"

Day took a moment to consider the question. He assumed that at the time, the police investigation would have found out if the two teenagers had known each other. Seven years on, Norton had revealed himself as a cold-blooded killer. When he went missing, it was assumed he was nothing more sinister than a teenage runaway. Was it possible the girl was his first victim?

"The fact that the girl disappeared around the same time as Norton ran away from the home isn't proof of anything, is it?" Shields said.

Day shook his head. He so wanted to agree with her, but deep down, he knew better. "Considering what we know about Norton now, do you really think that's likely?"

Shields kept her eyes on the bumper of the car ahead and said nothing, her silence answer enough.

Day closed his eyes and tried to picture Norton as a fresh-faced, happy-go-lucky teenager. No chance.

"I bet there are plenty of files stashed away in the care system on Norton's mental state as a youngster. I'm guessing the children's home would have laid on therapy sessions for him and he would have lapped up the attention. I'd like you to dig them out and we can get a psychological profiler to take a look at them. See what they come up with."

Shields nodded and Day turned back to the window. Somewhere out there, he thought, on a bleak south London housing estate, Mary Freeman's parents were probably still sipping tea, or numbing the pain with something stronger, as they waited for a call from the police.

All these years on, the best they could hope for would be that their little girl had despised them so much, she'd decided that running away would be a good option, that she'd survived, built herself a new life, and that she couldn't be bothered to ease their suffering by letting them know she was alive and well.

Day knew that was an unlikely scenario. His time as a detective had taught him a lot about the dark side of the human psyche and that when it came to missing teenage girls to always assume the worst. Something told him that fifteen-year-old Mary Freeman never celebrated her sixteenth birthday.

41

FIGHT

THE REPORTER

Matt Revell sat on the edge of the glass conference table and stared up at one of the three televisions suspended from the ceiling in the center of the newsroom.

A bright-red breaking news banner slid along the bottom of the screen followed by text revealing that a murder investigation had been launched after the body of a lawyer had been found on the floor of his office in central London.

The newsreader, a brunette in her late thirties, announced that Drew Bentley had been working late at the employment law firm Stone and Maddox when an intruder broke into the building and choked him to death.

Revell was intrigued. He'd received the press release from the New Scotland Yard press office about an hour ago and had realized straightaway that the victim was Gem Golding's boyfriend. So far, not one news outlet had mentioned the connection. Maybe the police weren't linking the two crimes.

Even if that was the case, Revell knew another big story had fallen into his lap, and he needed to get going on it before someone beat him to it. His news editor had accused him of missing the scoop of the year by letting Golding's carjacker get away before the police arrived. *I'm a writer, not a fighter,* he'd told her. You'd have to be pretty stupid to take on that psycho. *Avenging Angel's Boyfriend Murdered.* It was one of those headlines that wrote itself. That should get him back in Duffield's good books. All he needed now was a few good quotes from the grieving girlfriend.

Revell pressed the doorbell and waited, the fluttering in his stomach excitement, not nerves. He'd doorstepped a lot of grieving relatives over the years and knew that many people found talking about a recently lost loved one therapeutic.

The door opened, and he found himself looking down at a stocky woman with dark wavy hair wearing a gray skirt and dark-green jacket. He should have guessed the police would have arranged for a family liaison officer to babysit.

"Good evening," he said. "I was wondering if I could have a word with Gem."

The woman pursed her full lips. "And you are?"

"My name is Matt. I work for the *Daily News.*"

"Miss Golding is not feeling well enough to speak to anybody at the moment, especially not the press."

Matt smiled. Being polite but firm was always the best tactic in situations like this. "I understand, but we do know each other. I'd appreciate it if you would let her know that I'm here and let her make up her own mind."

The police officer glared at him and took a step back to give herself room to shut the door. Over her shoulder, Revell spotted

Gem Golding standing at the far end of the hall, wrapped in a fluffy blue dressing gown.

"It's all right, Carol," she said. "You can let him in."

Before the police officer had a chance to argue, Revell ducked past her and followed Gem into the living room. She sat on one of the two large leather armchairs, and he took a seat on the sofa. He took his phone out of his pocket, switched on the recording app, and showed Gem the screen before placing it on the seat beside him. She nodded to confirm she knew their chat would be recorded.

"I'm so sorry about your boyfriend," Revell said. "I couldn't believe it when I saw the press release."

Gem didn't answer. She crossed her arms and hugged herself. She wore no makeup, her cheeks were pink and blotchy, her eyes puffy and bloodshot. Under the dressing gown, she wore blue jeans and a black sweater.

"Have the police any idea why anyone would want to murder Drew?" Revell asked.

Gem rubbed the tops of her arms with her hands and shivered. "I'm cold. It's very chilly in here. Are you cold?"

Revell shook his head. It was a mild spring evening, and the central heating system seemed to be throwing out an awful lot of heat.

"I wish I'd never done that interview about the carjacking with you," Gem said. "That was the biggest mistake I've ever made. I'm not saying that I lied about what happened. I told the truth, and I did so to try to help other women who find themselves in the same awful situation, to get them to think about how they should or would react. To be prepared, at least. There is no right or wrong way to respond, is there? I suppose if you survive, then you've made the right choice, but if I had kept quiet, then maybe things would have turned out differently."

Revell could hear the family liaison officer talking in hushed tones on her cell phone. He suspected that at least a couple of uniformed officers were on their way and decided to push harder than he usually would when interviewing a grieving woman.

"Are you saying that our story about how you fought off an attacker is connected to the murder? Do the police think the same man killed your boyfriend?"

Gem shook her head. "They're not saying it officially, but it's obvious, isn't it? Since the article was published in the *Daily News*, I've been getting threatening phone calls, I've been followed in the street, and now Drew is dead."

Elation pulsed through Revell, and he shifted forward in his seat. He had his story and didn't want to jeopardize it, but he needed to give Gem the chance to think carefully about what she was doing.

"If you think speaking out about the carjacking provoked your attacker to commit murder, then is it sensible to do another interview? You're grieving, and I don't want you to do or say anything you'll regret."

Gem took a deep breath, raised her chin, and looked directly at Revell. "There's no cure for grief, but I'm hoping to sidetrack it, at least for a while. The strongest emotion I'm feeling right now is anger. I want Drew's killer to pay for what he's done. I've looked him in the eye. I know he's evil, and I know deep down, under all that arrogance, he's weak."

Whether she was right or not about the killer being the man who'd attacked her, she obviously believed it, and Revell was entitled to report that. The police wouldn't appreciate him jumping the gun, but that had never stopped him before.

The family liaison officer ended her telephone call and stood in the doorway glaring across the room at him. Making sure she couldn't see what he was doing, he slipped his phone back into his jacket pocket. It was time to change tack, make his excuses, and leave.

"Like I said before, Gem, I'm so sorry about what's happened. Let's hope the killer is caught soon. Have you got any family members nearby who can help you through this?"

Gem blinked back tears and swallowed hard. "It's just my mum and me. She lives in Wales, but I'm hoping she's coming to stay with me soon."

Revell stood up. "That's good," he said. "It always helps to have family around you at a time like this. Thank you for talking to me, and take care."

He headed for the door where the family liaison officer stood blocking his way. At the last second, she stepped aside to let him pass. He hurried down the hall, opened the door, and stepped out as a marked police patrol car pulled up outside the house. Revell smiled and waved at the two police constables as he strode away.

THE DETECTIVE

Day sat at a corner table in the station canteen and stared at the beige folder on the table. He'd sent the video footage of the attack on Shields and the killing of Drew Bentley to a psychologist he'd worked with on the murder squad and asked her to provide a full offender profile as well as give her thoughts on what Norton was using the coin for.

As he'd expected, Shields had shown amazing resilience since her return to work. It helped that the details of the attack had not yet been released to the press, but once Norton was caught, she would have to give evidence at his trial.

Normally, Shields would be sent a copy of the profile at the same time as he received his, but he'd asked for a delay so he could check it out first. He flipped the folder open and started to read:

Offender Profile Report by Criminal Psychologist Danni York

After studying the videos of the offender in action, I have come to the conclusion that he can be categorized as a full-blown psychopath. For that reason, I find it surprising that he doesn't appear on any of the national databases of criminal offenders. It is unlikely that he hasn't been involved in criminal activity from his early teens onward, so it would be logical to assume that he is particularly adept at avoiding being caught.

Psychopaths typically display fearlessness, lack of empathy, narcissism, an inability to cope with rejection or humiliation, and an obsession with power and control. This offender appears to display all these traits. He certainly would have been humiliated by the media coverage of the carjacking, and this could have acted as a trigger for the subsequent sudden escalation of violence.

The way he toyed with the female detective and the murder victim Bentley, seemingly giving them the opportunity to fight back or to submit, demonstrates the offender's desire to impose his will and control those around him. Studies have shown that psychopaths' brains release unusually large quantities of dopamine, a reward or pleasure chemical, when they commit extreme acts.

It is my opinion that he uses the coin to make himself the master of the "game." Although it appears that the coin flip decides the fate of the victims, it is more complex than that. For example, if the coin lands on heads and heads means resist, then the victim must choose to fight back to be allowed to survive. If it lands on tails, then the victims must submit to live. I think Norton derives immense satisfaction from controlling the game, especially as he has more influence than you might think. He's the one who has to offer the victim the opportunity to fight back or not. He can choose how long he turns his back for, how quickly he retrieves the knife after dropping it. So the outcome is not truly down to the flip of a coin.

The fight or submit rules make it a win-win situation for the offender. He controls the game. If the victim chooses the predetermined "right" course of action, then he gets to let them live. That can make someone like him feel just as powerful as when he gets to take a life because the victim made the "wrong" decision.

It is possible that the game was devised after the carjacking attempt and may have been inspired by the media coverage, but it could be more deep-rooted.

What is in no doubt is that the offender is totally fixated on the intended carjacking victim, Gem Golding. Detective Shields was abducted after leaving Golding's home, and, of course, the murdered man was Golding's boyfriend.

As for the offender's likely background, I would hazard a guess that he had a troubled upbringing. By that I don't mean to suggest that this would have caused his psychopathy. I mean that he would have been a troubled child anyway. Psychopathy is now thought to owe more to genetics and brain abnormality than environment, but childhood trauma of some kind can often switch it on.

I am convinced that the offender's ultimate target will be Golding, the woman who refused to bow to his will and then chose to publicly humiliate him by giving an interview to a newspaper. In my opinion, it's simply a question of time.

Note on how victims react to the trauma of violence.

Victims of crime react in one of three ways. Fight, flight, or freeze. All are instinctive, and the freeze response is the most primitive. Nobody should feel shame or be blamed for an instinctive response they have no control over.

Day closed the folder. Norton's deadly coin "game" made him feel sick to his stomach. He'd arrange for Shields to be sent a copy of the profile straightaway. He knew her well enough now to trust her to handle it.

He wondered whether her training and experience on the force had given her the ability to read the situation and reach the conclusion that if she did as she was ordered, if she didn't take any risks, she'd walk away and have the satisfaction of locking the bastard up another day. Or had she frozen in fear, while the killer's twisted brain bathed in pleasure chemicals?

42

SURRENDER

GEM THE VICTIM

Gem Golding sat sideways on her chair, her arms folded and her legs crossed. Despite yesterday afternoon's menacing telephone call, she felt stronger than she had for a while. She was damaged but nowhere near broken.

Detective Inspector Day walked into the interview room accompanied by a petite, dark-haired woman wearing black trousers and a three-quarter-length burgundy coat. They both sat opposite Gem and placed the files they were carrying on the table.

"This is Danni York," said Day. "She's a criminal psychologist who is experienced at offender profiling. She's had a look at your statement about the telephone conversation you had with the suspect, and I thought you might like to hear her conclusions."

Gem nodded at York. The psychologist offered her a brief smile as she opened the folder in front of her and smoothed it down on the table. Gem wasn't sure she'd be that interested in a psychological profile. The man was a cold-hearted killer. What else needed to be said? She tilted her head and raised an eyebrow. York took that as a cue to speak.

"The suspect clearly has psychopathic traits, but as far as his interest in you is concerned, he is showing all the signs of delusional, obsessive, and distorted thinking. Since the carjacking, he has undoubtedly developed a twisted fascination with you. He wants to possess you, be with you, and almost certainly believes that you feel the same way."

Gem's face flushed. "That's absurd. This is nonsense."

York raised a calming hand. "Don't misunderstand me," she said. "I'm not suggesting any of this is true on your part. I'm explaining what the suspect is thinking, how his mind is distorting the truth. This is important because it might help us, DI Day and myself, to anticipate what the suspect might do next."

York turned to Day, and he nodded his agreement. "Offender profiles can turn out to be extremely useful in a case like this," he said. "Anything that might help us catch this man and then make sure he is held to justice for his crimes has got to be a good thing."

Gem wanted Drew's killer caught more than anybody. "All right. I understand."

York glanced briefly down at the copy of her profile and pressed on. "The suspect's delusional feeling and obsession with you lead him to make excuses for you not responding in the way he wants you to. He convinces himself that outside influences, other people are to blame, stopping you doing what you really want. Unfortunately, this can put family members, police officers, partners in danger."

Gem thought about Drew and clenched her jaw to stop herself letting out a groan. Day pulled a wad of tissues from his pocket and offered them to her. "No, thank you," she said. "I'm fine. Please carry on."

"It is likely that his obsession was triggered during the carjacking incident," York said. "Something you said or did, or even something that he imagined you said or did, sowed a seed in his mind, allowing the delusion to grow."

"Like what? What do you mean?" Gem interrupted.

"Maybe you smiled at him to try to let him see you were not a threat or agreed with something he said to calm him down. It could be as simple as that. His mind would have seized on it as proof that you had a special connection."

Gem closed her eyes and thought back to that night. All she had wanted to do was get out of that parking lot alive. She put her left hand on the right sleeve of her sweater and rubbed the cast on her wrist. The plaster had softened and was starting to crack. She had an appointment later that day to have it removed. If only shame, guilt, and grief could be removed as easily.

"I didn't smile at him, no way," she said. "I was too terrified to smile. But I did tell him that he could take the car, that I'd like him to have it, and that I wouldn't even report it to the police. I desperately wanted him to leave."

York looked across at Day and gave him a nod that Gem interpreted as "I told you so." *Are they judging me?* she wondered. It felt as if they were, and she didn't like it one little bit.

"Are you saying that because I tried to appease him, because I was desperate for him not to hurt me, he took that as meaning I felt some connection with him?"

"No one is blaming you for anything," Day said, shaking his head. "It's not the details of what you did or said that matter. It's what your attacker wanted it to mean."

Gem bowed her head and covered her face with her hands. *Stay strong*, she told herself. *You've got to stay strong now.*

"There is something else," she said. "I left it out of my original statement after the carjacking because I was embarrassed, but he pressed himself against me and touched me."

York pulled a pen from her pocket and scribbled furiously in the margin of her report. Day pressed his lips together and gave Gem a look of concern. She was relieved to see no hint of disapproval or pity. The psychologist stopped writing and dropped the pen on the table. "Let me stress that there is no criticism of your actions here," she said. "I honestly don't know how I'd react in that situation, but because there was no resistance and then no mention of sexual assault in the police appeal for information, the suspect could easily have convinced himself that you were keeping it secret because you had feelings for him."

Gem uncrossed her legs and dropped her elbows onto her thighs as if she was about to throw up. *How had this madness happened? This twisted killer thinks we have a special bond. He took Drew's life because he thought that deep down, that's what I wanted.*

"If I'd tried to fight him off, if I'd been honest with you about the groping, do you think Drew would still be alive?"

"Don't torture yourself," Day said. "No one will ever know what might have happened. If you'd resisted, then maybe you would have been seriously injured or worse."

Gem sat up slowly and straightened her shoulders. "Let me send him a message," she said, the thought scary and exciting in equal measure. "I'd like to make it clear that any suggestion that I want to be with him is absurd."

Across the table, Day and York exchanged doubtful glances, but Gem knew that she had to do this. The strength of her certainty surprised her.

"The media weren't that interested in me before. I was just a sad victim. The story is so much bigger now. I'll do anything you think will help catch this man, talk to the papers, do a TV appeal for information. I need to leave him in no doubt that I want him punished for what he's done." She took a deep breath and sat back.

Day was the first to respond. "There is a chance that a big publicity campaign will help us. It may well prompt someone's memory, someone might recognize him, and we could get some valuable information out of it. I'd have to clear it with New Scotland Yard, because there will be a new team investigating the murders."

Gem shook her head. "They can do what they have to do, but I only want to deal with you on this."

Day smiled. "I'll see what I can do. It's possible, because the carjacking is still my case. We could focus any TV appeal around that investigation."

York had been silent for a while. She picked up her pen and tapped it pensively on the table. "I can see the benefits, but I have to warn you that the whole thing is fraught with danger. The offender has created this fantasy about you and him belonging together, and he's prepared to do anything to make that happen. He has objectified you. He's not seeing you as a human being but as an object that he wants to possess and control."

"But I don't care what he thinks about me or what his sick mind needs, and I want to let him know that."

"That's the point," York said. "I'm sure this won't surprise you, but psychopaths don't tend to take rejection well. If he thinks that you set out to deliberately humiliate him publicly, he'll almost certainly feel he's been unforgivably betrayed."

"I don't give a shit about his feelings," Gem snapped. "In fact, I want to humiliate him, I want the sicko to think I've betrayed him, I want to hurt him in every possible way I can, and I want him to pay for what he's done."

York held up both her hands. "Please calm down and listen, would you? It's important that you understand what I'm saying. All this time, the offender will have told himself that deep down, you want to be with him. A TV appearance in which you go out of your way to condemn him is likely to be a tipping point. Once he believes that you have rejected him, when his carefully constructed delusion has been shattered, things will change. It won't be friends or family who will be in danger then. He'll want to make you suffer. There's a good chance he'll come after you."

Gem looked at Day and then back at York. She'd appeased this monster before and look where that had gotten her. For a moment, the psychologist's warning sent her mind back to that night in the parking lot when she had looked into those eyes and saw the darkness inside. The memory made her shiver.

"Let's do it," she said. "I'm ready."

43
FIGHT

THE MASTERMIND

Norton sat at a table in the center of the budget hotel's cramped breakfast room and stared down at the front page of that morning's *Daily News*. The splash headline screamed *Warrior for Women's Boyfriend Killed by Psycho Carjacker*. Underneath it, the byline read *Exclusive by Matt Revell*.

The reporter had used Gem Golding's assertion that the killer was the same man who'd attacked her as the new angle for his story, padding the article out by repeating the lurid details of the earlier incident, explaining how she'd fought him off and run him down with her car. A young couple at an adjacent table glanced briefly in Norton's direction before exchanging whispers and returning their attention to their fried eggs and beans on toast.

He pulled the peak of his baseball cap down, drained his mug of coffee, and read the news report for the third time. The murder of Drew Bentley was described as "an evil act of revenge." According to Revell, the carjacker had killed the lawyer to get back at Gem Golding for publicly humiliating him. The final paragraph spelled

out to the readers that New Scotland Yard had been given the chance
to confirm or deny the story, but the press office had responded
with a curt "No comment."

The whole article contained just one fresh quote from Golding.
"I want Drew's killer to pay for what he's done. I've looked him
in the eye. I know he's evil, and I know deep down, under all that
arrogance, he's weak."

Norton clenched his teeth. The muscles in his jaw twitched. He
rarely allowed himself to show anger, unless it was to make a point
or to manipulate a situation to his advantage, but he had to call on
all his inner strength to stay calm.

He took a couple of long, deep breaths and waited for his rage to
subside. When he was able to think straight again, he started to draw
up a plan of action. The time was coming when Golding would pay
dearly for the insults, the accusations, the disrespect.

Any sensible human being would have learned by now to keep
their mouth shut, but not her. She insisted on stirring up trouble.
Even Bentley's death hadn't silenced her. Norton thought for a
moment, then smiled to himself as the details of what he needed to
do fell into place.

Everyone had underestimated his talents. In the children's home,
Bentley had truly thought he was the smartest kid, the leader, and
Norton the grateful follower. He allowed himself a smile as he
recalled how easy it had been to plant ideas in the idiot's head. One
afternoon, they stole a dozen cans of beer from a grocery store,
laughing as they outran the overweight security guard, their hoods
hiding their faces. Back at the children's home, Bentley had laughed
as he bragged to the other kids about how he'd decided to rob the
place on the spur of the moment. Just for the hell of it. He truly
believed the whole thing had been his idea.

Norton shook his head. He'd visited the store as a customer

three times before that day. He'd checked out the positioning of the CCTV cameras and noted that the big-bellied security guard always spent several hours in a nearby pub before starting his afternoon shift.

Being misjudged made everything so much easier. Never underestimate the power of being underestimated. The police, the media, that bitch Golding, they were doing it too. If only they knew what kind of mind they were dealing with.

THE DETECTIVE

Day pulled up in the car parking space below his office window and switched off the engine. He looked at the unopened letter lying on the passenger seat and considered tearing it up into tiny pieces and throwing it out the window.

He'd been pushing it to the back of his mind since the mailman had shoved it through his letterbox. He had a good idea what the envelope contained, and he didn't want to touch it, let alone read it. A killer was on the loose in the city, and he needed to concentrate on catching him, not sit around reading letters from his wife's lawyer. She'd never had a lawyer while they were together; she had never needed one. No doubt Hardy had encouraged her to engage a shit-hot operator. The bastard would be only too happy to pay for it.

Day snatched the envelope up, ripped it open, and pulled out the letter. He read it through quickly, just once, screwed it into a ball, and tossed it over his shoulder onto the back seat. Leaning forward, he pressed his forehead against the top of the steering wheel.

Opening the letter had been a big mistake. The morning briefing was due to start in twenty minutes, and he needed to pull himself together. He was trying to refocus his mind on work when the front passenger door opened and Shields slipped onto the seat.

"So, you've got a secret admirer who sends you fan mail," she said with a smile. "There's no need to beat yourself up about it."

Day sat up straight. "What are you talking about?"

"That letter. You should show more respect to your fans."

"It's from Amy. Well, it's from a solicitor on behalf of Amy. She wants a divorce. A quick one."

"Oh, right. I didn't know. I'm sorry."

"There's no need to be. It's not your fault."

"Are you all right?"

Day didn't reply. He was the complete opposite of all right, but he didn't think he should admit that to his sergeant.

After a few moments, Shields filled the awkward silence. "I don't suppose this news has come as a big surprise though, has it? She left you to move in with another man, didn't she? You must have seen this coming."

Her bluntness stung, like a slap to his face. But she was right. "It seems a bit hasty, that's all. I still harbored hopes that I could get them both to come home, Tom and Amy. Put my family back together. Get back to how it used to be. Once I'd achieved that, I was going to concentrate on earning myself a return to the murder squad. That was the plan."

"You'd have her back, Boss? Forgive her if she asked you to?"

"I don't know. Maybe. Probably. Once she's divorced, then she can marry Hardy."

"Tell me to mind my own business, but why would you want things back the way they were? They obviously weren't good, or this never would have happened."

Day stifled an urge to tell Shields that she'd been right, that it was none of her business. He wasn't comfortable discussing his private life with a colleague, but in the short time they'd worked together, he'd come to value her way of looking at things.

"If we divorced, she can remarry, and Hardy will officially be Tom's stepdad. I'm worried I'll lose my son as well. I'm already making a mess of everything, letting him down when we should be spending time together."

Shields half opened the car door and shifted her weight toward it. "Right now, you're working every hour of every day trying to bring a killer to justice. Surely they understand that?"

Day shrugged. "I think they do, but understanding what being a detective means to me is obviously not enough. Not for Amy anyway." He looked at his watch and shouldered his door open. "We're going to be late if we don't get a move on. Let's go."

They walked into the squad room together to find Stock sitting with his feet up on his desk chewing on a sandwich. He looked crumpled and unshaven. The young detective had been trawling through databases when they'd left the previous night, and Day suspected he hadn't been home.

As they approached, Stock slid his feet off the desk, put his half-eaten sandwich in his jacket pocket, and brushed crumbs from the creases in the front of his shirt.

"You look like you've been here all night," Shields said. "I hope it was worth it."

Stock stood up and smiled. "I did find something interesting." Next to his desk stood a whiteboard. Across the top were photographs of Gem Golding and Drew Bentley and a grainy CCTV image of Connor Norton.

Stock tapped the photograph of Bentley. "Andrew Bentley spent several years in a children's home in Croydon after being taken from his drug addict mother. I found a couple of old newspaper articles describing him as a poster boy for the foster care system. A shining example of a children's home resident made good."

Day shrugged, failing to hide his disappointment. "Good victim background, I suppose," he said. "But it doesn't get us any nearer to finding Connor Norton."

Stock's shoulders slumped. He picked a copy of the *Daily News* off his desk and held it out to Day. "The information line has been getting quite a few calls this morning in response to this. We're already checking out a few people who have reported sightings of Norton."

Day took the paper and read the splash headline. *Warrior for Women's Boyfriend Killed by Psycho Carjacker.* He kept his face expressionless as he read the lead article, but it wasn't easy. "Why didn't anyone tell me that this was being published?" he demanded.

Stock looked vacantly at Shields, desperately hoping that she'd come to his rescue.

"I don't think anybody knew about it, Boss," she said.

Day turned around and walked out of the squad room. The morning had started off badly. Things were going downhill fast.

44
SURRENDER

THE MASTERMIND

Norton threw his head back and drained half a bottle of beer in one go. The televised police appeal had been running for a couple of minutes, and he watched with a wry smile as Detective Inspector Elliot Day explained how he wanted anybody who had information about the whereabouts of the suspect to call the confidential police telephone line.

He'd been intrigued to see and assess the man who was spectacularly failing to track him down. Day appeared to be fairly intelligent, physically fit, and relatively young for a senior detective, but Norton quickly came to the conclusion that, intellectually, he had nothing to worry about.

The detective's ramblings soon started to bore him. He was impatient to hear from the main act, the star of the show. He slid off the sofa and knelt on the thick carpet to get a closer look at the woman sitting to the right of the detective.

He watched Gem Golding reach for a glass of water on the table in front of her and remembered how her body had pressed hard against his. She took a nervous sip, trying desperately not to make eye contact with a camera. Norton understood why her mouth was dry. She was being forced to take part in the appeal against her will. She'd eventually caved in to what must have been enormous pressure, and he wasn't going to think badly of her for that.

The opposite was true. Seeing her paraded in front of the TV cameras, pale and vulnerable under the studio lights, made him want to protect her, take control, and whisk her off somewhere safe so she didn't have to pretend any longer.

He heard movement behind him and turned slowly. Alice stood in the doorway, waiting for permission to enter. He waved the beer bottle at her, and she scurried back into the kitchen. Norton reached for the TV remote and turned up the volume. Day was starting to say something interesting.

"In addition to the carjacking incident, the suspect is wanted for questioning in connection with at least one other serious crime. I'm afraid I can't release any details yet. We want to hear from anybody who can tell us anything about him, but I want to stress that he should not be approached. If you see him or know where he is, I repeat, do not try to approach him. This man is extremely dangerous and almost certainly armed."

Norton finished off his beer and threw the empty bottle onto the sofa. He was starting to warm to Detective Inspector Day. The man knew what he was talking about.

Day finished speaking, and the camera panned in for a close-up of Gem Golding. She glanced down at the script the police had prepared for her and then looked directly down the lens of the camera.

Norton edged nearer the television, fascinated. It was almost as if she were in the room with him.

"When this man attacked me, tried to strangle me, broke my wrist, and took my car, I was treated for my injuries in the hospital and then sent home. Of course, I was still in shock. I didn't want to talk about what had happened to me. I wanted to put it all behind me and get on with my life. Now I know that was the wrong approach to take. The wrong approach for me. I consider myself fortunate to have survived. I should have spoken out sooner." She hesitated, licked her lips, and took a deep breath. "This man needs to be caught before he harms another innocent person. Evil will thrive if we don't challenge it. That's why I'm speaking out now. Please, please, call the police if you think you have information that will help them put this monster behind bars."

The camera panned even closer until Gem's face filled the whole screen. Her cheeks had more color than when she'd started speaking, and her eyes seemed to stare defiantly at Norton.

He didn't want to believe it, but there was no denying what he'd heard, no other way of interpreting her words. The rage that drove him rose inside him like an icy mist. They'd gotten to her, turned her against him. She would pay for her betrayal.

Norton clenched his fists, then uncurled his fingers slowly. His anger gave him power, as long as he kept it cold, controlled.

He stood up and swung his right boot at the television. The screen shattered, exploding like gunshot, spraying bullets of glass onto the carpet. He heard a gasp behind and turned. Alice stood trembling in the doorway, a freshly opened bottle of beer in her hand.

Norton reached out, took the beer, and gave her his broadest smile. "There's so much crap on TV these days," he said.

GEM THE VICTIM

Gem slid the key into the lock, pushed the front door open, and stepped inside. Detective Sergeant Shields had told her that she would be arranging for a police patrol car to be parked overnight outside the house for the foreseeable future.

She closed the door, making sure it was double-locked. The promise of a police guard was reassuring, but she still wasn't expecting to get a lot of sleep. The house was far too big for one person. The space and the silence put her on edge. She walked into the kitchen and opened the fridge, her stomach grumbling. Nerves had made it impossible for her to even think about eating before the TV appeal, but now she was famished. Typically, her mother had made a point of stocking up with ready-made meals before going back to Wales. Gem unwrapped a cottage pie for one, put it in the microwave, and set the timer for eight minutes.

The microwave hummed as she poured herself a large glass of white wine and sat at the kitchen table. The police had been pleased with the way the appeal had been received by the viewing public. People had started calling in to report sightings of Norton within minutes of the broadcast ending.

Gem sipped her drink and closed her eyes, tension flowing from her body. Drew would have complained that the wine was too cold to taste of anything. He'd always insisted that a bottle of white straight from the fridge needed to be left to warm a fraction before serving. She took another, larger sip. She definitely preferred her vino icy.

The microwave pinged. Gem used an oven glove to carry the steaming meal to the table. She picked up a fork and dug into the mash, which had the consistency and color of gluey tapioca.

Her first and—hopefully—last television appearance hadn't been as scary as she'd expected. She'd started off shaky but had soon gotten into her stride. She put a forkful of mash and minced beef into her mouth. It was hot, salty, and incredibly bland, but she was hungry enough not to care.

Publicly condemning her attacker had given her a lot of satisfaction. Telling the world about what he'd done to her felt liberating. Refilling her glass, she wondered whether he'd watched the broadcast. She needed him to understand how much she despised him. She hoped with all her heart that he'd gotten the message, that she'd shattered his sick fantasy once and for all.

Gem pushed the half-eaten meal away, picked up her glass of wine, and walked through into the living room. She heard a vehicle pull up outside and crossed to the window. Shields had been true to her word. She sighed with relief at the sight of the uniformed officer sitting behind the wheel of the patrol car.

The criminal psychologist's warning had been clear. Gem knew that if she'd achieved what she'd set out to do, then she'd put herself in serious danger.

45

FIGHT

THE DETECTIVE

Day hadn't been back to New Scotland Yard since his disciplinary hearing. Riding the elevator to the fourth floor, he had mixed feelings. He'd always felt privileged to work at the Yard. The place had a purposeful buzz about it, a feeling that everybody knew what they were doing and why they were doing it. But he was back today because he'd been called in, like a schoolboy summoned to the principal's office.

The elevator door opened, and he stepped out into the corridor. Detective Chief Superintendent Sherri Cox's office door was closed, and he could hear the soft murmur of voices inside.

He knocked once and entered without waiting to be invited in. Cox looked up, surprised, from behind her large oak desk. "Good afternoon, Elliot," she said with a tight smile. "It's been a long time."

The only empty chair was positioned next to the other police officer in the room. He was the last person Day wanted to see. Detective Chief Inspector Rob Hardy gave him a curt nod.

Day slid the chair away from Hardy to the far edge of the

desk before sitting down. Cox rolled her eyes, brought her hands together, and clasped them tightly.

"I know that you two have a serious personal issue, but I would be grateful if you would both keep this discussion strictly professional," she said. "In fact, scrub that. I'm not asking you to behave professionally. I damn well insist on it."

Day kept his eyes fixed on Cox. At least ten years his senior, she wore a smart, dark jacket and skirt, and her jaw-length bob appeared several shades blonder than when he had last seen her.

"I'd like to know what I'm doing here," he said.

Cox sighed and leaned forward, resting her elbows on the desk. "I've called you in because I want to remind you that the Drew Bentley case is now officially being investigated by the eastern murder investigation team and that DCI Hardy is heading the inquiry."

"I don't need to be reminded about that," Day said. "My team have already passed on everything we have on Bentley's death."

Cox's lips twitched in irritation. "The problem is you are still pushing hard on the carjacking involving Bentley's girlfriend. Rob feels that as the same suspect is involved in both crimes, it makes sense for you to drop the carjacking case."

Day glanced across at Hardy, whose thin lips had twisted into a sneer. He imagined him sitting at the dinner table with Tom, telling him that his incompetent father had been called to the Yard to have his ass kicked.

"I don't see any problem with my team following up leads generated by the hard work they've already done. If something turns up that eventually results in Bentley's killer being caught, then surely that's a good thing?"

Hardy snorted loudly and shook his head. "I don't want you and your team of amateurs stomping clumsily all over my operation. A murder inquiry takes priority. Forget about the carjacking, and let me get on with catching Bentley's killer."

Day stifled a strong desire to carry out his previous threat to hurl Hardy out a window. The fact that he'd have a high-ranking officer as a witness made it easier to stifle that urge.

Refusing to address Hardy directly, he turned back to Cox. "If you're ordering me to close the carjacking inquiry, then I have to say I don't think it's a good idea. The work we've put into the investigation is starting to bring leads in, and I assure you that everything will be handed over to the MIT."

Cox unclasped her hands and drummed her fingers on the desk. "I'm happy for you to keep the case open, but I don't want you getting in the way of the murder investigation. Any information you receive that could lead to an arrest must be passed on to Rob and his squad. Is that clear?"

Day forced himself not to look at Hardy. The briefest glimpse of that reptilian smile would threaten his already severely tested self-control. Permission to keep the Gem Golding inquiry open counted as a minor victory, and he'd settle for that.

"You can rest assured that I will never do anything that will jeopardize the chances of bringing Drew Bentley's killer to justice," he said.

46

SURRENDER

GEM THE VICTIM

Gem slept for longer than she had for weeks, but tiredness still pinned her limbs to the bed. The sleep had been fitful, her dreams haunted by Drew. He'd appeared before her, his presence vivid but mundane. Drew walking purposefully past her, unresponsive as she called his name. Drew sitting on the side of their bed wearing his best work suit, staring at the screen of his cell phone.

She rolled out of bed and headed for the shower, pausing briefly to check her reflection as she passed the mirror. She looked pale and drawn, but then she was never at her best first thing in the morning.

A few minutes under the hot spray perked her up, and for the first time in weeks, her stomach felt settled enough for her to think about eating breakfast. After dressing for work, she put the kettle on and dropped a couple of slices of white bread in the toaster, walked to the front door, slid back the bolt, and opened it. The police car was still parked right in front of the house.

Gem stepped outside and tapped the front passenger window.

The noise made the police constable jump. He lowered the window and leaned toward her.

"Is everything all right?" he asked.

Gem bent down to get a better look at the officer. She guessed he was about her age, and considering he'd been on duty all night, he looked remarkably fresh.

"I was wondering if I could get you a coffee or tea and some breakfast," she said.

The constable smiled and shook his head. "Very kind, but no thanks." He pointed at a large, hot drink flask on the seat beside him. "I still have some coffee left, and I'm off to the station canteen in a few minutes. I'll be back on guard duty this evening though."

"That's good to hear," Gem said. "Can I ask you your name?"

The constable smiled, and Gem detected a faint blush on his cheeks.

"I'm PC Weaver. PC Mark Weaver."

"Well, PC Weaver," Gem said. "Thank you. It's nice to know you're going to be out here tonight."

The constable gave an embarrassed nod and reached for the button to raise the window. "Just doing my job," he said.

Gem used her phone app to order a taxi, and it arrived outside her door fifteen minutes later. She climbed into the back seat and double-checked that the driver knew their destination. The journey to Covent Garden usually took around half an hour, and she'd gotten into the habit of using that time to plan her workday.

Paying for a taxi to and from the office wasn't cheap, but after what had happened to Drew, there was no way she was going anywhere near a Tube station platform. She was optimistic that she'd be able to get back behind the wheel of a car soon.

As the taxi turned right into City Road, Gem's cell phone rang. She checked the caller ID and was surprised to see it was Detective Inspector Day.

He got straight down to business. "There are a couple of things I need to speak to you about."

Gem waited, sensing the detective was making an effort to pick his words carefully.

"We may have made some progress in the hunt for Norton. We suspect he may have been staying at a guesthouse in Stepney. We've had an anonymous call to our helpline claiming that someone matching his description has been seen near Stepney Green Tube station, and we know he was once in a relationship with the owner of the guesthouse."

Gem's heart missed a beat. Stepney was no more than three and a half miles from Shoreditch. She'd taken comfort in the fact that London was a sprawling city of nearly nine million people. Finding out he'd been so close made her feel physically sick.

"Should I be worried?"

"No, there isn't any reason for you to panic. There is going to be a patrol car parked outside your house every night until this is sorted."

Gem swallowed hard. "Yes, it was a comfort to know it was there last night."

"Good," Day said. "The other thing I wanted to mention was that our inquiries into Mr. Bentley's background have turned up a few interesting facts. We now know that he was a resident at Greenhills children's home in south London at the same time as Connor Norton and that they were close friends. They even shared a room."

"You can't be serious."

"It's true."

Gem couldn't make sense of what she was hearing. She knew Drew had spent some time in the childcare system, and he'd occasionally joked about not having a family to share his success with, but he'd always made it clear that he didn't want to talk about those times. The past was the past, he'd insisted.

"You're telling me Drew used to be friends with the man who killed him? The man who attacked me?"

"It's looking that way. Norton ran away from the home and was put on the missing persons list. Around the same time, a local fifteen-year-old girl vanished. Police feared Mary Freeman had been abducted. They never found a body."

Gem found this revelation confusing. What was the detective trying to say? What had this to do with her and Drew?

"Why would Norton surface after all these years and set out to destroy our lives?"

"I don't know," Day said. "As far as you can remember, did Drew ever mentioned the missing girl, Mary Freeman?"

"No, never. Why should he?"

"I don't know, but we have to explore every avenue. If you think of anything else Mr. Bentley may have said about his time in the children's home, then please let me know."

Gem slipped her phone back into her bag and stared out the window at the snaking traffic, her thoughts still occupied by the mention of a missing girl and Drew's time in a children's home. None of it made sense.

THE DETECTIVE

Day clicked the Play button and listened to the recording of the anonymous caller one more time.

The woman spoke so fast, her words blurred. "The man you're after, the carjacker, I'm sure I saw him standing outside Stepney Green Tube station last night. He was wearing a dark baseball cap and a hooded top. It was definitely the man I saw on television. I'm certain of it."

It wasn't much to go on, but the Underground station was only a ten-minute walk from the Roman Villa guesthouse. More significantly, Day thought, the anonymous caller sounded like Alice Shelton.

On his way out to the parking lot, he looked in on the squad room. Shields had taken a well-deserved day off. Only three of the seven desks in the room were occupied, two of them by civilian support workers he'd asked to dig up everything they could find on the investigation by Croydon police into the disappearance of Mary Freeman.

Thirty minutes later, he pressed the guesthouse doorbell and held it down for several seconds. After a minute or so, he rapped hard on the door with his knuckles. He was about to try the bell again when the door opened slowly.

Alice Shelton's left eye resembled a ripe plum, shiny, purple, and swollen to a slit. Her lower lip was fat, split, and encrusted with dried blood. Day peered down the hall and dug out his cell phone, but Shelton held up a hand.

"He's not here," she said, her voice distorted by her swollen lip. "He's gone."

Day stepped into the house, put a hand gently on Shelton's shoulder, and walked with her into the back room. He sat her down on the sofa, glancing at the shattered television screen and the glass scattered on the carpet.

"I think I should call an ambulance," he said. "It looks to me like you might need stitches."

Shelton shook her head. "There's no need. I'll be all right. I've got plenty of painkillers. To be honest with you, I'm just pleased that he's gone."

Day looked at the television again and then at the mess Norton had made of Shelton's face. *What sort of creature is this man?* he wondered.

"It was the television appeal by that Gem Golding woman," Shelton said. "He was watching her, calmly drinking beer, then he kicked the screen in."

"How long had Norton been staying here?" Day asked.

Shelton bowed her head and said nothing.

"Was he already with you when I came around with Detective Sergeant Shields?"

Shelton nodded. "I was too scared to say anything. He was standing in the utility room, listening to our conversation."

Day choked down his frustration. If she'd given Norton up straightaway, they'd have him in jail, awaiting trial.

"When did he do that to you?"

Shelton lifted a shaky hand to her face, touched the swollen flesh, and winced. "The lip straight after smashing the television, the eye after getting up early this morning before he left. A little farewell gift is what he said. Something to remember him by."

Day shook his head in despair. This could have been avoided. "Was it you who called the helpline with the anonymous tip-off? I'm right, aren't I?"

Shelton tried a rueful smile, but her lip split open again, leaking fresh blood. She took a tissue from her pocket and dabbed her mouth gently. "I just wanted him gone and thought you'd suspect he was here if he'd been seen nearby. It's almost as if he's got some kind of sixth sense about these things. I wish I could have been braver sooner. I wish I'd had the courage to speak out like the woman on the television."

47

FIGHT

THE MASTERMIND

Dusk fell like a gray mist, silhouetting east London's jagged skyline. Above the city, threatening clouds scudded low. Driving west along Whitechapel Road, Norton passed the Victorian façade of the infamous Blind Beggar pub.

The van stank of cigarette smoke and stale sweat. Norton wound down his window and took a deep breath. The air wasn't exactly fresh, but it was an improvement. He patted his jacket pocket, his fingers fondling the hilt of his knife.

He remembered the look of terror on the van owner's face as he handed over the keys and smiled. The knife was like a magic wand. All he had to do was wave it around, shout "Jump!" and people jumped.

He'd stayed far too long in the hotel. The woman on reception had been all smiles during the first few days, but recently, he'd noticed her fiddling with her eyebrow piercing and pretending not to look at him whenever he passed by. It would only be a matter of time before she'd whisper her suspicions to her boss or call the confidential police hotline.

The traffic slowed to a crawl as Norton passed the gold dome of the East London Mosque. He looked at his watch, drumming his fingers on the steering wheel. Now that he'd set his mind on a course of action, he was eager to get on with it.

He had a feeling that the police were closing in. He'd been so active in that part of London, stuck his head so far above the parapet, it was bound to happen. It was time for him to move on, find another dark corner of the city to hide in.

But he wouldn't be going meekly. That wasn't his style. He had a score to settle, a troublemaker to silence, and he'd always had a special talent for that kind of mission.

GEM THE WARRIOR

Gem pulled the hood of her coat over her head as the first fat drops of rain bounced on the sidewalk. The square clock tower of St. Leonard's Church loomed in the half-light to her right. She veered onto Hackney Road and started to run, determined to get home before the clouds burst.

She'd almost made the front door when the deluge hit. By the time she slipped the key in the lock, she was drenched. She took off her coat and hung it on the rack in the hall.

The family liaison officer had been unsure when Gem had announced she was going out for a walk, but Gem had dismissed her concerns. Since her last interview with the *Daily News* reporter, she'd felt like she was making progress. Summoning up the strength to denounce Norton again, despite the silent calls, despite the stalking, despite Drew's murder. She was proud of herself, and she hadn't been able to say that for a long time.

Perhaps this was a turning point. She could make it so, couldn't she? All she had to do was make that choice. If she could get back to her old self, be the woman who, before the night of the carjacking, felt capable of anything, then maybe she'd live up to the newspaper headlines and really be a warrior for women.

She walked into the kitchen where Carol was sitting at the table tapping away furiously at the keyboard of her laptop.

Carol looked up and smiled. "How was the walk?"

"It was good, but a little wet," Gem said. "I'm off upstairs to get dry, then how about I make you a coffee?"

Carol nodded and returned her attention to her laptop.

Gem left her to it and went upstairs. She hadn't had the chance to grieve properly, and grief couldn't be avoided forever. She knew there were tough times ahead, not least the funeral, but she felt more optimistic than she had for weeks.

THE DETECTIVE

"Norton's surfaced," Shields said, bursting into Day's office. "It looks like he's been staying at some dump of a hotel on the Mile End Road. About an hour ago, he checked out without paying his bill, driving off in a van he stole from the hotel parking lot."

Day looked up from his desk, his mind whirring. "Are we certain it's him?"

"Both the hotel manager and the owner of the van identified him from the e-fit and CCTV images."

Day could feel his sergeant's excitement but deliberately kept his voice calm, professional. "Get an automatic number-plate recognition trace on the van as soon as possible. There are plenty of cameras in this part of the city. Let's see if we can find out what he's up to."

Shields moved to leave but hesitated at the door. "What about the Yard?" she said. "By rights, we should inform the Bentley murder squad about the sighting. If we don't and things go wrong, there's going to be a shitstorm."

Day held up a hand. "I haven't suggested we keep this to

ourselves. But maybe we should give it an hour or so, wait until we have a better idea exactly what is going on. At this stage, we are only investigating the theft of a van, after all."

Shields shot him a stern look before heading back to the squad room. Day sat back in his chair and sighed. He'd had to beg to stay in the force after being kicked out of the murder squad. One more strike and he'd be out on civvy street, but the opportunity to put Norton behind bars, to show Hardy exactly how it was done, was too tempting to resist.

48
SURRENDER

GEM THE VICTIM

Gem sat at the kitchen table sipping her coffee, listening to the rain rattling against the window. She'd had a good day at the office. Melanie had asked her to take on two new product launches, and most of her colleagues had stopped treating her like someone likely to break down sobbing at any minute.

Keeping as busy as possible at work had helped her push thoughts of the future to one side. She knew she'd have to move on eventually, and she'd told herself that moment would come after Drew's funeral. But who knew when that would be? The police had shown no sign of being prepared to release his body soon.

She put the coffee down, rested her elbows on the table, and cupped her chin on her hands. *If Drew hadn't been killed, would we still be together?* she wondered. Probably not. No, definitely not. He'd been pressuring her into giving up her career so he could further his, lying to her, trying to manipulate her. She knew he was calculating, a little cold even, but what the police had told her about him needing a wife to become a partner at Stone and Maddox had shocked her to her core. She never would have forgiven him. She never would have tried.

On the journey back from the office, she'd found herself imagining moving out to a less expensive part of the city, allowed herself to think about her future without Drew.

She'd even thought about setting herself a career deadline: earn a promotion within twelve months or find herself a position with a bigger PR company. Her world had shifted on its axis, and she had to shift with it.

Norton would be caught soon. She had to believe that. He would stand trial and be locked up with no prospect of ever being released. Only then would it be over, and she would be ready to embrace life again, face it and all its uncertainties head-on.

When the taxi had dropped her home, she'd been relieved to see the police car already parked outside the house. She'd given PC Weaver a wave, and he'd responded by cheerfully tipping the peak of his cap.

It was reassuring to know that the police constable would be on duty throughout the night, but even so, Gem didn't like the feeling of being in the house on her own. It was much too big for one person. She resolved to telephone her mother before going to bed in the hope of persuading her to return sooner than planned.

The thought made her smile to herself, because she knew that she wouldn't have to do much persuading. If she asked the question, her mother would drop everything and come. She'd always been there when needed, and when she'd judged that Gem had grown into the strong and independent woman she'd wanted her to be, she'd been happy and proud to let her forge her own way in life.

Gem finished her coffee, walked into the living room, and pulled the curtains back a fraction. Darkness had fallen, and the shimmer of the streetlights reflected in the silvered puddles on the pavement.

Since she was a child, she'd always found the sound of raindrops drumming on a windowpane as soothing as a lullaby, especially when lying tucked up warm in her bed. She took a deep breath and promised herself that she would read that night, something she loved to do but hadn't done since the parking lot attack. Nothing new. She'd reread one of her old favorites.

The rain fell harder, pummeling the roof of the police car. Gem could just make out the blurred silhouette of PC Weaver in the driver's seat. She wondered how much a police constable would be paid and had a feeling it probably wasn't enough.

49
FIGHT

GEM THE WARRIOR

Gem took off her damp clothes and changed into a comfortable pair of blue tracksuit pants and a cream sweater. She sat on the edge of her bed, listening to the rain beating against the window. It was a sound she'd found comforting since she was a little girl.

She looked across the room at the silver framed photograph of her and Drew on their first holiday together. *What would he think of me now?* she wondered.

Gem stood up, walked over to Drew's wardrobe. She smiled ruefully at his love of order and routine, even when it came to hanging up his clothes. He insisted on wearing a different suit for every working day of the week. She reached out and gently touched the only empty coat hanger. The suit he was wearing on the day he was killed was probably folded up and labeled inside a plastic evidence bag.

She closed the wardrobe door and went downstairs. Carol still sat at the kitchen table working on her laptop. She glanced up at Gem and smiled.

When she'd first introduced herself, Carol had explained that her role as a family liaison officer involved offering emotional support as well as acting as a link with the investigation team. More than anything, Gem was grateful for her company.

"I suppose you get used to dealing with people who have lost loved ones?" she said.

Carol shook her head, causing a lock of graying hair to fall over her right eye. She brushed it away with a flick of her finger. "I don't think you ever get used to it, but you do learn how to handle difficult situations. The truth is, I love helping people. That's why I volunteered to train for this role. You know you can ask me anything or tell me anything, don't you?"

Gem could tell that Carol's gentle manner was underpinned by a steely resolve to do good. She wanted to ask her if she'd ever been the victim of violent crime and if she had, how she had reacted, but decided against it. A question like that would be better left until they'd gotten to know each other a little better.

Gem glanced at her watch. "It's nearly 9:00 p.m. How much longer are you staying for?"

Carol checked her watch and hurriedly switched her laptop off. "I've got to leave in a few minutes, actually. I've a partner and two young teenagers waiting for me at home."

Gem tried to hide her disappointment but failed miserably.

Carol tucked the laptop under one arm and touched Gem gently on the elbow. "No need to worry," she said. "Detective Sergeant Shields is doing everything she can to arrange for a patrol car to be stationed outside the house overnight. They're all busy on calls right now, but I'm told that the first car that becomes available will be assigned to guard duty."

Gem nodded. *Thank God for Detective Shields*, she thought as she led Carol down the hall. When the FLO stepped out into the rain, Gem slammed the door shut and drew back the security bolts.

50

SURRENDER

GEM THE VICTIM

Gem sat on the sofa, a glass of white wine in one hand, Donna Tartt's *The Secret History* in the other. She'd read the book so many times, it had become like an old friend. She always found something new that made her think, and tonight was no different. She read the sentence again. *Psychology is only another word for what the ancients called fate.*

As she carefully placed the wineglass on the coffee table, the doorbell chimed. She closed the book and put it down, trying to think who would be calling at that time of night. Whoever it was had made it past PC Weaver unless, of course, it was the police constable himself.

Gem walked over to the window and pulled back the curtain. The police car was there, the rain bouncing off its roof, but she couldn't see any sign of PC Weaver inside. She let out a sigh of relief. *He's probably run out of hot coffee or just wants to check in*, she thought. The doorbell chimed again, and then for a third time. Gem closed the curtains and hurried to the door. The poor man would be getting drenched.

As she reached for the security bolts, she hesitated and pressed an eye to the glass peephole. Her view of the figure standing side on to the door was distorted by the rain, but she could clearly see the shiny black peak of PC Weaver's cap.

She slid back the bolts and opened the door. A sudden gust of wind sprayed rain in her face, and the curved blade of a hunting knife gleamed like silver.

51
FIGHT

THE MASTERMIND

Norton braked and pulled up at the curb outside an Italian restaurant. Leaving the engine running and the headlights on, he climbed out of the van, crossed the busy road, and started walking back toward London Bridge Underground station.

He turned the collar of his jacket up and pulled the peak of his baseball cap down. It wouldn't be long before the police received a call about the abandoned vehicle.

Some people might describe it as a diversion tactic. He'd say it was all part of the game. By the time the white van was identified as having been reported stolen, he'd be back north of the river making a special house call.

Standing outside the Tube station, Norton lifted his head to stare at the Shard, slicing into the dark sky as it towered above the Thames. The rain stung his face, but he kept his eyes on the skyscraper. To him, it was a symbol of ambition, a stark reminder of his failure to make a mark on the world.

He often wondered what someone with his talents might have

achieved given the chance. It pained him to think about everything he'd missed out on. Most people clung to the idea that you get what you deserve. Norton knew that was far from true. But things were changing. He'd show everybody, all the ordinary people out there, exactly how extraordinary he could be. Let the world watch out.

He dragged his gaze away from the skyline, took a one-pound coin from his jacket pocket, and flipped it. As the coin descended, he caught it in his right palm and slapped it onto the back of his left hand.

52

SURRENDER

GEM THE VICTIM

Gem lay curled up on her side, blinking in the darkness. Strips of gray duct tape sealed her mouth and bound her ankles and wrists.

The trunk of the patrol car smelled of sweat, fear, and fresh blood. As far as she could tell, she wasn't injured. That meant PC Weaver must be bleeding. One of his knees dug painfully into her lower back. The other pressed against her left shoulder. He wasn't moving at all, and she prayed that he was still alive.

Gem took a deep breath through her nose, determined to keep her lungs oxygenated. She closed her eyes, gritted her teeth, and used every ounce of strength she could muster to try to pull her wrists apart, but the tape held fast.

The patrol car slowed, veered left, then drew to a halt. Gem heard the crunch of the handbrake. The vehicle rocked to one side, and Gem heard the driver's door slam shut with a crunch.

The rain thrummed loudly on the bodywork of the car. Gem couldn't hear Norton's footsteps, but she knew he was coming for her. A siren wailed in the distance, and for a split second, she allowed herself to imagine that help was on its way.

THE DETECTIVE

Shields turned in surprise at the clang of a trash can being kicked high into the air. It landed in the center of the squad room and spun like a top, spewing its crumpled contents across the gray carpet tiles.

"Golding's been taken," Day said, striding toward the map of the city on the wall next to Shields's desk. "And the police constable guarding her house is missing too."

Shields stood up and joined him. "What do you mean taken?"

Day shot her a withering look. He wasn't going to waste time explaining the obvious. He picked up a marker pen and circled a spot on Hackney Road, Shoreditch. "She was snatched from her home about twenty minutes ago. When the uniform didn't respond to a routine radio check, another patrol car was sent to the house. The front door was open, there was a puddle of rainwater on the floor, and there was no sign of Golding, PC Weaver, or the patrol car. I want as many officers as we can get knocking on neighbors' doors. Someone must have seen something."

Shields nodded. "If we think Norton's got them, then we need to let the Yard know, Boss. We can't do this on our own."

"It's Norton. It's him all right. I've already informed the MIT, and every patrol car in London is going to be out looking for them."

Day took a moment to think, his heart thudding against his ribs. It was easy to make bad decisions in the grip of an adrenaline high. He covered his face with his hands and massaged his temples. Where would Norton take his victim? If he was going to kill her, why didn't he do it there and then on the doorstep of her home? Maybe he had a special location in mind. He fished his phone out of his jacket pocket, searched his contacts, and dialed. The call went to voicemail.

"Hi, Danni. It's DI Day. Sorry to call so late, but we've got a live kidnap and potential murder situation going on. It's Connor

Norton, the offender you've already profiled for us. I really need you down here as soon as possible. Preferably sooner."

GEM THE VICTIM

The trunk of the patrol car opened, and Gem looked up to see Norton smiling down at her through a curtain of rain. He'd discarded his baseball cap, and his dark hair was plastered flat against his scalp.

He bent down, put his hands under her armpits, and lifted her out with ease. He laid her on her back on the ground, slammed the trunk shut, then crouched beside her. In one swift movement, he ripped the tape off her mouth, taking a layer of skin with it. Making an effort not to cry out, she clamped her lips together and tasted blood.

She kept her eyes on Norton. He stared impassively back and said nothing. *We're only here for one reason*, Gem told herself.

"The police constable needs urgent medical help," she said. "You need to get him to the hospital as soon as possible."

Norton shrugged, and Gem knew he wasn't playacting. He really didn't care whether Weaver lived or died. Her brain whirred as she tried to work out the best way to talk Norton around. Should she grovel, try to reason with him, or appeal to his ego? *Speak the truth*, she told herself. *Whether he likes it or not.*

"You killed Drew, pushed him under a train," she said. "What did he ever do to you?"

Norton threw back his head and bellowed with laughter. "Andrew Bentley. What a man he was. The children's home boy made good. An example to us all. I did the biggest favor anyone can do for another person. He had big ideas, and I made sure that girl didn't ruin his life before it had even started properly. Then he betrayed me, disowned me. Is that enough for you?"

Gem remembered Day's revelation about the girl who went missing at the same time that Norton fled the children's home. She stayed silent, hoping for an explanation. A fat raindrop spilled from Norton's hairline into his right eye. He shook his head, spraying her face with tiny droplets.

"I guess he never told you about the girl in the woods."

Gem said nothing.

"Mary Freeman. She was a looker. We both liked her, but she preferred Andrew. Nobody knew what was going on except me. Then the silly bitch got pregnant, didn't she? Of course, Andrew didn't want to know. He had big plans. He asked me to reason with her. Persuade her to get rid of the baby. I always did his dirty work for him. He said I had a talent for persuading people to do things they didn't want to do and that people should always capitalize on their talents. The funny thing is he really believed that he had manipulated me into taking care of things when all the time, I'd already made my mind up, had already decided what needed to be done. I was in control. I made up the rules."

Gem's mind raced. *Keep calm and be ready.* "What did you do to her?"

"I did what needed doing. Afterward, he suggested that I should run. Said kids ran from children's homes all the time and that the police wouldn't connect my disappearance with hers. He was right about that."

"I don't believe you," Gem said. "You're making this up."

Norton shook his head and grinned. "Why would I do that? You asked me why I killed Drew, and I'm telling you. I found it so easy to hide in London. This city is such a faceless, wriggling mass of humanity. I did what I needed to do to survive, waiting for Andrew, so we could team up again. But when he got his big job in the city, the little snake didn't want to know me. The slimy bastard. After everything I'd done for him."

Gem licked her lips. They were still sore and bloody. *These are the ramblings of a madman*, she told herself. *Don't be taken in by a pathological liar.* She was jolted from her thoughts by the sight of Norton pulling a knife from his waistband. He sliced swiftly through the tape binding her ankles and wrists.

"Let's move," he said.

Gem pushed herself up and followed, unsteady on her feet, her limbs stiff. She stamped the ground to try to get the blood flowing in her legs and looked around. Despite the darkness, she instantly realized that she was in the parking lot where it had all begun. There were no other vehicles around, and the store was unlit and shuttered. It had to be after midnight.

Norton walked her at knifepoint until they stood in front of the patrol car. The engine was still running, the headlights cutting through the darkness. Norton moved toward her until she could feel his breath on her face, the blade digging in her ribs.

"Here we are again," he said. "Back where we first met. How about that? Who said romance was dead?"

53
FIGHT

THE DETECTIVE

"The van Norton stole from the hotel has been found," Shields announced, marching into Day's office. "It was abandoned south of the river, on Union Street, Southwark."

Day looked up from the report he was reading. "No sign of Norton, I suppose?" "No sign. Forensics are going over it right now, but we know it was Norton, don't we? What we don't know is where the hell he is now."

Day shared his sergeant's frustration. Norton seemed to have the knack of always being one step ahead of them. "Why do you think he'd steal a van, drive it to Southwark, and dump it? It's a long way from his stomping ground."

Shields sat down in the chair opposite her boss and took a moment to think before answering. "I don't know for sure, but I'm not prepared to believe he's lost interest in Gem Golding. The white van may be in south London, but he could be anywhere by now. I've been trying to get a patrol car assigned to guard duty outside her home, but the uniforms are so short-staffed, it's proving difficult. If it doesn't happen soon, I'm going to take one of our unmarked cars and do it myself."

Day didn't think that having his best detective sit outside a house all night on guard duty was a good use of resources, but he didn't have the heart tell her that he disapproved.

"Get someone to check with the city's camera control rooms to see if they can tell us what Norton was doing with the van before he dumped it. Maybe that will give us an idea what he's up to."

GEM THE WARRIOR

Gem checked the front and back doors one more time. Then she went into the kitchen and poured herself a glass of wine. After downing it in two gulps, she took the largest carving knife she could find from the cutlery drawer.

The weight of the knife felt alien in her hand as she walked up the stairs, went into her bedroom, and slipped it under her pillow. Would she be able to use it if she had to? She didn't have an answer, but she felt slightly better knowing that it was there.

She moved over to the window and peered through the blinds out onto the road. She had been promised a police patrol car, but there was no sign of it yet. She grabbed her phone from the bedside table and checked the time. It had gone midnight. There was no way she'd sleep tonight.

Shields had said she could call her if she needed anything. Well, she did. She needed to stop feeling terrified. She found the detective's number and pressed Dial. The call went to voicemail. She was about to leave a message when the sound of breaking glass stopped her in her tracks.

Gem's blood runs cold. Her throat tightens. She walks quickly to the bedroom door and presses an ear to it. She can hear someone moving about in the bathroom, and her heart jackhammers against her ribs. She starts to dial 999, but it's too late. The bedroom door flies open, crashing into her arm and knocking the phone out of her hand and onto the carpet.

Norton stands on the threshold wearing dark trousers, a dark jacket, and a dark smile. He strides into the room, and Gem takes a step back.

Did I bring this all on myself? *she wonders.* If I hadn't challenged him, if I'd simply handed him the car keys and let him drive away, maybe he wouldn't be here now.

As if reading her mind, Norton nods thoughtfully. "You should have stayed silent. Shown me the respect I deserve. Even then, we'd still be here, wouldn't we? The game has to be completed."

Gem takes a sideways step, moving closer to the bed, closer to the pillow. She needs to distract him, keep him talking.

"Why did you have to kill Drew? He didn't do anything to you. In fact, he was the only one who tried to talk me out of going to the newspaper. He didn't want me to speak to the press about the carjacking."

"I bet he didn't," Norton says, his smile widening.

Gem doesn't understand. "Drew was a decent man. He didn't deserve to die like that."

Norton laughs. "I know you probably think you and Andrew Bentley were perfect for each other, but I can assure you that I knew him a lot better than you ever did. The real Andrew Bentley was not a decent man. He arranged the carjacking. The whole thing. Paid me to do it. That's how much he cared about you."

Gem shakes her head. "No, you're lying. You're crazy."

"It's all true," Norton gloats. "What do you think of your precious Drew now?"

Gem takes another step sideways and sits on the bed, her hand resting on the pillow.

"Stand up," Norton says. "Do not defy me again." He moves toward her, slips his right hand around to the small of his back, and produces his hunting knife. "I told you to stand up," he says, his voice strangely calm.

This is the moment, *Gem thinks*. This monster wants to destroy me, but I don't have to take it. I've stood up to him before. Can I do it again? Should I do it again? *Her brain doesn't have the answer, but her gut does.*

She slides her hand under the pillow and pulls out the carving knife. Norton moves closer, and she instinctively swings the blade at his right arm, slashing through the soft underside of his wrist.

The hunting knife falls from his fingers. Norton's blood splashes onto the carpet. He groans loudly and sinks to his knees.

The whole of Gem's body trembles as she points the carving knife at Norton's face. The blood is still flowing from his wound, but he gets to his feet. She is preparing to strike again when he launches himself at her. The impact knocks her back onto the bed. Norton grabs the carving knife with his good hand and hurls it across the room.

Gem tries to push him away, but even though he's wounded, he is far too strong for her. He uses his weight to hold her down and presses his left forearm hard across the base of her throat. His eyes are rolling. The blood loss is taking its toll, but Gem knows that by the time he is weak enough for her to fight him off, it will be too late.

"You made the wrong choice," Norton whispers. "You lose."

54

SURRENDER

THE DETECTIVE

Day and Danni York stood side by side facing the map on the squad room wall. The psychologist had arrived shortly after midnight, dressed casually in jeans and a baggy sweater.

"I don't think he'll leave London," York said. "Not yet. Not until he's done what he intends to do with his victim. He's a predator, and the city's his hunting ground, his killing field."

Day flinched at the phrase *killing field*, but he knew she was right. If they didn't track the patrol car down soon, they might as well start searching for a body. Two bodies. He scanned the map, looking for answers, his eyes flitting from the city center to the mass of urban sprawl.

"There are so many shadowy backstreets and dark corners in this city," he said. "So many places to hide."

York turned away from the map and perched herself on the edge of an unoccupied desk. "Norton will have planned exactly where he wants to go. As far as Gem Golding is concerned, there will be no random choices. Since the carjacking, he's been obsessed with her one way or the other. In his mind, everything revolves around her, and everything stems from the carjacking: the murders, his stalking, his desire for revenge. For people like him, life is one big game of violence, control, and manipulation. He has to be the winner, and he'll do whatever it takes."

Day was nodding his agreement when Shields called across the room. "We've had a camera hit. The stolen patrol car was picked up heading east on Old Ford Road, Bethnal Green about thirty minutes ago."

Day stared at the map, tracing the route Norton had taken. If he continued driving east, along the southern perimeter of Victoria Park, any right turn would take him into Bow, back where it all started.

"I think he's gone full circle. Maybe he's taking her to the parking lot where their paths first crossed." He looked at York, inviting her opinion.

"That sounds like a good call," she said. "He'd definitely see that as poetic justice. It was during the carjacking that he first imagined that they had a secret bond. Returning to the scene would be fitting. It would be the perfect place to punish her for what he sees as her betrayal."

Day jabbed a finger at a uniformed officer at the back of the room. "I want an alert put out to every car and foot patrol we have in the area."

Turning swiftly, he headed for the door, beckoning Shields with a wave. "Come on, Cat. Let's go. You're driving."

55
SURRENDER

GEM THE VICTIM

The parking lot is darker than Gem remembers. She looks up and notices that the single security light is no longer working. Norton lowers the knife but stands too close for her to consider making a run for it. She looks directly at him and feels a surge of contempt.

"You are nothing but a coward," she says.

Norton looks momentarily shocked by her boldness. He tilts his head to one side and grins. "What about your Drew? He was the biggest fucking coward I've ever met. Crafty though. I'll give him that."

Gem lifts her chin. "He was a good man. He was in the same children's home as you but didn't let his circumstances drag him down. He built a good life for himself."

Norton walks slowly around her, encircling her like a wolf moving in for the kill. "Your precious Drew set the whole carjacking thing up," he says. "He telephoned me that night and told me you'd be stopping here to buy painkillers."

Gem opens her mouth to speak, but the words stick in her throat. She swallows them down and tries again. "That's a lie. You're lying."

Norton stops prowling and pushes his face so close to hers, the tips of their noses touch. "I never lie," he hisses. "Unless I have to."

She backs away, and he gives her space.

"I told you he didn't want to know me, but it was easy to find out which fancy law firm he worked for. I needed money, and Andrew owed me big time. He agreed to pay me if I did a little job for him. Two thousand before and two thousand when completed. He wanted you scared a little. Just enough to help him persuade you to give up work. Like I said, he was cowardly but cunning."

Gem shakes her head. "No, no, no. I don't believe you. This is fantasy. Your crazy mind working overtime."

Norton laughs again. "Why the hell would I make this stuff up?" he says. "He said I'd fucked up. I was supposed to just take the car. I couldn't let that go. Anyway, he had to die to make way for us. There was no choice to make. He never had a chance."

"You're deluded. There was no us. Never."

Norton shakes his head slowly. "You know there was something special there. Until you betrayed me as well."

Gem's heart flutters like a trapped bird. She remembers the arguments she and Drew had about her working late. She can't let herself believe he would do such a thing, but suspicion gnaws at her brain.

"What's the matter?" Norton teases. "Lost for words?" When she doesn't reply, he steps forward and points the knife at her stomach. "Get on your knees."

Gem doesn't move. Don't do anything rash, *she tells herself.* There's too much at stake.

Norton hesitates, then pulls a coin from his trouser pocket and flips it. It spins in the darkness and lands between his feet. He bends down, peering, his dark eyes narrowing to slits. "Tails," he says. "Interesting. If you do what I say, I won't hurt you."

Nothing this man says or docs makes sense, *Gem thinks. She looks down at the coin, and her mind flashes back to the last time she was in the parking lot. A memory jolts her, a vivid snapshot of her cell phone, her lipstick, and a pound coin on the ground. She'd thought the coin had rolled out of her bag.*

"All I want is a little show of humility," Norton says. "That's not too much to ask, is it? Now, get on your knees."

Gem stays where she is. She can hear the patrol car's engine idling behind her, and that's when it hits her, the reason Norton wants the headlights on. He wants to make sure it's bright enough for the parking lot's security cameras to capture his performance. He needs the world to see his triumph. He's not there to let her walk away.

He puts a hand around the back of her neck, grabs a handful of hair, and starts to force her down.

"Don't," she says. "I'm pregnant."

He yanks her hair so hard, she has no choice but to drop to her knees.

"You've tried that lie before, remember? How stupid do you think I am?"

"I'm not lying. I'm not. I'm pregnant with Drew's baby."

He draws back his right foot and kicks her hard in the stomach. Gem cries out and falls on her side, instinctively curling into the fetal position.

She is gasping loudly, as if the kick has driven the air from her lungs, but she's not as breathless as she appears. She clutches her hands to her stomach and thinks. She sees Norton shape up to lash out again.

Something clicks in her head, and she knows. This time, it will be different. She is different. Whatever happens, she will not be his victim again. As he lifts his foot, she kicks out at his standing leg, jamming her heel as hard as she can into his knee. She hears something crack, like a twig snapping, and knows she's done some serious damage.

Norton cries out, and his leg gives way. He topples to the ground, his arms outstretched to cushion his fall. The impact jars the knife from his grasp.

Gem snatches it up and scrambles to her feet, ready to run. She hesitates and looks down at Norton. This has to end here, *she thinks.*

Norton tries to get up, but the knee gives way again, and he rolls onto his back. Gem shifts the knife from one hand to the other, then back again, feeling its weight.

Norton glares up at her. "You haven't got it in you," he says.

"You'd be surprised what I can do if I've got a good enough reason."

Norton grimaces as he pushes himself up into a half-sitting position. "If you're going to do it, then get on with it," he snarls.

Gem looks at the knife for a second, then sprints to the patrol car and climbs into the driver's seat. She has to get PC Weaver to a hospital, but she isn't finished with Norton yet.

She hears another siren, the wailing getting closer every second. She revs the engine a few times before reversing, keeping her eyes on Norton. He has rolled onto his front and is slowly hauling himself toward the car, like a wounded soldier crawling through mud.

Gem stops and shifts the gear stick out of reverse. She can end this now, she tells herself. Make sure that Norton never taints her life again. She can make the city a safer place for everybody. The sirens sound very close now. She has to make a decision. The patrol car's headlights encase Norton in a tunnel of light. She thinks she can see him smiling, daring her to do it.

She puts her foot on the accelerator, holding the steering wheel steady as the engine roars. She sees no sign of fear in Norton's eyes, only surprise.

At the last second, she slams her foot hard on the brake, but the ground is wet, and the patrol car skids, tires screeching. A police car, siren screaming and blue lights flashing, speeds into the parking lot. An unmarked vehicle follows. Shields leaps out from behind the wheel and sprints to Norton.

Day and two uniformed officers hurry over, and the police constables drag Norton away. Gem climbs out from behind the steering wheel and staggers over to Day. "PC Weaver's in the trunk," she says. "I think he's badly hurt."

An ambulance pulls into the parking lot, and Day waves it over. He and Gem watch the paramedics lift the police constable gently onto a stretcher.

Gem's legs wobble, and Day offers her a hand. She grips it and steadies herself.

"It's over," he says.

Gem doubles over and clutches her stomach. "Is it really?" she gasps.

56

SURRENDER

THE DETECTIVE

"I hate this smell," Shields said, striding along the hospital corridor. "The scent of sickness, decay, and death."

Day stepped to his left to allow a nurse pushing a pajama-clad woman in a wheelchair to pass. "You're in a sparkling mood this morning, I see," he said. "Look at it another way. It may be an unpleasant odor, but think of it as the scent of healing, caring, and hope."

Shields shot her boss a suspicious look. "What's got you all warm and cuddly today?"

Day allowed himself a smile. Two days had passed since Norton's arrest. The media coverage was in full swing, the tabloids splashing the story across their front pages. A Matt Revell exclusive revealed that the arrest had been made by Hackney CID, and he'd given Day and Shields full credit for taking a serial killer off the streets. Hardy would be foaming at the mouth.

"I'm just happy that we've got Norton locked up, that's all," he said.

"I suppose you'll have a bit more time to try to save your marriage now."

Day shook his head. He'd usually shy away from discussing his personal life with colleagues, but Shields was different. He didn't know why; she just was.

"No, the divorce is happening. I accept that. I'm taking a leaf out of your book, focusing on work and forgetting about relationships. Except for Tom, of course."

At the end of the corridor, they stopped outside the entrance to the ward. "Are you ready?" Shields asked.

Day nodded, and she pressed the buzzer.

57

SURRENDER

GEM THE VICTIM

Gem tore her eyes away from the television beside her hospital bed as Day and Shields entered the room.

The detectives both glanced at the screen. Beneath footage showing sniffer dogs searching an area of woodland near Croydon, a scrolling red banner announced *Breaking news: Shallow grave of missing girl found in woods*. Gem adjusted her pillow and sat up straighter, pulling the crisp white sheet above her waist.

"It's so sad for her parents, isn't it?" she said. "After all this time."

"At least they know for sure now," Day said. "It must have been torture for them, clinging desperately to the hope that their daughter was still alive."

Gem couldn't imagine how anyone could go on with life, day after day, fearing the worst but never knowing.

"Now you'll be able to charge Norton with her murder, won't you?" Gem asked.

Day sighed and nodded slightly. "We hope so, yes…and with the murder of her unborn child."

Gem closed her eyes and dropped her chin to her chest. *How can one person cause so much evil?* she wondered. "Is Norton talking to you, admitting what he's done?"

Day stepped closer to the bed. "He's not admitting anything at the moment, but I think he will. People like him believe they are cleverer than the rest of us, and they can't resist letting us know how they outsmarted us."

Gem frowned and levered herself up into a higher sitting position, nodding at him to go on.

"The evidence you gave us about Norton flipping a coin has intrigued the psychological profiler working on the case. We don't have any details yet, but she believes that he has devised some kind of twisted game, using a coin to decide whether his victims live or die, depending on whether they submit to him or try to fight back."

Gem caught her breath. In her mind, she saw the coin spinning in the darkness.

"That's so sick," she said.

Day's phone trilled. He pulled it from his pocket and checked the screen. "Sorry, I have to take this," he said and hurried out of the room, his phone clamped to his ear.

When he'd gone, Shields sat down beside the bed. "How have you been sleeping?" she asked.

Gem smiled. "I think I've had more sleep the last two nights than in two weeks. They're discharging me later today. I can't wait to get home, put all this behind me, and get back to work."

"How's the bump?" Shields said.

Gem couldn't help but beam at the detective. "They tell me that everything's fine. I've had a scan, and apparently, it's all good. I've got extensive bruising around my stomach, but it's all external."

"Did Drew have any idea that you were pregnant?"

Gem rubbed her eyes. "No, he didn't. I didn't even know myself at first. I was late, but with all that had happened, the stress and everything, I thought… Well, I'm not sure exactly what I thought."

Day reentered the room, his expression a mixture of shock and excitement. "When the forensic team started exhuming Mary Freeman's remains this morning, they found a coin on her skull."

Gem looked at Shields, then back at Day. "What does that mean?"

"It means we have a direct link between Norton's attacks on you and the killing of Mary Freeman. It also means that we are going to have to reexamine every unsolved murder and every missing person case over the last seven years. It looks like Norton's been playing his murderous game for a long, long time."

When the detectives left, Gem pushed the sheet back, climbed out of the bed, and walked to the window. Small, wispy clouds raced across the sky, matching the hustle and bustle of the city.

The thought of a teenage Norton squatting by Mary Freeman's body with a coin in his hand turned her stomach. She shook her head to push the image away. It was immediately replaced by the realization that the choice she'd made on the night of the carjacking had changed everything.

She'd lost a lot but gained so much. She had a career to restart and a new life to build. There was no need to overthink it. *I'll never be anybody's victim again*, she told herself. *And neither will my baby.*

Read on for a look at *Don't Look Now* by Max Manning
Available now from Sourcebooks Landmark

PROLOGUE

She hears herself breathing, quick and shallow. She knows what's coming, and there's nothing she can do.

Tears sting, and she blinks hard. Dusk is falling like a gray shroud, and the undergrowth is thick with gloom. It's an unseasonably warm September evening, but still she shivers.

He smiles and holds his phone up in his right hand. She can't tell whether he's taking a photograph of her or a selfie. All her attention is focused on his other hand.

He steps around and behind her, moving so swiftly, it makes her head spin. The heat of his body burns through the thin fabric of her dress. He positions the phone in front of her face so she can get a good look at the screen.

It takes her a second to recognize the woman in the photograph. Her skin is paler than usual against her short, dark hair, the blue eyes startlingly wide.

"You're very photogenic, but you should have smiled," he says. "You've got a beautiful smile."

Her heart races, and rivulets of sweat run down her spine. Maybe, she thinks, maybe there is still a way out of this.

"Why me?" she says, her voice part whisper, part sob.

He laughs softly, and she feels his breath hot on the back of her neck. "This is so much bigger than you."

She wants to run, but her legs are shaking so badly, she can barely stand. She opens her mouth wide. The scream doesn't come. Her breath has been sucked from her lungs. She tries to step away, but he grabs her right forearm, his fingers digging into the flesh.

He releases his grip and stands so still, so silently, she lets herself believe, for a fraction of a second, that he has gone. But all hope dies in a moment. He's there, and the stillness and the silence mean he's ready.

Hot tears spill down her cheeks. Her vision blurs, but she sees. She sees a dark-haired child learning to ride her first bicycle, her father cheering her on as he runs, arms outstretched, ready to catch her should she fall.

She recalls the excitement of her first kiss, the tenderness of her last kiss. She regrets the precious days she's wasted, never saying the things she wanted to say. She feels the warmth of her mother's hand.

ONE

Detective Chief Inspector Dan Fenton thought he'd seen it all. He stared at the images on the computer screen and shook his head in despair. It was the first time he'd looked into the eyes of someone who knew they were about to be murdered.

A second picture, taken later at a side angle and low to the ground, showed the same woman on her back, her arms splayed, her torso slick with blood and her legs crossed neatly at her ankles. In the background, the faint silhouette of a line of trees snaked into the distance.

A message typed next to the photographs read:

The world certainly looks different through the eyes of a killer. #IKiller

Fenton lifted a hand and massaged the back of his neck. They had a murder, showcased online. Before and after pictures of the victim. An email sent by the killer, generously providing a link to his handiwork. What they didn't have was a body.

Yet.

His thoughts were interrupted when the office door swung open. Detective Sergeant Marie Daly paused to tug at her ponytail before stepping in.

"The online team is trying to trace the source of the email," she said. Daly never used more words than necessary. Fenton valued that. He also trusted her to make good decisions under pressure.

"How long is it going to take to get this stuff taken down?" he said.

Daly shrugged. "It's a fake Instagram account, Boss. Created in the UK with the username @IKiller. We've put in a request, but it could take twenty-four hours. It's already been viewed by several hundred people."

Fenton glanced at his watch and swore under his breath. Another long night at the office. Another broken promise. He slid his chair back and stood, resting his hands on the desk.

"Whoever did this couldn't wait to flaunt it." He jabbed a finger at the computer. "We need teams searching every park in the city, every open space large enough for that many trees. Cancel all leave, and get every available officer out there looking. I want that body found."

Daly nodded and left the room. Fenton sat down, lifted his hands to his face, and rubbed his eyes gently with the tips of his fingers. *What kind of mind could do that to another human being? God help us all*, he thought.

TWO

The key to everything was finding her. I'd been searching for a long time without knowing exactly who I was looking for.

That was a great moment for me. Strike that. The word *great* is far too weak. It was a prodigious, life-changing moment.

I'm still feeling the joy. Yes, that's the word. The public loves my work. I knew they would. It's hard to resist a glimpse into the darkness.

I can't blame myself for what I've done, for what I have yet to do. Guilt is a concept I've never understood. It gets in the way of true creativity, stops you from doing things you want to do. Imagine not having a conscience. Think about it. Wouldn't life be so much easier? Admit it.

A veil has been lifted. Life promises so much more for me now. I'm free to follow my path.

THREE

Fenton pushed through the journalists, ignoring their shouted questions and turning his face from the flashing cameras.

Two police constables guarded the Gore Road entrance into Victoria Park. As Fenton approached the iron gates, a photographer wearing a beanie and leather jacket stepped in front of him and raised his camera.

Fenton swerved slightly and turned his left shoulder, knocking the pressman off balance, forcing him to step aside. The discovery of the body hadn't been made public, yet the media had arrived en masse. Fenton would make it his business to find out how the news had been leaked.

Passing through the gate, he stressed to the uniforms that on no account should any reporters be allowed in. To the left, about fifty yards away, a constable stood by a line of crime scene tape sealing off a triangular area of undergrowth that filled the gap between two towering plane trees.

As Fenton walked towards the constable, he was struck by how fresh-faced she looked. *Probably a new recruit*, he thought.

He flashed his badge and a smile. "You're the one who found the body?" he asked.

The constable's face reddened. "That's right, sir."

Fenton nodded, ducked under the tape, and edged through a narrow gap in the shrubbery. The woman lay on her back in a small clearing. He moved close to her feet, putting himself where the killer must have stood to take the photograph. The coppery smell of blood turned his stomach as he moved beside the body and squatted to take a closer look. The victim appeared to be in her late twenties. Her eyes stared at the sky, lifeless and shiny. Like a doll. Fenton resisted a sudden urge to walk away. He needed to do his job properly.

This was somebody's child. Somebody's baby. When he'd first joined the force, arresting the bad guys, doing his bit for society, felt good. It was all about winning and proving yourself. After the birth of his daughter, that changed. One day, she'd be out there on her own. Taking bad guys off the streets had become even more important. It felt personal.

Dragging his eyes away from the woman's face, he checked her hands. They were small and clean. No obvious defense wounds. No attempt to fend off the blade. Her dark-blue skirt was hitched up around her thighs. He could see no sign of sexual assault, but the pathologist's report would provide the details.

He stood up and slipped through the undergrowth back onto the path. The police constable stood at attention. Fenton lifted a hand to acknowledge her and started walking back to the gate. After a dozen or so strides, he paused, took a few deep breaths to clear the smell of death from his airways, and gazed across the park.

The morning sun hovered low over East London's tower blocks, its rays glinting off the surface of the boating lake. A thin line of mature oaks curved north to south across the green space, their leaves already changing color. At that time of day, the park would normally be bustling with people.

A white van approached through the trees. It turned onto the grass and pulled up beside Fenton. Ronnie Oliver, New Scotland Yard's most experienced crime scene manager, and a younger, taller woman climbed out, both already wearing white forensic overalls.

Built like a pit bull, Oliver squared up to Fenton, his jutting jaw level with the detective's chest. "Don't tell me you've contaminated my crime scene," he said.

Fenton shrugged. "Okay, I won't. I had a quick look. That's all."

Oliver curled his upper lip and glanced at his colleague. She turned away and stared at the scenery. Fenton guessed she'd seen her boss lose it before. He admired Oliver's passion for his job and his obsession with protocol and, most of the time, was prepared to indulge his tantrums. "I had a look, but I didn't touch anything. I'm in charge of this investigation, remember."

Oliver scowled. "You could be the prime minister for all I care. Don't come near my crime scene again unless you're wearing a fucking forensic suit." With that, he strode off, his colleague scurrying after him.

It was going to be another long day and, unless they struck lucky, an even longer night. Fenton pulled his cell phone out of his jacket pocket. The call was answered after the sixth ring.

His neighbor sounded flustered. "Bad timing," she said. "We're late for school."

"Tina, I need a favor." Fenton paused, hoping for a positive response. He didn't get one. "Something's come up, and I'm going to be late. Very late. Can she sleep over?"

The silence on the other end stretched. When his neighbor finally spoke, her words sounded clipped. "It's early. How do you know you're going to be so late?"

"You'll see it on the news. It can't be helped. I'm sorry."

"You know this can't go on, don't you? It's not fair."

"I'll sort it out. I'll call the agency."

Fenton waited for at least thirty seconds before he realized the call had been terminated. He took that as a yes.

He was staring at his cell phone's blank screen, momentarily paralyzed by guilt, when he heard footsteps. He turned to see a pale, frowning face, topped with cropped reddish hair.

"Everything all right, sir?"

Detective Constable Ince had been on the team for less than six months. In that time, Fenton had come to appreciate his youthful enthusiasm. "You were the first detective on the scene?" Fenton said. It came out more as a statement than a question.

Ince nodded. "Ten minutes after the uniforms found her. Made sure the area was sealed off straightaway." He paused for a few seconds, running the fingers of his left hand across the stubble on his head as he tried to come up with something to impress his boss. "I think she's probably been there all night, because the park closes at dusk and the gates are locked. I remember thinking there was a lot of blood."

Fenton kept the disappointment off his face. He was good at that. He'd had a lot of practice. Sometimes first sight of the body can provide a gem, a little nugget of information that can help break a case. Not this time.

Ince rubbed his head harder and pressed on. "She wouldn't have been visible from Gore Street or from inside the park because of the undergrowth, but she would probably have been found by a dog walker if we hadn't gotten there first."

"We need the victim's ID confirmed," Fenton said. "I know I can trust you to get it done quickly." He watched as Ince walked away, a spring in his step, his head held a little higher.

READING GROUP GUIDE

1. At the opening of *The Victim*, we see Gem fall prey to what appears to be a carjacking. If you were in Gem's shoes, how would you react? Do you think you would submit, or would you try to fight back?

2. Compare Gem throughout these two scenarios—Gem the victim versus Gem the warrior. What differences do you see? Do you think the decisions we make fundamentally change us as humans?

3. What do you make of Drew? Do you think he got what he deserved in the end? Why or why not?

4. Describe the role fate and choice play in the story. What do you think has the most influence: fate or the choices we make? Or is it a combination of both?

5. Con Norton is the mastermind behind the story. Why do you think he is obsessed with this game? What drives him to act in both story lines?

6. Describe Detective Day. What are some of his strengths? What faults does he fall victim to? Do you think his demotion was warranted?

7. At one point, Revell asks Gem what advice she would give to women who found themselves in the same situation. What advice would you give?

8. What drives Norton's fascination with Gem? What does it say about him as a character?

9. Detective Day says he doesn't believe in good luck or bad luck; rather, he believes in good people and bad people. Do you agree with this? Why or why not?

10. What is Gem's relationship with her job in both scenarios? Imagine you were in Gem's shoes. What do you think your reaction would be? Would you want to go back to work, or would you make a different lifestyle choice?

11. What happened in Norton's childhood that influenced the person he became? Do you think he was "born bad," or was he a victim of his circumstances?

12. Describe the connection between Norton and Drew. What do you think brought them together? What set the wheels of this game in motion?

13. How do the choices Gem makes ultimately influence her fate?

A CONVERSATION
WITH THE AUTHOR

The Victim is a taut and gripping thriller. What was your inspiration for the story?

The idea for the plot of *The Victim* came to me while I was halfway through my first crime thriller, *Don't Look Now*. I spent many years covering crime incidents as a news reporter, and when considering the plight of victims, I'd often wondered if things might have turned out better or worse for them if they'd made different choices. What if they'd gone to a different bar that night? What if they hadn't turned down that street? What if they'd handed over their money straightaway? Of course, where there is a victim, there is also a criminal, and he or she has choices to make too.

The narrative structure you've created is extremely unique. What made you want to write a story with two opposing threads?

I decided that I needed to write a story with two threads to emphasize how powerful the choices we make are when it comes to determining who we become. I wanted to explore how our moments of decision can shape our personal futures. Gem has to make a split-second decision at the beginning of *The Victim*. At that point, the story divides into alternating threads and leads to very different outcomes.

Were there any challenges to writing in this format? How did you overcome them?

Writing two parallel story lines is definitely a challenge! I had to make a lot of notes to keep track of each thread. They had to be different but not too different, complex but not too complex. I wanted each of the story lines to be entertaining and gripping in their own way.

Which character was the most fun to write? Which presented the greatest challenge?

I thoroughly enjoyed writing the character of Con Norton, the mastermind behind the Fight or Submit game that runs through *The Victim*. I always find trying to delve deep into the mind of a psychopath a fascinating and sometimes deeply satisfying exercise. But there is no need to be alarmed! There is an immense amount of research material available on the workings of a psychopath's mind, and imagination can be more powerful than knowledge. Gem was great fun to write, too, but definitely challenging, especially as her character developed differently in each thread.

Gem as the victim is almost a completely different character compared to Gem as the warrior. Was this intentional? How did you keep them so different yet still connected?

The whole point of the separate threads is to explore how the choices we make can determine who we become. The lives of Gem the victim and Gem the warrior take different twists and turns, and their characters develop differently in response. At the same time, Gem the victim and Gem the warrior are the same woman. It's just that they respond differently in a moment of crisis, and that takes them on different journeys.

What do you think ultimately drives our lives—choice, fate, or a little bit of both?

This is a big question! I think maybe it's a little bit of both, with choice being the more powerful of the two. It's how we respond to what fate puts in front of us that shapes our future. Certainly, as a crime thriller writer, I would warn the characters in my books to shape their own destinies, or someone else will take control and do it for them!

What does your writing process look like?

My writing process may appear pretty chaotic, but I've come to realize that I have quite a rigid routine. I am not a morning person and never start writing until mid- to late afternoon and go on until I hit my daily word target. I always know how the story begins and how I want it to end. The hardest part is finding my way through the maze in the middle. I write via a laptop, and as ideas often pop into my head, I scribble them down on Post-it Notes and stick them on the wall of my office. I rarely look at the notes again, and probably wouldn't be able to read them anyway because my handwriting is so untidy.

If you could give one piece of advice to future thriller writers, what would it be?

Above all else, once you start to write, focus on getting the first draft finished. Don't obsess about rewriting or editing your work as you go along. It will slow you down, confuse and demoralize you.

Getting the first draft completed is so important. Once you have it, then you can rewrite, rewrite, edit, edit, edit.

When you're not writing, how do you spend your time?

When I'm not at my desk writing, I'm often reading. Also, because being a writer involves spending so many hours sitting down in an office, I like to spend time outdoors. I love walking, especially coastal walks, and cycling.

ACKNOWLEDGMENTS

By the time a novel is out there on the shelves, it is never the work of just one person. I'm truly grateful to everybody who has helped this one on its way.

My editor, Shana Drehs, the talented editorial director at Sourcebooks, has been fantastic, along with her editing team, including MJ Johnston, Heather Hall, and Sabrina Baskey.

I also want to express my gratitude to my amazing agent, Madeleine Milburn, of the Madeleine Milburn Ltd. literary, TV, and film agency, whose insights have, as always, been invaluable.

A thank-you is due to my brother, Patrick, a former long-serving police detective, who answered several questions I had regarding investigation protocol. Any mistakes are, of course, down to me.

The encouragement of those close to you is vital in the early days, especially when an author is trying to get to grips with a first draft. I consider myself so lucky to have the incredible love and support of my family, and special mention must go to my wife, Valerie, a dedicated and valued reader.

ABOUT THE AUTHOR

Max Manning started his career in journalism in the UK, where he worked at the *Daily Express* and the *Daily Telegraph*. He is the author of *Don't Look Now*. He lives in London.